REVIEWERS RAVE OVER
SUZANNE SIMMONS!

NO ORDINARY MAN

"Suzanne Simmons is on a roll! For passion, romance, humor, and a touch of intrigue, you can't do better than NO ORDINARY MAN!"

—*Romantic Times*

"NO ORDINARY MAN is extraordinary romance."

—Jayne Ann Krentz

"There is nothing ordinary about Suzanne Simmons' sensational books and NO ORDINARY MAN is no exception."

—Stella Cameron

"Simmons has wit, sizzle, and a wicked way with plots . . . Sheer reading pleasure."

—Elizabeth Lowell

"A diverting adventure with clever clues."

—*Publishers Weekly*

"A fun read with many elements sure to please romance fans."

—*Booklist*

"A sizzling, provocative story filled with plenty of humor and passion. Romance fans should definitely find a space on their bookshelves for this gem."

—*Rendezvous*

More . . .

"Passion becomes entwined with danger and mystery as Ms. Simmons sweeps readers into an incomparable sensuous adventure . . . a wonderful book!"

—*Old Book Barn Gazette*

"This is pure romance! A little magic, a lot of glamour, an age old family feud, a wicked stepmother all mixed together on a mysterious island off the coast of Scotland. Enjoy!"

—*Calico Trails*

THE PARADISE MAN

"THE PARADISE MAN is a sinful pleasure."

—Elizabeth Lowell

"A fabulous fantasy, an utterly wonderful romance."

—Stella Cameron

"Suzanne Simmons always delivers what romance readers love best. THE PARADISE MAN is no exception. I loved it!"

—Jayne Ann Krentz

"Get ready to savor a witty, sexy, adventure-filled romp from the captivating imagination of author Suzanne Simmons. THE PARADISE MAN is a tropical treat!"

—*Romantic Times*

"Ms. Simmons has written a true romance with adventure and mystery thrown in for good measure. The sensuality of her love scenes is breathtaking . . . This promises to be an excellent 'Man' series!"

—*Rendezvous*

"THE PARADISE MAN is a decadent pleasure."

—*Under the Covers* (Very Highly Recommended)

Lady's Man

SUZANNE SIMMONS

St. Martin's Paperbacks

LADY'S MAN

ISBN: 0-312-96825-6

Printed in the United States of America

St. Martin's Paperbacks edition / February 1999

St. Martin's Paperbacks are published by St. Martin's Press, 175 Fifth Avenue, New York, NY 10010.

10 9 8 7 6 5 4 3 2 1

This one is for Liz and John Johnson:
the best of times,
the best of friends.

"Take him and cut him out in stars
and he will make the face of heaven so fine
all the world will fall in love
with the night."

Juliet of Romeo
—*Romeo and Juliet*

"*I have in me something dangerous...*"

Hamlet of himself
—*Hamlet*

One

Coleman Worth remembered when he didn't have a pot to piss in.

The one he was staring down into at the moment was low, sleek, probably European and without a doubt expensive.

Everything about the Sonoran was expensive, everything was the best and he could afford the very best. The fifty-two-hundred-dollar-a-night presidential suite provided all the comforts of home: four televisions, eleven telephones and a Steinway baby-grand piano.

Not that he played.

The master bath, in addition to the expensive European toilet and matching bidet, was filled with polished mirrors, pure white marble from Carrara, Italy (marble of such high quality had previously been used only for sculptures) and twenty-four-carat gold fixtures.

The suite also had a full kitchen—not that he cooked—and a separate service entrance.

What more could a man want?

A butler, of course.

Head butler William Regen had been assigned to pro-

vide him with around-the-clock service. No request was
too large or too small or beyond the call of duty, Cole
had been assured by the distinguished gentleman when
he'd met him at the airport earlier in the week.

On the drive from Phoenix's Sky Harbor to the luxury resort in the foothills of the Sonoran Desert, William
Regen had made it clear that he would be only too happy
to run faxes out to Mr. Worth if he was playing golf,
serve three meals a day in the formal dining room of the
suite or look after the children at the pool.

Not that Cole had any children.

Regen would also take care of the dry cleaning or
arrange for an upscale department store to stay open after regular closing for a special fitting. He would even
have the furniture in the suite moved if Mr. Worth didn't
like how it was arranged.

Not that Cole gave a sweet damn about the furniture.

The Sonoran's butler program took service to another
level, enthused William Regen. By way of illustration,
he mentioned that one guest had rung him at three
o'clock in the morning and requested that the drapes in
his suite be changed, "because he didn't like the color."
It had been seen to immediately.

"Nothing is impossible," was the head butler's
motto.

Which was just another way of saying what Cole believed: if you wanted something in this life so bad you
could taste it, you'd find a way to get it.

Cole stripped off his evening clothes and stepped into
the opulent, room-size shower. He pressed a button on
the wall and hot, steamy water precisely the temperature
he preferred instantly pulsated from the showerhead.

There were three things that Coleman Worth always
did. He always told a woman up-front that he wasn't the
marrying kind. He always slept in the nude. And he

always sang "Home on the Range" in the shower. He understood the reasons for the first two, if not the latter.

Maybe that particular song had something to do with his past. Although these days he didn't think much about the past. It wasn't that he had forgotten it; he just didn't dwell on it. The past had gotten him where he was—here—and that's all he needed to know.

Cole stopped singing for a minute and asked aloud, "Where in the hell is *here*?"

When he started talking to himself that was a sure sign he was bored or restless or—God forbid—both. That meant it was time to get away for a while.

Once he had sailed to a deserted island north of Key West. He had lain on the beach for two weeks, never shaving, never showering, except for a long swim in the waters of the Gulf of Mexico every morning. He had lived off the land: eating coconuts, fish he'd caught himself and the occasional crab.

Another time Cole had hired a biplane to drop him off near Great Bear Lake in the Northwest Territories. He had only the clothes on his back and the supplies he could carry. The pilot had been kind of nervous about leaving him in the middle of nowhere and wanted to arrange a rendezvous point in case anything went wrong. Cole had insisted on having his own way. A week later he'd walked out of the Canadian wilderness and into the nearest town: population 27, including a dozen huskies and a resident moose.

Yup, sometimes when it got to be too much for him, there was only one thing to do: take a sabbatical from the rest of civilization.

Cole always came back a new man.

" 'Home, home on the range. Where the deer and the antelope play. Where seldom is heard a discouraging word and the skies are not cloudy all day.' "

He finished his song, turned off the shower, wrapped a towel around his hips, grabbed a cold beer from the bar—Regen had made certain the fridge was stocked with Cole's favorite brand, Coors Light—flipped off the lights inside the suite with the push of another button and wandered out onto the patio.

He stood there in the dark and gazed out over the city of Phoenix and the surrounding valley.

It was one of those spring nights that seemed to happen only in Arizona: warm but not too warm, a million stars in the sky overhead, a million lights in the valley below, the distinctive outline of Camelback Mountain over a distant adobe wall, the air filled with the scent of roses, bougainvillea and orange blossoms.

There was a faint breeze off the desert tonight; it stirred the palm trees lining the driveway and the lighted swimming pool into a swaying dancelike movement.

Cole raised the can of ice-cold beer to his mouth and took a drink. His business dealings in Phoenix had gone exactly as planned. Worth Industries had made yet another shrewd acquisition. The end result: his company had tripled in size in the past five years alone. He had more money now than he would ever need.

Since when had need been a consideration when it came to making money?

Maybe back in the beginning, Cole reflected. Maybe back when he didn't have two nickels to rub together, or a pot to piss in. But after he'd made his first million or two, money had become nothing more than a way to keep score. It was a game and he played it well, certainly better than most: with a cool head and a cold heart, with ruthless intent and always, always to win.

Winning used to give him a bigger thrill than it did these days, Cole acknowledged.

Maybe he was getting too old to play games.

''You were thirty-seven on your last birthday, Worth. You're in the goddamned prime of life.''

A life that was becoming predictable.

Almost as predictable as his hostess hitting on him earlier tonight when he'd wandered out into the desert garden behind the sprawling Santa Barbara–style house—how much square footage did it take before a house became a mansion?—to admire the cacti in bloom.

He'd managed to extricate himself from an awkward situation without offending the lady—he used the term *lady* loosely—and had left the party as soon as it wasn't obvious to anyone, especially the lady's husband, that he was trying to make a getaway.

Cole absently rubbed one hand back and forth across his bare abdomen.

He was getting too old to have to contend with errant wives: it neither amused nor flattered him. Maybe he'd call Martin first thing in the morning and let his second-in-command at Worth Industries know that he was taking off again for parts unknown. It wouldn't be the first time that he asked Martin Davis to take over while he got some R & R, and it wouldn't be the last.

Sometimes a man had to get away from it all. Sometimes a man had to be alone.

Hell, he was always alone. Always had been. Always would be. He didn't need anyone. He didn't intend to ever need anyone. He had been on his own since the age of fourteen when he'd run away from an abusive foster home: the third one in a row the system had placed him in.

It was also the last one, as it turned out.

After that, he had done whatever it took to survive. Some of it he wasn't real proud of.

Cole raised the can of beer to his mouth and took another long swallow.

There was no sense in having regrets. No sense in brooding about it. The past was the past. His past was like anyone else's: it couldn't be changed. And since no one was promised a future, that left only the present. So he concentrated on living in the here and now.

His ruminations were interrupted when he heard what sounded like a key turning in a lock. Then the door to the service entrance slammed open behind him. He hadn't rung for William Regen, and he wasn't expecting company.

"What the—?" Cole muttered under his breath.

He set the can of beer down and, moving quickly and quietly, melted into the shadows. It was a trick he'd learned a long time ago when the ability to make himself invisible might mean the difference between life and death: his life and death.

As he slipped from shadow to shadow, he could hear someone stumbling around in the dark.

Cole had excellent night vision. In the back hallway between the kitchen and pantry, he could make out a human form bent over at the waist, arms clenched to its midsection, gasping for air and not even trying to be quiet about it.

Who was in his suite?

Why was someone in his suite?

He positioned himself behind the figure. There wasn't any weapon visible. While he still had the element of surprise in his favor, Cole reached out and flipped on the light switch.

"Sonofa..." he swore softly.

It was a woman dressed in a tuxedo.

She straightened and stared at him with eyes that were huge and wild and decidedly green. Between gulps, she managed to get his name out. "Mr. Worth."

She had him at a disadvantage: she evidently knew

who he was and he didn't have a clue as to her identity.

Coleman Worth had never liked being at a disadvantage. He ran his fingers through the still-damp hair at his nape. "I know who I am. Who are you?"

"The butler," she replied.

Fear.

For the first time in her life Georgiana understood on the most basic level what that primitive emotion really was. Well, perhaps not for the first time; the first time she had been truly afraid was the night her mother and father had told her the money was gone: every last dollar, pound and franc of it.

This was fear of a different kind, however. This was fear of the unknown, the hunted at the mercy of the hunter, the pursued stalked by the pursuer. Her breath came in gulps. Her hands and feet were ice-cold. Her mind was alert, while her body seemed paralyzed. It was like a nightmare, only she was wide awake.

Her instinct was to run.

So she ran.

To the suite next door.

Georgiana stood in the back hallway, gasping for air, and stared at the man wearing only a towel around his waist. The old adage about jumping from the frying pan into the fire came to mind.

"You know who I am," he said.

She nodded her head and recited by rote: "Coleman Worth. CEO, Worth Industries. Wichita Falls, Texas. Multimillionaire. Presidential suite. Coors Light. Steaks rare. Home fries. Coffee strong and black. Wears cowboy boots with everything."

Except a towel, of course.

"Ms. . . . ?"

"Burne-Jones."

That produced a raised eyebrow. "Hyphenated?"

"Yes."

Mr. Coleman Worth of Wichita Falls, Texas, frowned. "Why?"

Georgiana blinked. "It was my parents' idea. My mother's maiden name was Burne and——"

"And your father's was Jones," the man finished for her. "That isn't what I meant."

Of course that wasn't what he'd meant, she realized belatedly. He was referring to her knowledge of his vital statistics, as they called them in the hotel business. "In case I need to take over for Mr. Regen at a moment's notice. I'm one of the underbutlers."

Coleman Worth shook his head. "Why are you in my suite, Ms. Burne-Jones?"

Her mouth formed a perfectly round O. She should have known. She should have guessed that's what he would ask. What was she going to tell him?

Georgiana licked her lips—they were parched like the desert—and wiped her palms on the legs of her trousers. That was when she noticed the blood on her hands.

All of a sudden she was feeling light-headed.

"You'd better sit down, Ms. Burne-Jones. You look like you've seen a ghost."

"Not a ghost," she rasped as she sank into the chair he provided. "A body."

Coleman Worth glanced down, as if to make certain the towel around his hips was still covering him with some degree of modesty. "Surely seeing a man's body isn't that much of a shock for you."

"Not your body, Mr. Worth." Georgiana felt a sudden and terrible urge to laugh hysterically. She shivered despite the warmth of the night. Her lips were numb when she said, "A dead body."

"In that case, you'd better have a drink, too."

Two

The whiskey burned all the way down.

Cole could tell from the expression on Ms. Burne-Jones's face: a face that would, no doubt, under normal circumstances be considered damned attractive.

As it was, she looked like death warmed over.

"Would you like another shot?" he inquired, indicating her empty glass.

The young woman nodded her head and handed the crystal glass back to him.

Cole noticed her hands were trembling. They were also stained with what appeared to be blood. He should have found out right off the bat if she was injured. "Are you hurt?"

Ms. Burne-Jones blinked in bewilderment. "Hurt?"

He had to ask. "Is that your blood?"

It was some time before she slowly moved her head from side to side—light brown hair, once neatly arranged into an efficient bun at her nape, had started to come unraveled, allowing stray wisps to fall around her face—and responded, "I don't think so."

If it wasn't her blood, Cole assumed it belonged to the dead body she'd mentioned.

Life was suddenly not quite so predictable.

He poured another shot of whiskey into the imported crystal glass and, as long as he was behind the bar, dampened a kitchen towel. He made his way back across the living room and held the towel out to his unexpected guest. She stared up at him with a blank expression. Cole wondered if Ms. Burne-Jones was in shock.

He set the glass of whiskey on the table beside her, went down on his haunches—luckily the Sonoran supplied its guests with the finest oversize Egyptian cotton bath towels, so his dignity, among other things, remained intact—took her hands in his and gently wiped them off as one would a child's.

Not that he ever remembered washing a child's hands.

Once that was taken care of, Cole gave her the whiskey and watched as she raised the glass to her lips. She was still shaking like a leaf.

He didn't think he should risk leaving the room, even long enough to pull on a pair of pants, so he retrieved his can of beer and plunked himself down in the chair directly opposite Ms. Burne-Jones. "Want to talk about it?"

She shook her head.

Cole couldn't say he blamed her. Obviously the young woman didn't *want* to talk about it.

He decided to take a different tack with her. "Don't you think you should tell me what happened?"

Ms. Burne-Jones huddled around her glass. "All right," she finally said, taking another sip of whiskey.

"From the beginning," he prompted.

Then he waited.

For a man who had literally moved mountains in his

meteoric rise to the top of the business world, Cole could be remarkably patient. He knew what was said about him: God had created the heavens and the earth in six days; Coleman Worth could have done it in five. But, despite what people said or thought, he was good at waiting.

It was some time before she murmured, " 'In this world we walk on the roof of hell gazing at flowers.' " Then she looked up at him; her face pale, her eyes dark, dark green like a dense forest after a drenching rain. "I read that somewhere once. I don't think I understood what it meant until tonight."

Cole went on waiting.

"There is . . ." She paused and made a fresh start. "There *was* a Mr. Paul Isherwood in the suite next to yours. He is . . . he *was* some kind of financier."

"Never heard of him."

"Neither had I until he checked into the Sonoran five days ago." She rolled the nearly empty glass back and forth between her palms. When she spoke her voice was raspy. "I was assigned as butler to Mr. Isherwood. He wasn't much trouble. Quiet. Undemanding. Very few special requests in the beginning."

"In the beginning?"

"Two days ago Mr. Isherwood informed me, on rather short notice, that he was entertaining guests that evening. He instructed me to stock the bar in his suite and have plenty of food on hand. He also wanted me to greet his guests as they arrived. Since his requests were reasonable and well within the range of services a butler at the Sonoran is expected to provide, I agreed."

Cole sat back in the chair and took a sip of his beer. "So you were to act as a kind of hostess."

Ms. Burne-Jones nodded and took a slow, deep

breath. "At eight o'clock sharp a dozen men in dark business suits showed up."

That brought a raised eyebrow from him.

She gave a small smile that wasn't really a smile. "You're right, of course. We don't see many dark suits here in the valley unless they're tuxedos."

Cole had to admit he was fascinated by the woman's story. Or maybe it was her voice that enthralled him: it was warm and smooth, yet slightly husky like the whiskey she was drinking. Maybe it was the story *and* her voice.

"Go on," he urged, noting that she'd finally stopped shaking. The alcohol had done its job.

"I should backtrack for a moment and explain to you that Mr. Isherwood had also requested that I tend bar." She breathed in and out. "Which I did."

"I assume you would usually bring in a separate bartender for that duty."

"You assume correctly. In addition, Mr. Isherwood had asked me to oversee the buffet table, although I would normally schedule at least one waiter for a party of thirteen people."

From behind his Coors Light, Cole muttered, "Curious."

"It gets curiouser and curiouser, Mr. Worth. Just before his guests arrived—I remember I was arranging the shrimp cocktail on a mound of shaved ice—Mr. Isherwood took me aside and said I was to be like those monkeys."

Cole scowled. "Monkeys?"

"That was precisely my reaction," said Ms. Burne-Jones, staring down into her glass. Then she raised her head and recited, " 'Hear no evil, see no evil, speak no evil.' "

"Ah, *those* monkeys."

"Yes, those monkeys."

"The legend of the three wise monkeys carved over the door of the Sacred Stable in Nikko, Japan."

A tremulous smile flitted across a soft, feminine mouth. "Somehow I doubt if Mr. Isherwood knew anything about the legend of the three monkeys." Ms. Burne-Jones brushed at the pants leg of her tuxedo. "Discretion, however, is the hallmark of my profession. That's what I assured Mr. Isherwood."

Cole digressed for a moment. "A butler must see and hear just about anything and everything in the line of duty."

"We do, but, naturally, we never talk about it."

Until now, Cole nearly said.

Aloud he ventured, "You must get some strange requests."

She concurred. "We're trained not to be judgmental. We are responsible, after all, for providing the ultimate in personal service. We will cater to every whim of our guests as long as it's not illegal. As Mr. Regen reminds us on a daily basis, 'Ours is not to reason why. Ours is but to do or—' "

" '—die,' " he finished for her.

She raised the glass to her lips and took another— and final—swallow of whiskey.

Cole recapped the story so far. "So two nights ago, at eight o'clock sharp, twelve men in dark business suits showed up at the door of Mr. Isherwood's suite."

"Exactly."

"What did you do?"

"Mostly I tended bar. Whenever I had the chance I restocked the buffet table and removed dirty plates and glasses. It wasn't difficult to ignore the conversations around me, as Mr. Isherwood had instructed. There was always something that needed to be done, since I was working the party alone.''

Suddenly Ms. Burne-Jones became absolutely still.

''What is it?''

She gave herself a shake. ''I'm not certain. From the start it was an unusual evening. The mood was somber. The guests ate very little. They talked even less.'' She paused. ''I've just realized that while the gentlemen present rarely spoke to one another, each of them in turn had a lengthy conversation with Mr. Isherwood.''

''Odd.''

''Very odd, now that I stop and think about it.''

''Can you recall overhearing any of their conversations? Any individual words or names?''

She leaned back and closed her eyes.

Cole waited.

Dark, regretful eyes blinked open. She shook her head. ''I'm sorry, Mr. Worth.''

''The name is Cole. And you don't have to apologize, Ms. Burne-Jones.''

''The name is Georgiana.'' Georgiana Burne-Jones seemed to brace herself to finish the story. ''The party ended promptly at midnight. After everyone had left I started cleaning up. Mr. Isherwood thanked me, handed me a sealed envelope with what he said was my tip inside and disappeared into one of the other rooms. Before I had finished tidying he returned to the living room. He was dressed in his bathrobe.''

''How much was your tip?''

Her expression was one of utter distaste. ''At that point I hadn't looked in the envelope.''

''Not kosher to peek, huh?''

She hesitated. ''I had a job to finish.''

''I take it you and Mr. Isherwood were of two opinions about what that job entailed.''

Her voice was a strangled whisper. "Yes."

"He made a pass at you."

She nodded.

"Rebuffing unwanted attentions"—what an old-fashioned phrase he had chosen to use, Cole realized—"must be part of standard butler training."

"It is."

"So this wasn't the first time you'd found yourself in a similar situation."

"It wasn't. In fact, I can usually see it coming and avert any unpleasantness." There was a short, brittle silence. "It was strange because Mr. Isherwood didn't seem like the type to me. Although I guess you can never tell."

"I guess not," Cole said dryly. "How did Mr. Isherwood take your rejection?"

"As if he'd expected it."

"And your tip?"

"I tried to leave the envelope on the bar, but he insisted that it was only for the job I had done at the party."

"So you took it."

"Yes." Her mouth was a grim line. "I reported the incident to Mr. Regen that same night before I left the grounds. It's required by the Sonoran. Mr. Regen asked if I wanted to be relieved of my duties in regards to Mr. Isherwood."

"Did you agree to be relieved?"

"No. There are six men and two women currently working as butlers at the Sonoran. As Mr. Regen frequently reminds us, the hotel is always looking for a reason not to include women in the butler program, so I didn't want to fail him or myself or the other female butler."

"Understandable." Cole ran a hand through his hair. "So what happened tonight?"

"Mr. Isherwood ordered his favorite dinner: filet mignon rare, baked potato with sour cream and chives, asparagus with a side of Hollandaise and crème brulée for dessert. He requested that I personally deliver room service to his suite."

"Was Mr. Regen aware of this request?"

"Yes." Her face was tight. "Mr. Regen was also present tonight when I finally remembered to open the envelope Mr. Isherwood had given me after the party."

"The envelope containing your tip?"

She moved her head.

Cole watched her closely. "And . . ."

She gave a soft sound of dismay. "There were crisp, brand-new one-hundred-dollar bills inside."

Cole was starting to get a strange feeling in his gut. "How many?"

"Thirty," she said in a whisper.

"Three thousand dollars." He gave a low whistle under his breath. "Some tip."

"I told Mr. Regen that I didn't want to keep the money, that I wanted to return it to Mr. Isherwood."

"What did he say to that?"

"He said it was my decision." Georgiana Burne-Jones moistened her lips. "But when I delivered dinner to Mr. Isherwood's suite, the money completely slipped my mind."

"Why?"

"Mr. Isherwood was already seated at the dining room table, and frankly he seemed to be in a daze. In fact, he was so pale that I wondered if he was ill. I inquired if he needed any help. He said yes."

"What kind of help did he need?"

"He asked me to cut his filet mignon for him using

the steak knife. So that's what I did. Then he told me to leave and return in one hour.''

Cole was intrigued. ''Did you?''

She nodded and tried to swallow. ''I returned exactly fifty-nine minutes later and I couldn't believe my eyes. The suite, especially the bedroom, looked as if a struggle had taken place: lamps were tipped over, sofa cushions were knocked to the floor, paintings on the walls were askew, furniture was out of place. I picked up the telephone to call security and that's when I noticed Mr. Isherwood.''

''Where was he?''

Her voice was reed-thin. ''On the floor behind the sofa.''

Cole waited.

She added, ''There was a knife stuck in his chest.''

''The steak knife?''

Tear-filled eyes met his. ''How did you know?''

Cole shrugged. ''Lucky guess.''

''Mr. Isherwood was dead.''

Cole didn't doubt that for an instant.

Her voice sounded strangely disembodied. ''His eyes were wide open and he was staring at the ceiling. There was a red stain on his shirt.'' She glanced down at her hands. ''It must have been blood.''

''Did you touch anything?''

Tension clung to her sharply drawn features. ''The telephone, of course.''

''Anything else?''

''I don't think so. I hung up without speaking to the security guard on duty and stood there for a minute, maybe longer, trying to understand what was going on . . . what had gone on. Then I noticed that Mr. Isherwood hadn't eaten a single bite of his dinner. The dining room table was exactly as I had left it.''

"Except for the steak knife," he pointed out.

"Except for the steak knife." Fine nostrils flared. "I'm not sure when it occurred to me that the fingerprints on the steak knife were probably mine."

Bits and pieces.

Pieces and bits.

Cole summed it up. "Hotel guest makes pass at pretty female butler. Butler informs her superior and the incident is officially on record. Nevertheless, butler declines to forego her duties. Guest tips butler a very generous amount of money, perhaps expecting something extra from her in terms of service. Guest makes a second and more physically forceful pass at pretty female butler. A struggle ensues. In the process lamps and furniture are knocked over. Butler grabs steak knife and stabs obnoxious guest in self-defense."

"But that's not the way it happened," Georgiana Burne-Jones countered in her own defense.

"But that's the way it might look."

The young woman sank deeper into the chair cushion and herself. "Oh, dear God."

She was in it right up to her neck . . . and they both knew it.

Cole did his thinking out loud. "I wonder why Mr. Isherwood was so pale when you brought in his dinner."

"I don't know." She made a gesture in the air. "Maybe he really was ill."

"Or maybe someone else was already there."

"In his suite?"

"Yes."

"Who?"

He was glad she was sitting down. "The real murderer."

She shuddered, and the color drained from her face.

Cole double-checked. "Did you search the suite?"

"No."

He had a pretty good idea, but he asked anyway. "What did you do?"

"I ran."

"You ran directly here?"

"Yes. I have a key to this suite, as well. All I could think about was getting away from that . . . that place. I wanted time to collect myself, time to think."

"And you didn't speak with security?"

Her eyes were huge. "No, but a call from Mr. Isherwood's suite would still have registered on the security monitor." She stared down at her hands as if she were trying to ascertain where the bloodstains could have come from. Then she looked up. "I want you to know I didn't kill Mr. Isherwood."

Was she telling him the truth?

Or was he the one being set up?

If Ms. Burne-Jones had been subjected to an extreme form of sexual harassment and had retaliated, then it was likely that Isherwood's death would be ruled self-defense.

If the entire horrible incident had happened exactly as she had described, then Ms. Burne-Jones was as much a victim of the crime as Isherwood. The problem was how to prove her innocence.

If he helped her, that made him an accessory to a crime, guilty of aiding and abetting, harboring a fugitive and breaking several dozen laws in the process.

Not that he hadn't broken a few in his day.

The funny thing was, Cole believed her story. He didn't know why. He was fairly skeptical about people in general and women in particular, and beautiful women even more so. It had been his experience that beautiful women often felt exempt somehow from those rules which applied to ordinary folks.

Ms. Burne-Jones was beautiful, but Cole was pretty sure she was indifferent to the fact. She certainly didn't play her looks up. She was dressed in a tailored black tuxedo. Her light brown hair had been pulled straight back from her face—at least until it had started to come undone—and her makeup was subtle to nonexistent.

He finally said to her, "I believe you're innocent."

She exhaled. "Thank you."

"Don't thank me until you hear what else I think," Cole advised her.

Her eyes narrowed. "What else do you think?"

Coleman Worth knew damned well the lady wasn't going to like what he had to say. "I think it's possible you were set up."

Her tone was one of incredulity. "You mean someone deliberately arranged the evidence to put the blame on me?"

That was what he meant.

She was stunned. Her mouth opened and closed. Then she managed to ask, "Am I in big trouble, Mr. Worth?"

"Cole," he reminded her.

"Am I in big trouble, Cole?"

He wasn't going to lie to her. He leaned forward in his chair. "About as big as it gets, Georgiana."

Three

Georgiana knew she had committed the ultimate sin, for a butler: she had been indiscreet.

She had involved a guest staying at the Sonoran in affairs that were none of his affair. She had gossiped about one guest with another. (It hadn't really been gossip, but she had talked about Mr. Isherwood to Coleman Worth.) She had entered a hotel room without permission and without being summoned.

She'd had her reasons, of course. They were even good reasons. But that was still no excuse.

Instead of panicking and running to the presidential suite next door, why hadn't she talked to security or gone straight to Mr. Regen's office and told the head butler everything that had transpired?

Georgiana answered her own question. Because she had panicked. Because she had been badly frightened. Because she hadn't been thinking clearly.

She was thinking clearly now. Well, as clearly as could be expected under the circumstances *and* after several straight shots of eighty-proof alcohol. She couldn't undo what she had done—her conduct would not be overlooked by the hotel; she was certain it would cost her her job—but she could exercise a certain amount of damage control.

Georgiana started to rise from the overstuffed chair: the woven jacquard fabric was from Clarence House; the pattern was the playful figure of Kokopelli, the ancient flute-playing god of the Anasazi. "I'm sorry, Mr. Worth."

"Cole."

"I shouldn't have come here, Cole." She shouldn't be addressing him as Cole, either. "I had no right to intrude on your privacy or to involve you in this unsavory business."

The man was philosophical. "What's done is done."

Georgiana stood, brushed a nonexistent speck of lint from the lapel of her tuxedo jacket, tucked an errant strand of hair behind her ear and squared her shoulders. "Please accept my apologies."

"You don't have to apologize."

She disagreed with him. "I shouldn't have told you about Mr. Isherwood."

"Why not?"

"For one thing, it was indiscreet. For another, it was unfair to you," she explained.

"Under the circumstances I think any indiscretion can be forgiven. And I'll be the judge of whether it was fair or unfair to me," Coleman Worth informed her.

It was only then that something else occurred to her. "I may have put you in harm's way."

He seemed unconcerned about the possibility. "It wouldn't be the first time. It won't be the last."

Georgiana stared at him in disbelief. Mr. Worth was either a very cool customer or he was an utter fool. She assumed he was the former and not the latter. "I'm not

talking about something relatively innocuous like a corporate takeover."

"Neither am I."

She spelled it out for him. "I think there may be real
physical danger involved."

"So do I."

"But—?"

"There aren't any buts about it, Georgiana. I've had
far more experience with this kind of thing than you
have."

She didn't want to think about it, yet she had to.
"With what kind of thing? With cold-blooded murder?"

"Not murder per se. But I've certainly encountered
more than one life-threatening situation in my time."
Coleman Worth nonchalantly finished his beer and then
ventured, "You're not usually involved with murder, either, are you?"

"No," came out low and in a whisper.

"You need help."

"Yes."

That seemed to cinch it for him. "Whether you realize it or not, you've come to the right place."

Georgiana was bewildered. "Why would you want to
help me? You don't know anything about me."

"I know you're in trouble." She watched as he
crushed the empty beer can with his bare hand. "The
authorities might believe you acted in self-defense. Or
they might decide to book you on a charge of man-
slaughter or even second-degree murder." They both
heard her sharp intake of air. "Are you willing to risk
it?"

Of course she wasn't.

What if he was right? What if she was blamed for
something she didn't do? What if no one believed her

story but this man? What if they locked her up and threw away the key?

Georgiana sank back down into the designer chair she had just vacated. Unseeing, she stared straight ahead. "What should I do?"

"You should stay right where you are until I figure out what our next move is."

She swallowed the tears at the back of her throat. "I still don't understand why you're helping me."

There was an expression on Coleman Worth's handsome face that was too ruthless to be amusement. "Let's just say that I had my share of run-ins with the law when I was younger. I respect the law in principle, but I know damn well the innocent often go unprotected and the guilty frequently go free."

"That's the reason you're helping me?"

"It's one reason."

"What's another one?"

Dark blue eyes were raised to meet hers. "Lately life has become too predictable."

Georgiana didn't know whether to laugh or cry. "You're helping me because you're bored?"

He didn't dress up the truth. "That's about the size of it," he admitted.

Georgiana opened her mouth to tell the man from Texas exactly what she thought of him when there was a loud knock on the front door of his suite.

Coleman Worth raised his index finger to his lips and mouthed, "shhh." He pointed toward the master bedroom. She quickly got to her feet, steadied herself—her legs were the consistency of jelly—and slipped into the adjoining room.

The bedroom was pitch-black: there were no lights turned on and the blackout drapes were drawn in anticipation of tomorrow's fierce morning sun. Georgiana left the door ajar an inch or two and stepped back into the concealing cloak of darkness.

Coleman Worth whistled under his breath as he casually sauntered toward the door, bath towel hitched around his hips, crushed beer can in his hand.

He pressed the intercom button. "Yup."

"Coleman Worth?"

Cool as a cucumber he shot back with, "Who's asking?"

The gravelly baritone on the other end of the intercom replied, "Detective Mallory, Homicide."

The familiar voice of William Regen immediately interjected an apology. "Please forgive the intrusion at this late hour, Mr. Worth. The gentleman"—Regen sniffed and his tone clearly indicated that he considered the detective anything *but* a gentleman—"insists on speaking with you immediately."

Georgiana held her breath as Cole opened the door. There were two men standing in the hallway outside the presidential suite. One she recognized as William Regen. A distressed William Regen at that. The other she didn't know.

"Good evening, Mr. Worth," came the respectful greeting from the Sonoran's head butler.

"Regen." Then Coleman Worth turned his attention to the second man. "What can I do for you, Detective—?"

"Mallory." The no-nonsense officer got right to the point. "I was wondering if you heard anything tonight."

"Heard anything?"

The homicide detective clarified his question. "From the suite next to yours."

Cole shook his head. "The rooms at the Sonoran are supposed to be soundproof. I'd better not hear anything that goes on in the suite next to mine."

Detective Mallory was a bit of a bulldog. "Did you?"

"Nope."

The policeman was polite but persistent. "May I ask where you were this evening?"

"Now, see here, Officer—" sputtered William Regen, his face turning red.

Cole dismissed the objection voiced on his behalf. "It's all right, Regen. Detective Mallory is only doing his job. I was out most of the evening at a dinner party. Then I took a shower and I was just enjoying a cold beer." The towel around his hips and the empty can in his hand served to support his claim.

The detective in the rumpled suit asked, "Did you ever see or meet the guest next door?"

Cole was nonchalance itself. "Nope."

"I need to speak with one of the underbutlers. I was wondering if she might be here."

"She?"

Mallory flipped open a small notepad. "Female butler by the name of Georgiana Burne-Jones. Age: twenty-nine. Height: five feet six inches. Weight: approximately one hundred and twenty-five pounds. Light brown hair. Green eyes. Probably wearing a black tuxedo."

"Regen will tell you that he has been acting as my butler since my arrival at the Sonoran."

"It has been both a pleasure and a honor to serve Mr. Worth," piped up William Regen.

Coleman Worth leaned against the doorjamb. "What's this about, anyway?"

The detective dropped his voice to a more confidential level. "I'd like to ask Ms. Burne-Jones a few questions about the gentleman in the next suite."

"What about him?"

"Well, for one thing, he's dead."

"Did he die of natural causes?"

Detective Mallory shook his head. "Not unless you consider a steak knife through the heart a natural cause."

There was a certain irony in Coleman Worth's voice when he said, "Don't tell me you think the butler did it."

William Regen spoke up from behind the policeman. "Of course not. One of my staff would never do such a thing. It would go against everything that I've taught them about service."

"I wish I had your confidence, Mr. Regen," said Detective Mallory. He rummaged around in his suit jacket and produced a business card. "If you think of anything that might be of help, I'd appreciate a telephone call, Mr. Worth."

The head butler was crisp in his manner. "As Mr. Worth has already told you, he wouldn't have heard anything through the soundproof walls of the presidential suite."

A gray head nodded. "Just in case," he said and pressed his card into Cole's hand.

"Profuse apologies for the intrusion, Mr. Worth," William Regen said, clearly upset.

"It's okay, Regen."

"May I get you anything else tonight, sir?"

"Not a thing. Thanks all the same."

"Good night, then."

"Good night, gentlemen."

Coleman Worth closed the front door of the suite, turned the deadbolt and set the security lock.

Georgiana waited another minute or two—to make certain Mr. Regen and the detective were well on their way—before she ventured forth from the master bedroom.

She pitched her voice so only Cole could hear her.

"It didn't take the police long to get here."

"It never does when you don't want them to show up."

"They're looking for me."

"Yes."

Her lips were pressed tightly together. "You lied to protect me."

"I didn't actually lie," the man pointed out.

"You didn't tell the whole truth. That must make you some kind of accessory."

"I've been worse things."

"You could get into trouble." It was the understatement of the year.

"I've been in trouble before."

She was desperate enough to say, "Maybe I should turn myself in."

He dropped the crushed beer can into a nearby waste-paper basket. "I suppose you could."

Georgiana opened her mouth and swallowed air. "But you don't think it's a good idea."

A short silence followed.

"I think you're the only one who can decide what you have to do," he finally said.

Georgiana did her thinking out loud. "I'm afraid my fingerprints are on the murder weapon. I'm afraid the police will believe I had a motive. I'm afraid I'll be blamed. I'm plain afraid." She hesitated, then went on. "You volunteered to help me. Does the offer still stand?"

The man in the bath towel—she'd just realized that Coleman Worth was one of the best-looking men she had ever seen, in a rugged, larger-than-life kind of way—crossed his arms across his bare chest. "The offer still stands."

"What did you have in mind?"

"I'm leaving here early tomorrow morning. You could go with me," he proposed.

"Where are you going?"

Cole shrugged his broad shoulders. "I was thinking about heading out for parts unknown."

His statement surprised her. "Do you do this often?"

"Not often."

She was curious. "But you have done it before?"

"A few times."

She breathed in and out. "I'll bet you're good at being out there on your own."

He didn't blink. "Very good."

"I don't usually run away from my problems," she told him.

"Have your problems ever included being a murder suspect before?"

He had a point.

"No," she said.

"It'll buy us some time. Once we're safely away from here, I'll contact a friend of mine and have him look into Isherwood's background. Meanwhile, we'll head for a place where you'll be safe until we know who's who and what's what."

"Where is this safe haven?"

"North of Seattle."

"That's a long way from here."

"Yup."

"How do you know it's safe?"

"Because no one knows it exists besides me . . . and now you, of course."

From the frying pan into the fire: the thought once again crossed Georgiana's mind as she said to Coleman Worth, "I think we've just become partners in crime."

Four

"Hungry?"

His "partner in crime" shook her head, dislodging another stray wisp of light brown hair in the process.

Cole tried again. "Thirsty?"

Georgiana's voice was husky with weariness. "May I help myself to a glass of water?"

"Help yourself to anything you'd like." Cole briefly outlined his plans. "I'm going to throw some clothes on and make a telephone call." Hand splayed across his bare abdomen, he paused in the doorway between the living room and the master bedroom. "Just be sure to wash your glass thoroughly when you're finished, and wipe your fingerprints off any surface you touch."

Green eyes stared at him.

"You may think I'm being overly cautious, but I don't want to leave a shred of evidence behind that you were here in my suite," he admonished her.

"I see," she said emptily.

Cole had to make Georgiana Burne-Jones understand. "The longer it takes for the authorities to figure out that we're in this together, the longer it should take them to find us.''

Evidently she was beginning to get the picture. ''They'll be searching for a woman on her own, won't they?''

''Yes.'' After an interval he suggested, ''You might want to get some sleep. We'll be leaving early.''

Georgiana remained stoically immobile. ''How early?''

''Before dawn. I want to take advantage of the darkness when we have to make our way past the police or any Sonoran security guards posted outside.''

Ms. Burne-Jones suddenly appeared apprehensive.

Before he disappeared into his bedroom to dress, Cole felt compelled to reassure her. ''Don't worry. I'm very good in a crisis. We'll make it. I promise.''

He had always risen to the occasion before when the chips were down, he wanted to tell her. In fact, in many ways crisis management was his stock-in-trade.

Hell, he was never happier than when he was fighting his way through a corporate jungle, or pitting himself against the challenges of Mother Nature. And if he was completely honest with himself, he had to admit he was having the goddamned time of his life.

Cole wasted no time, however. He quickly pulled on a pair of shorts, followed by socks, jeans and a T-shirt. For some reason, he always thought better in jeans and a T-shirt.

When he returned to the living room—it couldn't have been more than five minutes since he'd left—Georgiana was perched on the edge of the sofa, sipping a glass of water.

He was straightforward with her. ''You look exhausted. Why don't you stretch out on the bed in the other room, or lie down right where you are? I'll wake you up when it's time to go.''

Her eyes were unfocused. ''I don't think I could fall asleep,'' she said in a flat voice.

Cole gave her a quick, penetrating look. ''You might surprise yourself.''

Apparently she decided he had a valid point. She kicked off her shoes and curled up on the sofa.

He had plans to make. He unlocked his executive briefcase and removed a special cellular telephone. He punched in a series of numbers and waited.

The telephone rang half a dozen times before a sleepy but familiar voice answered. ''Cole.''

''Martin.''

''How did business go today?''

''Predictably well.''

''What about the dinner party?''

''You were right about Quark's wife. She was well on her way to being smashed when she tried to corner me in the cactus garden between a prickly pear and a jumping cholla.''

''Ouch.''

''You can say that again,'' Cole related, allowing his mouth to curve up at the corners. He was barely exaggerating when he claimed, ''I was lucky to escape with my hide intact.''

''Not to mention your virtue.'' Once Martin Davis had stopped snickering he said, ''I did warn you.''

Cole expelled a breath of laughter. ''Yes, you did.''

''So you admit I was right about Mrs. Quark.''

''I admit you were right.'' His admission was only somewhat begrudgingly given.

''And I usually am right,'' his second-in-command stated without a trace of modesty.

"Which is why you're so valuable to Worth Industries and to me," Cole said.

Martin Davis might look like just another good ole boy from Texas, but he was as quick as a whip. Intelligent, too, and very quick. As Cole often reminded Martin, he was one shrewd sonofabitch.

Despite what many people in the corporate world had concluded, Martin Davis was not the yes-man at Worth Industries. As a matter of fact, he was one of the few people who had the smarts, the wherewithal and the guts to disagree with Cole. Maybe because he'd come up the hard way, too.

Cole rubbed his hand along the length of his jaw and paced back and forth in front of the massive stone fireplace—due to the lack of rain in the valley, there was a no-burn restriction in effect—as he spoke. "I've been thinking about taking some R & R."

"I'm not surprised," was the response from the other man. "You've been pushing yourself hard for the past six months without a single day off."

"With this business deal in Phoenix wrapped up, it seems like the perfect opportunity for me to get away," Cole said as if it were entirely logical.

"What can I do for you?"

That was one of the things Cole liked about Martin. The man never complained when he was called—and, no doubt, awakened from a sound sleep—in the middle of the night.

"I'll need a few things."

"Let me grab a pen." The sound of paper rustling could be heard. Then Martin returned and said, "Shoot."

Cole rattled off his list. "A blue pickup truck with an extended cab and a short bed. Extra gas tank filled and stowed in the rear. Supplies should include plenty of bottled water, food rations, first-aid kit, flashlight, a couple of canteens, a thermos of strong, black coffee, a secured cellular phone and some cash. Make sure the money is all in small bills, nothing larger than a twenty. And the usual clothes: jeans, shirts, a jacket, an extra pair of boots and a hat.''

''Anything else?''

''Two sleeping bags.''

''Two?''

''Two.''

''Consider it done,'' came the confident response.

That was another thing he liked about Martin Davis: he never told Cole something was impossible or that it couldn't be done.

Martin's next question was, ''When do you need the truck and the supplies ready?''

''In four hours.''

There was a low whistle on the other end of the telephone, and a raised eyebrow and a disbelieving look from the young woman stretched out on the designer sofa.

''Where do you want the truck left?''

Cole gave him directions. The location was on a quiet residential street near—but not too near—the Sonoran. ''Put the keys in the usual place.''

''Keys in the usual place,'' Martin repeated.

''I need another favor.''

''Name it.''

''I'd like you to check me out of the Sonoran tomorrow and pack up my belongings.''

''I'll fly in and see to it personally.''

''The name of the butler you'll be dealing with is William Regen.'' Cole sauntered across the room and gazed out at the starlit night. ''Try to make my abrupt departure seem reasonable, uneventful, like it's nothing out of the ordinary.''

"Like it's something an eccentric millionaire would do all the time?" was the rationale suggested by Martin.

"Exactly."

"Which means it's anything but ordinary." There was hesitation on the other end. "Are you on the secured phone?"

"Yup."

"Trouble?"

"Yup."

"Yours?"

Cole took a breath and reminded himself to relax his shoulders. "Indirectly."

"Ah . . ." It was a very telling *ah*. "Serious?"

He wasn't going to lie to Martin Davis. "Very."

"Yet you sound better than you have in weeks," said his friend. "Make that months." Cole could almost envision Martin sitting on the edge of his bed, shaking his prematurely balding head. "Trouble must agree with you."

"We both know it does."

"*It* does?" There was a moment of silence, followed by, "Or *she* does?"

Cole knew there was an unmistakable tone of excitement in his voice. "It's not like that."

Martin didn't press him. "Whatever you say, Cole."

He wasn't going into the subject of Georgiana Burne-Jones at this point in the game. "I'll call you with further instructions once I'm on the road."

Martin issued an unnecessary warning. "Watch your back."

"I intend to." Cole decided. "Put a little extra security under the front seat of the truck for me, too."

"One revolver under front seat."

"And a box of bullets."

"Box of bullets."

"Better make that two boxes."

"You're starting to make me nervous, Cole." They both knew it took a lot for Martin to get nervous.

"It's an uncertain world out there. We both know that. I'll be in some pretty desolate country. I may have to protect myself from all kinds of varmints."

"Two-legged as well as four-legged?"

"Not to mention those without any legs."

"I hate snakes," his second-in-command said vehemently.

"I know." Cole glanced down at the watch on his wrist. It was time to get a few other details taken care of. "Keep an eye on things for me while I'm gone."

"I always do."

"You're a good man, Martin."

"So are you, Cole. Take care of yourself."

Cole nodded. "Adios."

He punched another button, stowed the telephone in his briefcase and locked it up again. Then he placed the briefcase with the rest of the luggage Martin would collect on his behalf tomorrow.

When he finally checked to see if his guest needed anything, Cole was surprised—yet he really wasn't surprised—to discover that she had dozed off.

He stood over Georgiana Burne-Jones for several minutes and watched her. Asleep, she appeared younger, softer, prettier and definitely more vulnerable.

How old was she?

Twenty-nine, according to Detective Mallory.

Cole's first impressions were rarely wrong when it came to people. His gut instincts were telling him that Ms. Georgiana Burne-Jones had been in the wrong place at the wrong time. He didn't believe that she'd had anything to do with the death of Paul Isherwood. He did, however, think there was a whole lot more to Isherwood's mysterious death than met the eye.

He had his edge back. The short exchange with Detective Mallory had done wonders for his morale. He was definitely no longer bored. He'd get an hour or two of shut-eye himself after he saw to a couple of particulars.

Cole dug around in the kitchen until he found what he needed under the sink: a spray cleaner and a sponge. Then, starting with the doorknob of the service entrance, he wiped everything clean.

If for some reason—maybe by sheer process of elimination—the police suspected that Ms. Burne-Jones, the missing butler, may have hidden in his rooms, Cole was going to make certain they found nothing to support that supposition. Not one fingerprint. Not one speck of blood. Not a single thread of evidence to indicate she had ever been there.

The last item he took care of was the kitchen towel he had used to wash her hands. He rinsed the blood out and buried it under a dozen other damp towels at the bottom of the hamper in his bathroom. The maid would see to it first thing in the morning.

He did a thorough job.

He was a thorough man.

It was one of the reasons he was where he was today in the game of big business.

Cole softly whistled an old country western song under his breath. The title ran over and over again in his head: "It's All in the Game."

He loved the challenge. He loved the game. Despite their short acquaintance, he could almost hear Ms. Georgiana Burne-Jones correcting him in that elegant and slightly husky voice of hers: "But this isn't a game, Mr. Worth."

"Cole," he would have to remind the lady for the umpteenth time.

"This isn't a game, Cole," she would insist.

That was when he'd have to disagree with her. "It's all a game, Georgiana."

She awoke with a start.

Her heart was pounding. Her throat was dry. Her mouth tasted of stale whiskey. There was a sheen of perspiration covering her skin: her hair was slightly damp at her nape and there was a trickle of sweat sliding between her shoulder blades and down into the indentation at the small of her back.

For a heartbeat or two Georgiana didn't recognize, couldn't recall, wondered where she was.

Then it came all flooding back.

She groaned aloud. She was wide awake and yet she was still caught up in a nightmare.

She pushed herself into a sitting position on the sofa and peered out at the darkness. Now she remembered. She was in the presidential suite. Coleman Worth's suite. And in a few short, ugly minutes last night her entire life had been changed: irrevocably, without her consent, without her knowledge, against her wishes.

Her hands clenched into fists. It shouldn't have happened. She had simply been doing her job. A job she was proud of. A job she was very good at. She had been an innocent bystander; she had become a victim. It wasn't fair.

Life wasn't fair. Surely she had learned that lesson the hard way a long, long time ago.

Georgiana sighed and straightened.

A deep masculine voice came softly through the night. "You're awake."

She nearly jumped out of her skin. She hadn't heard Coleman Worth or seen him or sensed that he was even in the room. He was very quiet for a big man.

"I'm awake," she said, tasting the words.

Somehow his Texas drawl was more discernible in the dark: his voice was deep and his words slowly spaced. "Do you know where the powder room is located?"

"Yes."

"Can you find your way there without turning any lights on?"

"Yes."

"Then why don't you use the facilities and wash up before we head out?"

"I'll be careful about the fingerprints," she promised. Then she wondered, "What time is it?"

"Three-thirty."

She'd slept for several hours after informing Coleman Worth that she couldn't possibly fall asleep.

"I haven't thanked you yet, Mr. Worth," she said after taking care of her personal comforts.

"We're going to be together for the foreseeable future. I don't think we should stick to the formalities. I certainly have every intention of calling you Georgiana. Unless you have a nickname."

"I don't . . . Cole."

"Here's the plan, then."

She listened.

"I'll go scout around and locate where the security guards and police are on duty. Then I'll come back for you."

"That's the whole plan?"

"Not entirely. It'll help that you're dressed in black

and wearing sensible shoes,'' he said, as much to himself
as to her.

''Why?''

''We're going to cut through the nature preserve behind the Sonoran.''

Georgiana shuddered. She knew what that meant.

Cole went on, ''We'll move from scrub brush to
scrub brush, palm tree to palm tree, sticking to the shadows, making our way in the dark and hoping we don't
run into any two-legged or four-legged trouble.''

''Or the kind that slithers.''

''Rattlesnakes will at least give us warning, which is
more than I can say for some predators.''

Georgiana didn't want to think about what or who
those predators might be.

''We won't speak unless it's absolutely necessary and
only then in whispers. If you have any questions it
would be a good idea to ask them now.''

She was tired. She was hungry. She was strangely
chilled. And she was afraid. Yet Georgiana couldn't
think of a single question except why she had put her
life and her future in this man's hands.

Because her own had been trembling and covered
with blood when she had looked down at them a few
short hours ago.

Because Coleman Worth had believed her story. Because he was willing to help her. Because he had the
skills to survive out there. Because he had the means to
get them whatever they needed and wherever they
wanted to go.

He had telephoned someone named Martin and ordered a fully equipped pickup truck delivered to a pre-
arranged destination in the middle of the night.

Coleman Worth possessed power in ways she could
only begin to imagine.

"No questions?"

She licked her lips. "Just one."

"What is it?"

"You won't forget to come back for me, will you?"

A masculine hand gently brushed across her cheek. A masculine voice took on an almost caressing quality. "Don't worry, Georgiana. I'll be back for you. Just remember: stay close, stay quiet and do exactly what I tell you."

"Yes, Cole."

Then she watched as he opened the French doors that led onto the patio, stepped outside, closed the doors behind him, eased himself over the wrought-iron railing and disappeared into the night.

Five

It was just like the old days, Cole told himself as he crouched down and tried to make his six-foot-two-inch frame as unobtrusive as possible. Only this time he wasn't running away from a drunken foster parent hell-bent on beating him into submission, or an irate restaurant owner that he'd stolen used cooking grease from to sell for food.

He had been fourteen years old at that point in his life and quite literally starving. Stealing had been the means to a very good end: his survival.

This time he was going to be the knight in shining armor coming to the rescue of the damsel in distress.

Only maybe she was the one who had rescued him . . . from boredom.

Cole moved quickly and quietly for a man his size. It was a skill he'd learned at a relatively young age. He flattened himself against the wall. He waited and he watched.

Patience paid off.

He spotted an unmarked police car in the parking lot behind the main building: the standard-issue American sedan stuck out like a sore thumb among the Mercedes and the Range Rovers and the sleek, fancy sports cars.

Cole put his nose in the air.

Cigarette smoke. Nearby. Then he detected the tell-tale crunch of a shoe on crushed gravel as a cigarette butt was tossed to the ground and snuffed out underfoot.

He made his way in the opposite direction along the back of the hotel, looking for some kind—any kind—of cover between the building and a huge mound of boulders fifty yards away.

The scent of orange blossoms permeated the air. Suddenly the wind off the desert picked up considerably, tossing the fronds of the palm trees to and fro against the night sky. It was a bit of good luck: the sound of the wind would cover any noise he and Georgiana made.

Cole glanced up at the slim sliver of silvery light in the sky. Fortunately it was close to a new moon tonight. A full moon would have complicated things.

He fixed the landmarks in his memory.

Building to palm tree.

Palm tree to giant cactus.

Cactus to boulders.

Then over the rocky hill, down the other side, through a natural area, over a fence, behind an office building, across the street to a gas station, then around the corner to the pickup truck.

Cole closed his eyes and he could see the layout clearly in his mind's eye. It was a unique talent that had benefited him more than once in his day-to-day business as well as in his life. He had even been told by a grand master of the game that if he had any interest—which he didn't—he would have made a world-class chess player.

Chess wasn't his game.

Business was his game.

And sometimes life was a game.

Now it was time to go back for Ms. Burne-Jones. He hoped like hell she wasn't going to turn out to be a liability on this mission.

Cole materialized from the shadows on the patio outside his suite, knowing that Georgiana had neither seen nor heard him, nor, for that matter, even sensed his presence.

He opened the patio door, stepped inside and closed it soundlessly behind him. "Are you ready to go?"

"Yes," she whispered. Then she asked in a tension-filled tone, "Did you see anything?"

He told her the facts. "There's an unmarked police car in the parking lot behind the building and at least one officer in the bushes alongside the stone walk."

"What'll we do?"

"Avoid them."

There was concern in her voice. "I'm serious, Cole."

"So am I, Georgiana." He supposed he'd better reassure her. "You won't have anything to worry about as long as you stick to me like glue. If I stop, you stop. If I run, you run. And don't speak unless it's an emergency."

"I won't."

Adrenaline shot through Cole's veins like a narcotic. He was reveling in the feeling of matching wits—or guts—with whoever was out there. He was in his element, and he was eager to get started.

"We'll be moving fast and silent. Building to palm tree. Palm tree to giant cactus. Cactus to boulders. Then over the hill, down the other side, through a natural area, over a fence, behind an office building, across the street to a gas station, then around the corner to the pickup truck. You got that?"

He could hear the woman swallow nervously, followed by a somewhat tentative, "Yes."

"Any questions?"

"No."

He gave the order. "Let's go."

They moved quickly, quietly, without speaking, without making a single unnecessary sound. Darkness was their friend. They moved from shadow to shadow along the patio. Cole went over the railing first and Georgiana followed. Then they skirted the length of the building, making their way to a spot directly across from a grove of palm trees, palo verde and the red dash of blooming ocotillo. Beyond the grove was their intermediate target: a giant saguaro, arms raised skyward.

They moved stealthily. They blended in with the night. They saw no one and no one saw them. There was a dark shadow by the trunk of the first palm tree. Cole sprinted for it and flattened himself against its rough surface.

He turned his head. Georgiana had kept up. She was right beside him. He could hear her soft breathing.

Cole went down on his haunches and peered around the tree toward the saguaro and the small mountain of boulders beyond. This would be the tricky part: Once they left the protection of the palms, there wasn't much cover for at least twenty or thirty yards.

The ground was damp from the automatic sprinkling system that was timed to turn on at night. He tugged on the pants leg of her tuxedo and Georgiana hunched down beside him.

Camouflage.

He dipped his fingertips into what passed for mud in Arizona and began to smear the stuff in broad strokes down the sides of his face, across his cheekbones and along his forehead. Then he did the same to Georgiana before giving her the thumbs-up and motioning toward the saguaro. She nodded her head in understanding.

They were about to make a run for it when they heard a crunch in the nearby gravel.

Cole's hand shot out to stop her.

He raised his index finger to his lips, then pointed in the general direction of the sound.

There!

Georgiana froze. Apparently she had spotted something or someone as well. A human form materialized from the shadows not more than thirty feet from where they were crouched. Not knowing if it was a security guard, or a policeman, or even a hotel guest taking a very late—or a very early—stroll, they didn't dare move.

They waited until whoever it was had disappeared around the corner of the next building. Then Cole put his lips to her ear and urgently whispered, "Now."

He straightened and took off, hoping that she would be right behind him. When he reached the saguaro, he found she was beside him and barely out of breath.

This wasn't the time or the place to linger, however. The pile of boulders was next on the agenda.

Cole leaned toward her. "Ready?"

"Ready."

"Go!"

They ran side by side for the last twenty yards, then threw themselves against the north face of the rocks, safely out of sight of the elegant resort behind them.

Cole heard his companion's sigh of relief.

He couldn't blame her, but it was premature to be genuinely relieved. They'd made it out of the building into the palm trees, around the saguaro and behind the boulders without being seen. They still had a long way to go before daylight.

Cole tapped her on the shoulder and pointed toward the hill. They took off again. Georgiana followed without speaking.

Cole heard her stumble once or twice in the dark and realized that her night vision might not be as keen as his. He stopped and held out his hand to her.

She slipped hers trustingly into his.

It was the damnedest thing, Cole realized as they hiked across the desert terrain hand in hand. He was feeling downright protective of a young woman he had known for only a few short hours. Not only that, but he had staked his reputation, and a few other important things, on the belief that she was innocent of a gruesome murder.

This wasn't the time or place for reflection. He had done what he had done. He'd had his reasons and they had seemed like good reasons at the time.

For that matter, they still did.

They started across the natural ravine. Thank God there hadn't been any rain in the valley for weeks. Flash floods could be dangerous, even life-threatening, in the desert. They often occurred without any warning, as more than one unfortunate soul had discovered.

Cole gripped her hand. "Fence up ahead."

As he held the barbed wire down with his cowboy boot, she stepped over at the lowest point. The lighted street was no more than ten feet in front of them. Digging into the back pocket of his jeans, Cole took out a handkerchief.

He offered it to Georgiana. "You might want to wipe some of that mud off your face."

"Thank you."

She did the best job she could without a mirror or any water and handed the handkerchief back to him. Cole ran it over his own face a couple of times.

"We're going to walk to that small office complex, then across the street to the gas station and around the corner to where the pickup truck will be parked."

"What if the pickup isn't there?" Georgiana asked, measuring out her words.

"It will be."

She drew her delicately marked brows together. "You have a lot of faith in Martin, don't you?"

"Martin Davis has been my second-in-command at Worth Industries from the beginning. Let's just say that I have countless reasons to have confidence in him."

Cole could also have told her that Martin was one of the few people who had never let him down, that Martin was the closest thing he'd ever had to a friend, but he didn't.

His attention reverted to the business at hand. "Once we reach the pickup, I want you to remain inconspicuous."

"Remain inconspicuous."

"Just stand there by the truck while I retrieve the keys and unlock the cab."

"Just stand by the truck."

"Let's go."

The brand-new bright blue pickup truck was parked precisely where Cole's friend had promised it would be parked. It was only when she released an extended sigh of relief that Georgiana realized she had been holding her breath.

"There it is!" she exclaimed, grabbing Cole's forearm and squeezing hard.

He was more pragmatic. "The keys will be in a small magnetic box stashed under the right front bumper. As soon as I get the door unlocked on the driver's side, I want you to climb into the cab, scoot across to the passenger's seat and crouch down until I get us away from here.''

''Yessir.''

Georgiana imagined that Coleman Worth was used to giving orders and used to having them unquestioningly obeyed. There was a commanding presence about Cole that set him apart from the ordinary man . . . and set her teeth on edge.

However, under the circumstances, she could hardly refuse to do as he instructed.

The keys were located and the door unlocked. Georgiana stepped up into the pickup, quickly scrambled across to the far side of the bench seat, slid down until even the top of her head wasn't visible over the dash and waited for Cole to get in.

He started the engine and took off down the street.

''We did it!'' she exclaimed triumphantly and hugged herself.

''So far, so good,'' he allowed on a more conservative note, reaching behind the front seat for his cowboy hat and settling it comfortably on his head.

The look was a natural one for Coleman Worth, Georgiana realized. But then, the man was from Texas. He'd probably been born wearing a Stetson.

Once her initial exhilaration had died down, she thought to inquire, ''Where are we?''

''On Pima Road heading north toward Carefree,'' he replied. ''I'd like to get away from the city before daybreak.''

Georgiana leaned her head back against the leather seat and allowed her eyes to shut for a minute.

There was an unreal, even a surreal, quality to this entire escapade. In less than twenty-four hours, her entire life had been turned upside down. She had gone from being a respectable and hardworking young professional to a murder suspect. She had barged into the private suite of a handsome multimillionaire and blurted out her whole sordid story to him. Now they were on the run together from the law and heaven knows who else.

All of a sudden it occurred to Georgiana that the police might not be the only ones after them.

Her eyes flew open; they were wide with alarm. "Is anyone following us?"

Cole appeared almost blasé. He didn't even glance in the rearview mirror. "Not a soul."

She wasn't convinced. "Are you certain?"

He nodded, swept off his cowboy hat, ran the back of his hand along his forehead and then resettled the Stetson on his head. "I've had one eye on our backs since we left the Sonoran."

Were they thinking the same thing?

"You aren't just watching out for the police, are you?" Georgiana ventured.

"Nope," he confirmed.

"Someone else could be following us."

"They could be."

She blurted it out all at once. "I'm so sorry I got you involved in this mess, Cole."

The man behind the wheel reached out and patted her arm. "I'm not." Then he bit off an expletive.

Georgiana didn't want to ask him what was wrong, but she knew she had to. "What is it?"

"Roadblock straight ahead."

"What'll we do?"

"Make a U-turn," Cole said as he spun the steering wheel.

Georgiana realized that the loud sound she suddenly heard was the pounding of her own heart. It served no purpose to panic. She had to stay calm. She had to think . . . and quickly. "Are we still on Pima?"

Cole nodded.

She wetted her lips with her tongue and directed, "Turn west at the next cross street."

The man's tone was skeptical. "Would you like to tell me what you have in mind?"

"We're going to take the back way."

"Where?"

"As you'd originally planned: Carefree."

The sideways glance of deep blue eyes was disconcertingly shrewd. "Who do you know in Carefree?"

"Someone who will help us."

"Can they be trusted?"

"Implicitly."

Cole stared straight ahead. "Are you sure?"

"I'm sure."

"Are you willing to stake our lives on it?"

"I am."

"Mind if I ask who is it?"

"Crick."

Dark brows momentarily drew together. "Crick?"

"The gentleman's name is Alfred Crick and he is a very old friend of the family."

Six

"Miss Georgiana," greeted the distinguished, white-haired gentleman with the crisp English accent who opened the front door of the traditional Santa Fe–style house.

"Good morning, Crick."

He patted ineffectually at his tousled hair with one hand, while he attempted to straighten the collar of his bathrobe with the other. "Please forgive my appearance."

Cole didn't see anything wrong with the man's appearance. He was dressed in pajamas and a bathrobe, which was to be expected at five o'clock in the morning.

Georgiana tried to observe the proprieties as well, but her lips were turning white and she was trembling with fatigue. "I'm the one who should apologize for calling on you at this unforgivable hour, Crick. I'm sure we awakened you."

He hastened to put her fears to rest. "Not at all, Miss Georgiana. I'm still an early riser. I could never seem to get out of the habit even once I retired."

She swayed on her feet. Cole reached out and steadied her with a supportive hand under the elbow. "I'm sorry I couldn't telephone ahead to let you know I was coming," she said.

"*Mi casa, su casa,*" Crick proclaimed with a rather bad Spanish accent. Then the older man gave Cole a thorough looking-over. "Who might this gentleman be?"

There was exhaustion in Georgiana's voice. "Forgive me, Crick. I'm forgetting my manners. My only excuse is that it's been a very long and a very difficult night." She took a sustaining breath. "This is Coleman Worth. Cole, this gentleman is Mr. Alfred Crick."

Cole's Stetson was already clasped in his hand before he gave an acknowledging nod and repeated, "Mr. Crick."

"Just Crick will do." Shrewd eyes assessed him from the toes of his well-worn cowboy boots to the top of his hatless head. "Do you happen to be *the* Coleman Worth, sir?"

"I'm Coleman Worth."

"The Texas businessman?"

"Yes."

"Then I'm familiar with your name and reputation, Mr. Worth. I believe I read in the business section of the newspaper that you were here in the valley this week wrapping up a major merger with another company." Crick retreated several steps into the spacious Spanish-tiled foyer of his home. "Won't you please come in?" Then he added, "Frankly you both look like you could use a cup of coffee."

Cole glanced back at the pickup parked in the drive-way. "This may sound like a strange request, Crick, but could I pull my truck into your garage?"

Alfred Crick didn't so much as blink. "Of course you may, Mr. Worth. I'll open the garage door for you."

"Thanks."

The gentleman's attention reverted to Georgiana. "You come along with me, Miss Georgiana. I'm going to make you a cup of my special coffee."

After the automatic door had been raised, Cole pulled the pickup loaded with their supplies into the immaculate garage of the immaculate and beautiful house.

"Nice place you have here, Crick," he commented as he sauntered into the equally immaculate kitchen.

"I was very fortunate that in my maturity, Mr. Worth, I found and married a woman that I loved very much. It was icing on the cake that Mildred was also comfortably well off. She was a widow, you see, and had inherited a sizable estate from her first husband . . . although we never spoke of it, of course."

Of course.

Crick paused and counted aloud as he measured out precisely ten scoops of ground coffee beans into the sleek black cappuccino machine on the kitchen counter. He reached into the cupboard above his head for three porcelain mugs, a matching sugar bowl and a creamer.

It was only then that he resumed his story. "Since there were no children or other relatives, I became Mildred's family." Alfred Crick hesitated for a moment, perhaps wondering if saying any more would be considered bad form. "When my dear wife passed away a year ago"—his aging voice cracked with emotion—"I discovered she had left me everything."

Georgiana reached out and patted the old man's hand in a sympathetic manner.

Watery eyes fixed on her. "Why didn't . . . why don't you allow me to help you financially?"

She was gentle with him, but firm. "We both know why."

Suddenly Crick changed the subject and became all

business. "Have you two had any breakfast?"

Georgiana glanced up at the clock on the wall. "It's barely five o'clock."

"Hungry?"

Her answer was honest. "Starved."

As their host began to squeeze fresh orange juice, he glanced back over his shoulder. "You look a little the worse for wear, if you don't mind my saying so, Miss Georgiana."

She smiled at him with great affection. "You'll never stop calling me that, will you?"

Crick shook his head as he reached for three juice glasses. "I'm afraid it's too ingrained now. There's no sense in trying to teach this old dog any new tricks."

He set a small glass of juice in front of Georgiana, then watched with astonishment as she raised it to her mouth and drank it down in a single gulp.

Cole felt compelled to offer an explanation. "I don't think Georgiana had any dinner last night."

"Or a shower," she declared, apparently somewhat revitalized by the fresh orange juice.

"Why don't you use the facilities in the guest room, while I make breakfast and become acquainted with Mr. Worth? You know where to find everything you need."

"Thank you. I think I will," Georgiana said, accepting a mug of coffee from him.

Crick stared at her wrinkled and mud-streaked tuxedo. "I don't think any of Mildred's clothes would be suitable for you—she was half a foot shorter than you are—but I happen to have several boxes of jumbo I've been collecting for the church bazaar. Why don't you dig around and see if anything will fit you?"

As she left the kitchen, Cole called after her, "Make it jeans and a plain shirt if you can. We want to appear as normal and as inconspicuous as possible."

She indicated that she'd heard him and then inquired of Crick, "When is breakfast?"

"Thirty minutes," he replied. "That should give you plenty of time to clean up and to dig about for that pair of jeans Mr. Worth has sartorially recommended."

"I'll be back in twenty-five minutes," she promised before disappearing around the corner.

Cole watched her go and realized—to his amazement and bewilderment—how empty the room became the moment Georgiana left it. Admittedly she'd barely been out of his sight for more than a few minutes since that auspicious first meeting last night, but he couldn't imagine why he would feel her absence so profoundly.

Meanwhile Alfred Crick was busily preparing a breakfast that was going to consist of scrambled eggs, Canadian bacon and slices of perfectly browned toast. He rummaged around in his well-ordered refrigerator and emerged with a pot of marmalade.

"May I help?" Cole offered.

Crick was concise. "You may sit and talk to me."

Cole hung his hat on the back of a kitchen chair and sat down. "What about?"

"Miss Georgiana."

He decided to take it nice and easy until he got a better feel for the situation. "What about Georgiana?"

Melon, bananas and strawberries were expertly sliced into a large bowl. "How long have you known her?"

Cole glanced down at his watch. "Six hours." He looked up. "More or less."

The kitchen knife hovered for an instant in midair. "Six hours? You mean only since last night?"

"That's what I mean."

Crick turned his eyes on Cole in silent rebuke. "Miss Georgiana looks exhausted."

He told the gentleman the truth. "She is exhausted.

As far as I can ascertain the only sleep she's had was two hours on the sofa in my suite at the Sonoran.''

Alfred Crick summed up the situation. ''She hasn't slept. She hasn't eaten. She is still dressed in her professional uniform, although I must say that her tuxedo is uncharacteristically wrinkled and dirty. She has what appears to be mud smeared on her face.'' His voice sounded uneasy. ''But what bothers me the most is the expression in her eyes. She looks almost . . . haunted.''

Cole allowed his eyes to narrow to slits. ''*Hunted* is more like it,'' he said.

''Hunted by whom?''

He didn't like the answer he had to give Alfred Crick. ''The police, for one.''

The gentleman rinsed off the paring knife, carefully dried the sharp stainless steel blade, returned the knife to its appropriate slot in the butcher-block container beside the sink and then inquired, ''What is this all about, Mr. Worth?''

''Please call me Cole.'' He knew his own voice was husky with weariness. ''I think Georgiana should tell you herself what's happened in the past few hours. But let's just say that the lady needed help and I was the nearest help at hand.''

A mug of strong black coffee was placed in front of Cole. ''I think Miss Georgiana was very lucky you were the man at hand,'' Crick said distinctly.

''Thank you, sir.'' It was a vote of confidence. ''Now may I ask you a question?''

There was only the slightest hesitation before, ''Yes.''

Cole watched over the rim of his coffee mug. ''Why do you call her Miss Georgiana?''

A certain amount of surprise registered on the aging face. ''She hasn't told you?''

Cole's mouth twisted. "We haven't had time for that kind of chitchat."

"You don't know much about her, then, do you?"

"Enough."

That brought a raised eyebrow from Alfred Crick.

Cole explained, based on the experiences of the past few hours, his gut instincts and plain, old common sense. "Georgiana Burne-Jones seems to be a decent, honest and hardworking young woman. She isn't a whiner. We hiked through some pretty rough country last night and she never once complained, or faltered, or fell behind. She was very reluctant to involve me in her problems from the start. And I'd say that she's more vulnerable than she would like people to know."

Crick sighed. "That's Miss Georgiana."

"Which brings us back to my question. Why do you call her Miss Georgiana?"

Crick said, "Because for the first fourteen years of her life, I served as butler to her family."

Cole was trying to put two and two together and come up with four, but he wasn't succeeding. "Apparently that was before you met and married your wife."

"Marriage to Mildred came much later."

"Mind if I ask what happened?"

"To the Burne-Joneses?"

Cole nodded.

"There was—shall we discreetly say—a drastic change in the family's fortunes."

Tired as he was, Cole caught on quickly. "The Burne-Joneses lost their money."

Crick was blunt. "Every cent of it."

He wanted to ask why. He wanted to know how.

The former butler continued. "Miss Georgiana's parents were . . . are singular people."

"Singular in what way?"

"Although they both grew up with a great deal of money, they had—I suspect they still have—absolutely no concept of how to make money, how to invest money or how to preserve money. All they knew, or know, is how to spend money."

"Only now they don't have any money to spend."

"For the past fifteen years Maud and Jeremy Burne-Jones have been reduced to living like ordinary people. But, believe me, they aren't in the least ordinary."

"So Miss Georgiana became just plain Georgiana."

Apparently Crick did not take kindly to that comment, although Cole had meant it without any malice. "She will never be just plain Georgiana," he stated.

"You're absolutely right, of course." Cole took another drink from the coffee mug in front of him. He shook his head; the irony of the situation did not escape him. "Now she works as a butler and you live like a millionaire."

"I volunteered on several occasions to help Miss Georgiana, but she wouldn't hear of it. All I could do is teach her what I knew about being a butler." Crick added as an afterthought, "And, of course, I gave her a job reference."

Cole stiffened. "Did you give Georgiana a reference when she went to work for the Sonoran?"

"Yes."

"Damn."

"I beg your pardon, sir."

"Sorry, Crick. It's just that they'll make the connection sooner or later. Probably sooner."

"Who will?"

"The police."

"What you're saying is that they'll connect Miss Georgiana with me and they'll come looking for her here."

"That's what I'm saying." Cole drained the last of his coffee. "I'm afraid we won't be able to accept your hospitality for long. We'll basically have to eat and run."

Crick's mouth turned down at the corners. "The situation is serious, then?"

"It is."

The sideways glance was disconcertingly shrewd. "Do you know what you're doing, Mr. Worth?"

He thought so. He assumed so. He sure as hell hoped so. "Yes. I do."

Alfred Crick's only concern was for Georgiana. "You'll look after her?"

"Don't worry. I'll look after her." It was a solemn promise, Cole realized.

Crick apparently felt it necessary to tell him, "Miss Georgiana is very bright and very sweet and not nearly as tough as she would like people to believe. It's just that she's been hurt and she's been let down by the people she trusted most."

"Her parents."

"Yes."

Cole knew how she felt. The big difference between them was that Georgiana Burne-Jones at least knew who her parents were. Which is more than he could say for himself.

"Where are her parents now?"

"They live in a retirement community down by Tucson. They live well by normal standards. But there are no more big houses. No more staff. No more Rolls-Royces parked in the driveway."

"They live like most people."

"And they resent the fact. Maud is, or was, a society matron and Jeremy supposedly was, and supposedly still is, a poet. Maud was landed gentry and grew up in England. I came to this country with her when she married Jeremy Jones.'' He added as if it weren't in the least bit odd, ''I was a wedding gift from her parents.''

''You're not joking, are you?''

Crick shook his head.

Then something else occurred to Cole. ''Do they somehow blame Georgiana for the family's misfortunes?''

Alfred Crick thought about it for perhaps half a minute. ''I don't think they blame Miss Georgiana, but I do think they somehow expect her to restore their fortunes.''

''How?''

''The old-fashioned way, of course.''

Cole speared him with a long stare.

The gentleman explained, ''By marrying well.''

The sound of approaching footsteps brought their conversation to an abrupt end as Georgiana rejoined them.

''I could smell something delicious all the way upstairs,'' she exclaimed.

The kitchen was filled with the enticing aromas of brewed coffee and toasted bread, melted butter and orange marmalade, bacon and eggs.

Cole quickly spoke up. ''I see you found some clothes that fit.''

Georgiana did a pirouette in the middle of the kitchen and glanced in his direction for approval. ''How do I look?''

Her face was scrubbed clean. Her hair was wet and shiny and pulled back into a girlish ponytail. She was wearing jeans that clung to her derriere and legs in all the right places, and a plain white oxford-cloth shirt with the sleeves rolled up to the elbows.

Cole smiled in spite of himself. ''You look like you

couldn't be a day over sixteen. I'll no doubt be arrested for contributing to the delinquency of a minor.''

She smiled back at him. ''The important thing is, do I fade into the woodwork, so to speak, with this outfit?''

There was no way Georgiana Burne-Jones would ever fade into anything, he decided.

''Breakfast is served,'' Crick announced. ''Then we're going to have a little chat, Miss Georgiana, and you're going to tell me what has brought you to my house at the crack of dawn.''

Georgiana told him everything.

She'd always been able to confide in Crick in ways she could never talk to her parents. She told him the details of the night before and Coleman Worth sat quietly, sipping his coffee and listening, his dark blue eyes rarely leaving her face.

Once she had related the whole sordid affair, Crick reached across the kitchen table, patted her hand and commiserated, ''I am so sorry, my dear. What can I do to help?''

''You've already helped immeasurably,'' she said to him, finishing her coffee. ''You have fed me, clothed me, listened to me and revived my spirits.''

''I'm sorry to say that we can't stay,'' Cole spoke up. ''This is one of the first places the authorities will look for you, since Crick's name is on record at the Sonoran.''

''I'd forgotten all about the job reference you gave me,'' she admitted. Her voice was low and fervent. ''I hate to ask you to lie, Crick, but could you tell the police, or anyone one else who might ask, that you haven't seen us?''

His voice quavered. ''Of course, my dear.''

Coleman Worth made a suggestion. ''Why don't you

two talk for a few more minutes while I check the supplies in the pickup?'' He glanced down at her. ''You might see if there are several more changes of clothing in Crick's jumbo.''

''I've already picked out two more pairs of jeans and several shirts,'' she informed him. ''But I'll need to stop somewhere along the way and buy a few of the necessities.''

Alfred Crick spoke up. ''If you're going to complete your disguise as a cowgirl, Miss Georgiana, may I suggest that you wear a bit more makeup than usual?''

''Good idea,'' Cole agreed.

Crick had another suggestion. ''And since you possess a facility for languages, I think you should have Mr. Worth instruct you in the finer points of his Texas accent.''

''Another good idea,'' the big man said as he stood in the doorway between the kitchen and the garage. ''We'll also need to get rid of your tuxedo.''

''I'm going to the dry cleaner's later today with several suits of mine. I can include the tuxedo with my things. Any articles of clothing can be left for thirty days before they notify you to reclaim them.''

''You're an amazing man, Crick,'' Cole said.

''Isn't it you Americans who have a saying about that?''

Cole raised a quizzical brow. ''A saying?''

Their gracious host said, ''Something about not wanting to be up a crick without a paddle.''

Georgiana didn't have the heart to tell the sweet old man that the expression was ''up a creek.''

Once Cole had gone to see to the truck, Alfred Crick asked her, ''Do you know where you're headed?''

''North.'' She quickly folded up the extra clothing and stuffed it in a small valise he had insisted she take with her. "Do you think I'm doing the right thing?"

Sad and concerned eyes watched her. "I think it was your great misfortune to be in the wrong place at the wrong time."

She had to ask him. "Is Cole the wrong man?"

"I don't know. Maybe he's the right man and the wrong man." A question followed. "Do you require any money?"

"No." Georgiana suddenly remembered the three thousand dollars still stashed inside the breast pocket of her tuxedo. "There's an envelope containing some money in my tuxedo jacket. You might want to put it someplace safe."

Cole appeared in the doorway. "It's time."

Alfred Crick pressed a piece of paper into her hands. "I am acquainted with a wonderful couple who would be only too happy to help you out along the way. I've jotted down their name and address for you. Just tell them Crick sent you."

"Take care of yourself until we meet again," Georgiana said, fighting back tears.

"I will, my dear girl," the gentleman said, using an endearment Cole was certain he had never voiced before.

"Thank you for everything." Cole shook the man's hand. "Adios."

"Godspeed," Crick called to them as the blue pickup backed out of his garage and headed north.

Seven

"Do you know the difference between an optimist and a pessimist?" Cole asked her in an attempt to lighten their mood after they drove away from Alfred Crick's and were headed north on Highway 17 toward the Bradshaw Mountains and the town of Prescott, Arizona.

Georgiana managed to shake her head, but he could see that she was struggling to maintain her composure.

Cole gave it his best shot, although he'd never been much good at telling jokes. "An optimist thinks that life is one damned thing after another."

"And a pessimist?" the ponytailed woman beside him mumbled, obviously voicing the words with difficulty.

Cole frowned and drew his eyebrows together. He wished he'd never started, but he supposed he had to finish the joke now. He delivered the punch line. "A pessimist believes it's the same damned thing over and over again."

The resulting smile from his audience of one was fleeting.

"Why don't you close your eyes and try to get some

sleep?'' he suggested for the third time in the last half
hour.

"I couldn't," came the cryptic response.

"Why not?"

"It wouldn't be fair."

Cole's hands shifted on the steering wheel as he
tensed and then relaxed his back muscles. "To who?"

"To you."

Georgiana Burne-Jones was a hard woman to figure.
"How do you figure that?" he asked.

She stared straight ahead almost as if it were necessary to their forward progress that she keep her eyes
glued to the road. "Because you had even less sleep last
night than I did."

"Maybe I need less sleep than you do," he said, raising his chin a fraction.

It might be true.

It probably was true.

"You've been doing all the driving as well," she
pointed out as if that was a factor in the equation.

"We've gone less than seventy-five miles."

Georgiana took her eyes off the highway only long
enough to give him a quick, sideways glance. "Is that
all?"

"Yup."

"I thought we'd gone farther."

"Nope."

She exhaled on a drawn-out sigh. "It seems farther."

Hell, to him seventy-five miles was like a leisurely
drive around the block.

"I once jumped in a pickup truck and drove from
Wichita Falls, Texas, to Tijuana, Mexico," Cole said,
reminiscing . . . or as close to reminiscing as he ever allowed himself to get.

"By yourself?"

"By myself."

"Why?"

"I wanted to see the ocean," he told her.

"Hadn't you seen the ocean before?"

"Nope."

Georgiana lifted her ponytail off her neck. When she lowered it again, her hair was like deep shimmering gold—the color had appeared darker last night; but, then, everything had seemed darker to him last night—swinging back and forth in the sunlight.

"How long did the trip take you?" she asked, interested.

"I made it in less than two days."

"When did you sleep?"

"I didn't sleep," Cole explained. Well, that wasn't quite the whole truth. "I pulled off the highway once and grabbed an hour or two of shut-eye."

Georgiana turned and studied his profile. "May I ask how old you were at the time?"

She could ask. The question was, would he answer?

Cole ran his hand—the one not gripping the steering wheel—back and forth along his jawline. He could use a shave. His beard stubble was like sandpaper.

Her expression changed. "Of course, if you consider the question too personal you don't have to answer it," she assured him, using her best professional manner.

What the hell, he decided. "I was fifteen."

Cole could hear the dismay in Georgiana's voice when she said, "You were fifteen years old and you drove all that way alone?"

He set his jaw. "Yup."

She was a curious creature. "Were you even old enough to have a driver's license?"

He shrugged his shoulders and gave a noncommittal answer. "We drive pretty young in Texas."

Which wasn't *exactly* a lie. But then, it hadn't *exactly* been his pickup truck, either.

Ms. Georgiana Burne-Jones really did live by the letter of the law, Cole ruminated. No wonder the events of the previous evening had left her reeling.

"Where were your parents?" she blurted out.

He bit off the words. "Don't know."

His tone of voice should have warned her off, should have told her not to pursue that particular topic of conversation, but somehow it didn't deter the woman.

"*Don't* know?" she echoed.

Cole had to say something. He was tired of playing games, and he was tired of pussyfooting around the subject. "I didn't know then. I don't know now. I've never known."

She sank the serrated edges of her teeth into her bottom lip. Her hands were clasped tightly together in her lap. "I'm sorry, Cole." She swallowed with some difficulty. "It was none of my business and I forced you into giving me an answer."

That raised a sardonic smile on his lips. He spoke of himself in the third person. "Trust me, no one forces Coleman Worth to say or do anything he doesn't want to."

She was still contrite. "My only excuse for such a lapse in good manners is that I'm a little tired."

Which was where this conversation began, as he recalled.

"It's okay, Georgiana. I'm tired, too. What if I find a secluded spot where the pickup truck can't be seen from the road and we both get some shut-eye for a few hours?"

"I think it would be an excellent idea." Eyes squinted against the bright midday sun, Georgiana peered out the window on the passenger side. "Where are we, anyway?"

"Bumble Bee."

"Where?" She quickly turned and began to swat around with her hand.

Cole chuckled under his breath. "Not that kind of bumblebee. The town"—a slight exaggeration—"of Bumble Bee."

She slowly lowered her hand again. "Oh."

"It's where the saguaro stop."

Georgiana wrinkled up her forehead and inquired, "Where the saguaro stop?"

"We're heading into the mountains. The saguaro cactus won't grow above a certain altitude. Bumble Bee is on the Great Divide, so to speak." Now he was curious. "Where are you from originally, anyway?" It couldn't be Arizona.

"Boston."

That explained a lot.

Cole turned off the highway and headed cross-country for a mile or two. He knew he'd found the right place when he spotted a thicket of trees and underbrush that formed a natural leafy canopy. The pickup would be shaded from the heat of the midday sun. It would also be camouflaged from both the ground and the air. They could see out, but no one could see in.

It was perfect.

"You take the back seat," he proposed as he pushed the button to lower the truck window several inches. "Try to sleep for a few hours. I'll wake you up around five."

"How will you know when it's five o'clock?" Then Georgiana answered her own question. "Don't tell me. You're one of those people with a built-in internal clock, aren't you?"

Cole shook his head. "Nope. But I do have a built-in alarm clock on my watch."

That brought the first real smile to her lips, to her mouth, to her face that he had seen. Smiling transformed Ms. Georgiana Burne-Jones, Cole discovered.

"Sleep well, Cole."

"You, too, Georgiana."

"Pleasant dreams," he thought he heard her murmur as she stretched out on the back seat and closed her eyes.

It did her a world of good.

In fact, Georgiana felt like a new woman when Cole nudged her awake a few hours later.

Cole had a proposition for her. "Why don't we drive into Prescott and stop at one of those all-purpose superstores to buy the necessities you mentioned earlier today?"

"I need a comb and a hairbrush, deodorant, a toothbrush, toothpaste, some makeup," she began to rattle off the list of items. Then it hit her and she came to a dead stop.

"What's the matter?" Cole asked.

Georgiana groaned with dismay. "My wallet, my credit cards, even my bank card are all safely stowed in my handbag in my locker at the Sonoran. My checkbook is at my apartment."

"You couldn't have used them, anyway. Credit cards, bank cards, checks: they all leave a paper trail. One slip like that and it wouldn't take the police long to find us."

"I guess you're right." Then she groaned aloud again. "I left the whole three thousand dollars with Alfred. I should have brought at least some of the money with me."

Cole shook his head in disagreement. "You were smart *not* to bring any of Isherwood's money."

"I was?"

He spelled it out for her. "For two reasons. First, brand-new one-hundred-dollar bills may be too memorable in some of the small towns we'll be traveling through."

"And second?"

"The money could be marked."

"Marked money." Georgiana lightly slapped her forehead. She'd never considered the possibility that the money could be traced.

"Trust me, it's much safer for us if we stick to paying for everything with small, used bills."

She felt compelled to point out to Cole, "But I don't have any small, used bills."

"But I do," he told her.

Money was an emotional issue for her. It had been since the night she went from being rich to being poor within the space of a single heartbeat.

"I don't like using your money," Georgiana declared. After all, she had her pride.

"I know you don't," Coleman Worth said in an understanding tone. "So we'll consider it a loan. You can always repay me once we get ourselves out of this mess." He held out his hand. "Deal?"

"Deal," she said and they shook on it.

Then he suggested, "By the way, you might rummage around in the glove box and see what Martin has left for us."

Georgiana opened the compartment in front of her. There was a small package of tissues, several rolls of cherry Life Savers, a pack of sugar-free gum, two pairs of sunglasses—she immediately slipped one pair on and offered the other to Cole—and a portfolio of official-looking papers that included the car registration and license plate information.

Once again she wondered how Martin Davis was able to accomplish such an amazing feat in less than four hours and from a distant city.

Money, apparently, could move mountains.

At least when it was in combination with the kind of power that Coleman Worth wielded.

Georgiana finally came across a large black leather pouch.

''That will be the money in small, used bills that Martin secured for us at my request,'' Cole indicated. ''You can help yourself to as much as you need or want.''

Georgiana unzipped the pouch and the air she took into her lungs was a clearly audible gasp. ''My God, Cole, there must be thousands of dollars here.''

''There'd better be,'' he said, not in the least surprised. ''Never know how much cash we'll need on this trip, or when we'll have easy access again to money.''

Georgiana was stunned. ''I'll take forty dollars, if that's all right with you.''

''Better make it an even hundred for each of us,'' he advised. ''I understand the prices have gone up even at Wal-Mart.''

Eight

"What can I do for you, honey?" the saleswoman asked as Georgiana tentatively approached the cosmetics counter. Cole was two aisles over, checking out kerosene lanterns.

Georgiana wiped her palms on the legs of her jeans. "I need to buy some makeup."

The woman snapped her gum—the name tag pinned to the breast pocket of her blue cotton smock proclaimed her to be Ruby D.—and inquired, "Exactly what do you need?"

Georgiana suddenly wished that she had written down a list of items. "A compact."

"Loose or pressed powder?"

"Pressed powder."

Ruby D. peered across the counter at her. "You're pretty fair-complexioned."

"Yes, I am," she agreed.

"Tan?"

She didn't understand. "I beg your pardon."

"You gonna lay out in the sun and get a tan this summer? 'Cause if you are, you'll need a shade darker.

Of course, someday you'll also end up looking like a shriveled-up prune.'' Ruby D. chugged along like an old-fashioned steam locomotive.

"I never tan."

"Must not be from Arizona," the sales clerk stated as she slapped a pressed powder labeled "extra light" on the countertop.

"Not originally." Georgiana decided it might be wise to change the subject. "I also need mascara."

"What color?"

"What colors do you have?"

Ruby D. punctuated each reply with another snap of her gum. " 'Only After Midnight' black; 'Smoke Gets in Your Eyes' gray; 'Sherwood Forest' green; 'Lavender Dilly Dilly' blue; and 'Boy Toy' brown."

"The brown, I think."

"One 'Boy Toy' brown." The besmocked woman placed the tube of mascara next to the compact on the glass countertop between them. "Anything else?"

Georgiana licked her lips. "Lipstick?"

Ruby D. rolled her eyes. "Do you have a particular color of lipstick in mind, by any chance?"

Georgiana shook her head. "What colors do you have?"

The clerk pointed to a display case containing dozens and dozens of different lipsticks, perhaps as many as one hundred. "You name it, we got it. Pick your poison."

"I'd rather you helped me."

The champagne-bleached head moved from side to side. "That's the color of the lipstick. 'Pick Your Poison' pink."

"Oh."

"Then there's always the ever popular 'Brazen-berry.' "

"What do you think goes with my coloring?"

"Frankly, deary, you could use a little color, if you don't mind my saying so." Ruby D. studied her features intently. "Personally I think you should go with red."

"Red?" Georgiana swallowed and confessed, "I've never worn red lipstick before."

She usually dabbed on a subtle lip gloss with just the slightest suggestion of color while she was on the job. Her life outside of her job was practically nonexistent. In fact, she had spent so much time at the Sonoran during one guest's recent visit that she had given up her apartment for three months and moved into a room at the resort.

"You've got a nice mouth. You should play it up more. 'Moulin Rouge LaTrick' red would draw attention to your lips. Make them kissable, if you know what I mean? Men would find you irresistible. You'd have to fight them off."

That wasn't quite the effect Georgiana had in mind. "I don't really care for bright red lipstick," she finally admitted. Then quickly added, when she realized that Ruby D. was wearing 'Moulin Rouge LaTrick' herself, "On me, that is."

Ruby leaned closer and confided, "Honey, women never do. It's men that love bright red lipstick and skin-tight skirts and four-inch-high spike heels. Trust me on the lipstick."

Georgiana found herself nodding. "Do I need anything else?"

"Blush?"

She offered an explanation. "I try not to, naturally, but I do sometimes when I get embarrassed."

"I was suggesting the kind of blush that you brush on to give your skin some contouring and to highlight your cheekbones. You've got great cheekbones, by the way. You ought to flaunt them."

Georgiana wasn't going to argue with Ruby D. "I'll take some." Then she glanced at the stack of items that had accumulated on the counter. "How much is that, so far?"

"Well, let me see." The woman counted to herself and finally responded, "Give or take a few cents, and without sales tax, about twenty-three dollars."

"Twenty-three dollars?" Georgiana was astonished. She'd paid almost that much for one lipstick the last time she'd been in a department store in Phoenix.

"A little more than you wanted to spend, is it, dear?" Rudy D. said kindly. "I'll tell you what. There's a promotion going on with the other brand of cosmetics we carry. Supposedly if you spend fifteen dollars, you get a free blush. I'll just slip one of those into your bag and that will save you three bucks."

Georgiana was taken aback. "That's very kind of you, but—"

"No buts, honey. We women got to stick together in this cold, cruel world."

A pronounced Texas accent came from somewhere above and behind Georgiana's right shoulder as a strong, masculine arm was slipped around her waist. "How's it going, sugar?"

Sugar?

Georgiana turned her head. It was Cole, of course. "F-fine," she stammered.

"Finding everything you need?"

"Yes."

Rudy D. was suddenly all eyes and all ears as if this was a whole new and interesting development in her day. She even forgot to snap her gum.

"I'm going to mosey on over to camping equipment. How about we meet up in the shoe department in, say"—Cole glanced down at his watch—"twenty minutes?"

"Shoes?"

He gave her a squeeze. "Hey, I want to buy my favorite girl a new pair of boots."

Georgiana closed her mouth and checked her serviceable watch. "I'll be there on time."

Cole nuzzled her hair for a moment. "Twenty minutes, darlin' "

Darlin'?

After he'd left again, the woman behind the counter blew out her breath and began to fan herself with her hand. "Honey, I don't know what the question is, but he sure has got the answer."

Georgiana went so far as to say, "He is an attractive man."

"You can say that again." Ruby D. looked at the makeup stacked on the counter. "You can still buy all this stuff, of course, but you obviously don't need it."

"Oh, but I do."

Rudy D. shook her head and watched Coleman Worth until he disappeared from sight.

"Where is the shoe department?" Georgiana asked after she had paid for her purchases.

"Turn left at aisle nine, then right at aisle B and go all the way to the end."

"Thanks, Ruby."

"Good luck, honey." The woman laughed in that under-her-breath suggestive kind of way. "Although it doesn't look like you need it."

If Ruby D. only knew. . . .

Maybe it was nothing.

Then again, maybe it was something.

Cole had first spotted the black sedan four cars back

as he was driving into the town of Prescott with its hilly streets, historic courthouse square, picturesque—and now pricey—houses from the turn of the century, numerous antique and collectibles stores, coffeehouses and colorful local bars.

He'd caught a glimpse of the same black four-door cruising the parking lot of the superstore as he and Georgiana were headed inside to do their shopping.

And now the identical car was somewhere behind them as they inched along in the Friday night traffic that seemed to inflict even this otherwise quiet town.

Coincidence?

Cole wasn't sure he believed in coincidences. Coincidences made him nervous.

He wasn't going to take any chances. At the same time, he didn't want to unduly alarm Georgiana. She was sitting beside him, looking every inch a country girl instead of the city girl he knew her to be. Besides jeans and the white shirt she'd gotten from Crick's jumbo boxes, she was outfitted in cowboy boots—intentionally scuffed by him the minute they'd left the store—a brown leather vest with fringe dangling from the shoulders and the waist, a cheap knock-off of a Stetson, enough makeup—her lipstick was neon-red—to choke a horse and rather gaudy turquoise and silver dangle earrings.

It was a complete transformation.

"Hungry?"

"Yes."

"I asked back at the superstore where there was a good place to eat and they recommended Hal's."

"Sounds fine to me."

"Your accent is improving."

"Thanks, cowboy."

Cole couldn't help himself; he laughed out loud. But he kept one eye on the rearview mirror.

"Here we are," he said five minutes later as they pulled into a jammed parking lot.

Georgiana forgot her accent. "This is Hal's?"

"This is Hal's."

Hal's House of Honky Tonk was a remarkable establishment. It had started out life as a Texaco gas station back when the big Texaco star at the top of a sign had meant full service, including your front *and* back windshields washed, the use of a pristine bathroom and ice-cold bottled Cokes in a red refrigerated dispenser.

Somewhere along the way a mom-and-pop grocery had been tacked on in the form of a lean-to.

In its third reincarnation, there had been the addition of an automatic car wash. That was after gas station attendants in crisp brown uniforms had become a thing of the past.

Then some ambitious soul had apparently had an old gray barn moved onto the property from fifty yards down the road. That same ambitious soul had installed a few cheap tables and chairs, and opened a bar.

Hal had come onto the scene some years later, enterprisingly put the gas station, the lean-to, the car wash and the barn together, and the result was the best home-cooked food, the loudest bar, the hottest country western music this side of Nashville, and the most popular hangout in Yavapai County.

"They tell me this is the hottest spot in town."

Georgiana appeared skeptical. "It looks like the busiest."

Cole informed her, "Hey, I understand that they come all the way from Bagdad—"

She interrupted. "Bagdad?"

"Bagdad, Arizona. Just west of here. Population somewhere around two thousand." Then he went on. "They come over from Congress."

"Arizona?"

He nodded.

Georgiana smiled. "Population of Congress?"

"Eight hundred."

She seemed to be enjoying herself. "Where else do they hail from and all end up here at Hal's?"

"Skull Valley, the well-known Bumble Bee, Cherry, Clemenceau, and even as far distant as Happy Jack, which is in the next county."

"Hal must be one popular man."

"Don't know about Hal, but his food and drink sure are. And since we're hungry and thirsty . . ." Cole wasn't about to add, *and since we're being followed, this is a good place to lose the black sedan, too.*

He cruised the football-field-size parking lot three times before he found an available parking space.

Georgiana had been gazing out the window all the while. "I've spotted three pickup trucks identical to yours on this side of the building alone."

"Pickups are what make this country great."

She seemed to agree and gave a happy sigh. "I'm learning something new every day."

"Don't they have pickup trucks in Boston?"

She thought about it for a minute. "I don't think so."

"Well, that explains a lot."

That got a rise out of his passenger. "What is that supposed to mean?"

"It means I'm hungry and I'm thirsty. Let's go inside and grab ourselves something to eat and a cold beer."

The transformed woman beside him got an odd expression on her face.

"What's wrong?"

"I don't care for beer," she admitted in a small voice.

"What do you like to drink?"

"Perrier."

Cole managed to keep a straight face. "I don't think Hal's is going to have Perrier on the menu. Besides, you might surprise yourself. Coors Light is a treat for the taste buds."

He opened the door of the pickup and stepped down. Georgiana did the same and then hand in hand they headed into Hal's House of Honky Tonk.

Nine

It was a foreign country.

The blast of loud music, cacophonous noise and warm air hit Georgiana in the face like a shock wave.

The main room was cavernous. Originally it must have been the barn. The ceiling above them soared fifty feet and more into the air. She put her head back and gazed up. She could have sworn that she spotted a bird or two flying among the wooden rafters.

At one end of the roadhouse was a raised stage. There was a country western band set up with their guitars and fiddles and some kind of electronic keyboard. A female singer in a white hat and white leather outfit—the pants looked sprayed on—was standing behind a microphone belting out a mournful song about ''he was the right man until he done me wrong.''

On the far side of the room was the most impressive bar Georgiana had ever seen. It must have measured at least ninety feet from end to end, and every inch of space along it was occupied.

Behind the bar were smoky mirrors and flashing neon lights and placards. In big, bold lettering one sign warned, NO SPITTING. NO CUSSING. NO LOOSE WOMEN.

Hal's House of Honky Tonk was packed tonight, as no doubt it was on most Friday nights. The patrons appeared to come in every conceivable size, shape, age and sex, but they seemed to have one thing in common: they were having fun.

People were laughing and talking, eating and drinking and dancing. Dancing in pairs. Dancing in squares. Dancing in small groups and in makeshift lines. They were even dancing—and kissing and heaven knew what else—in the dark, secluded corners.

The smell of beer and cigarette smoke and tangy barbecue hung heavy in the air. Georgiana wrinkled her nose and turned to Cole to suggest that they look for someplace else to eat when she saw the expression on his face: he was grinning from ear to ear.

She couldn't believe it. He had scarcely smiled since they'd met. Occasionally he had chuckled, and very occasionally she had heard him laugh. But she had never seen him actually look happy.

Happiness transformed him.

Georgiana found herself staring at the man beside her. In fact, she took a really good look at Coleman Worth for the first time. He was tall: over six feet, even without the benefit of the standard heels on his cowboy boots.

He was broad-shouldered and slim-waisted and hard-muscled. He was tanned and lean and tough as nails. He gave an impression of strength. Not just an obvious physical strength, but strength of mind and strength of character, the kind that had resulted from testing one's self against all odds and coming out on top.

She doubted if Coleman Worth had ever come out anywhere else. Certainly never on the bottom. And she couldn't imagine that he would settle for anything in between.

Cole was one of those people who was determined—perhaps *driven* was the better word—to win the game. Period. In the global arena of high finance and big business, he evidently had won again and again. He was a very successful, very wealthy and very powerful man.

Yet Georgiana also believed him to be a man of his word. She didn't question for a minute that Cole would keep whatever promises he made: even if it was a vow to protect a woman he had known for scarcely twenty-four hours.

"Comin' through!"

Georgiana's musings were interrupted when a busy waitress elbowed by them, shouldering a tray of frosty beer bottles and enormous platters of barbecued ribs and charo beans.

Cole leaned over and shouted in her ear, "That looks delicious, doesn't it? Let's grab ourselves a table."

"Shouldn't we wait to be seated by the hostess?" she said, wondering where in the world the person who seated them was in the crush of human beings milling around the entrance.

"No hostess."

"No hostess?" Georgiana was taken aback. Then she inquired, "How do you know?"

Cole gave her one of those slightly amused looks of his that she was beginning to recognize. "You've never been in a place like Hal's before, have you?"

Georgiana shook her head.

"Well, I have," he told her. "Trust me, it's every man for himself." Then he added, "Stick with me."

So she did.

She didn't think anything of it, Georgiana realized later, when Cole tucked her into his side, slipped an arm around her lower rib cage and set out in search of an empty table.

There was none to be had.

It was on their third circle around the room that Georgiana felt a tug on her shirtsleeve. She glanced down and saw a pretty, and very pregnant, girl indicating two empty places at the table she was sitting at with a thin young man who was probably her husband. She mouthed the words, "We'll share."

Georgiana had been about to decline the offer when Cole stepped in, nodded his head, smiled down at the couple and shouted above the din, "Thanks, we'll take you up on the offer."

As they settled in, Cole extended his hand to his counterpart across the table. "The name's Cole Worth."

The younger man pumped his arm. "I'm Jacob Meyers. This is my wife, Sally."

Cole pulled Georgiana's chair closer to him and rested his arm along the back. "This is Georgiana."

"You two married?" Sally asked as she sipped from a bottle of nonalcoholic beer.

Before she had a chance to respond to the question, Cole spoke up and answered with his best Texas twang, "As a matter of fact, we're newlyweds."

Georgiana choked.

Sally's young face—she couldn't have been much more than eighteen or nineteen years old—brightened. "So are Jacob and me. We had to move the wedding date up when we found out that Jacob Junior was on the way." Sally Meyers was guileless, but curious. "How long have you two been married?"

Georgiana let Cole do the talking. He'd started this business; he could finish it. Besides, there must be some reason he'd thought it was necessary to concoct such a crazy story. "We've only been married a week. As a matter of fact, we're on our honeymoon," he claimed.

Jacob Meyers told them, "I promised Sally that we'll

have us a honeymoon as soon as the baby comes and
we can save up a little money to go away.''

Which might be never, by the less-than-prosperous
appearance of Sally and Jacob. Georgiana couldn't help
but notice that they were sharing a small plate of barbecued ribs. She wondered if it was from choice or necessity.

A waitress appeared tableside to take their order.

''What would you like, honey?'' inquired Cole.

''Whatever you're having is fine with me, darlin',''
said Georgiana, putting the ball right back in his court.

Cole smiled at the waitress—she seemed to blossom
under what passed for charm in his case—and said,
''We'll each have a Coors Light and a giant platter of
the ribs.''

Georgiana immediately leaned closer and whispered,
''I could never eat that much.''

The man beside her was suddenly quite serious. He
spoke out of the side of his mouth, ''I know.''

Cole was definitely up to something. Georgiana wondered what it could be.

''I don't think Georgiana cares much for Hal's ribs,''
Cole pointed out to their companions some time later.
She had meticulously removed several pieces of meat to
a smaller plate and nibbled on them. But the remainder
of her dinner was untouched . . . just as he'd expected it
would be. ''It's a shame to let good food go to waste.
How about splitting what's left with me, Jacob?''

''Don't mind if I do,'' the man answered, spearing a
slab of ribs from the platter in the middle of the table.

Sally Meyers confided, ''I've been off my food for
the past several months. Especially if it's real spicy.''

''I've never been one for spicy food, either,'' Georgiana admitted as she took another sip of her Coors Light.

Cole realized he'd have to keep an eye on her. She had eaten very little dinner, but it was her second beer. The last thing he needed on his hands tonight was an inebriated Georgiana Burne-Jones.

He turned back to the other man. "Tell me more about this souped-up pickup of yours, Jacob."

"Tinkering with engines has always been a hobby of mine, Cole. I bought Bessie from a junkyard for fifty bucks. I've been working on her off and on for two years."

"Jacob can work wonders with engines and transmissions and brakes and everything that has anything to do with cars and trucks," his wife stated with pride in her voice.

Jacob Meyers's youthful face was slightly flushed from the praise. "Bessie may not be much to look at on the outside, but she's a real beauty underneath where it counts."

"Looks can be deceiving," Cole said. The fleeting thought crossed his mind that they frequently were.

"I'd like to open my own garage someday," Jacob expanded. "Good mechanics are hard to find in Prescott."

"Good mechanics are hard to find anywhere," Cole observed. An idea was beginning to take shape somewhere in the back of his head. "I'd like to see your Bessie."

"Anytime," he agreed.

"Maybe a little later this evening. Right now I'd better dance with my better half." Cole winked at the younger man good-naturedly. "After all, we men have to keep our ladies happy, don't we?"

He got to his feet and held out his hand to Georgiana.

She stared at it.

"May I have this dance?" he asked.

It was touch and go for a minute.

"Yes, you may," she finally responded.

Georgiana placed her hand in his and allowed him to lead her to the crowded dance floor. It was wall-to-wall bodies. They made a small space for themselves and Cole took her into his arms.

At first she was stiff as a board and held her body aloof from his. But eventually she forgot herself, let out a sigh and placed her hands on Cole's shoulders.

They swayed in time to the slow twang-and-torch music along with the rest of the men and women dancing, each couple lost in their own little world, oblivious to the noise and the smoke and the crowd surrounding them.

Cole relaxed, leaned closer and found his lungs filled with the scent that clung to Georgiana's skin. It was subtle, surprisingly sensuous, slightly fruity, with a touch of musk.

He inhaled again. She made him think of something cool and crisp. Somehow she reminded him of rolling green hills and lush grass and deep blue skies.

After all she'd been through, how could the lady smell so damned good?

It was sometime later—Cole couldn't have said how much later—that he started to get a funny feeling.

Maybe it was the small hairs suddenly standing straight up on end at the back of his neck that first alerted him.

Maybe it was some kind of internal alarm system, some type of antennae for trouble, some sixth sense that forewarned him. Whatever it was, he swore it had saved his hide on more than one occasion over the years.

Or maybe it was the sudden blast of cool air from the

overworked air-conditioning system hitting his face that made him turn his head at just the right moment.

Whatever the reason, Cole glanced toward the front entrance of Hal's House of Honky Tonk just as three men in dark suits walked into the establishment. Among the swirl of colors and patterns in the huge room, they stuck out like sore thumbs. Their somber expressions were as much out of place as their attire.

Cole slowly maneuvered Georgiana until her back was to the newcomers and he was facing them. From beneath the brim of his Stetson, he waited and watched.

Who in the hell were they?

They didn't look like the police. They didn't look like the feds. They didn't look like DEA.

What they looked like were hired thugs.

They stood there and scanned the crowd. What were they looking for? *Who* were they looking for?

While he and Georgiana were in the superstore, he had sauntered into the electronics department. Under the pretext of comparison shopping, he had checked out the news on a row of television sets. There hadn't been one word about Paul Isherwood's death, not one mention of the Sonoran or of Georgiana.

He'd spent an equal amount of time scrutinizing the newspapers. There had been only one short article on the back page of the *Arizona Republic*. The facts had been sparse: a man's body had been found in his hotel room. Again, no mention of the Sonoran or Georgiana—someone at the posh resort had evidently pulled some strings to keep damage control to a minimum.

The three goons couldn't be looking for them, Cole tried to convince himself. No one even knew he and Georgiana were on the run together except Alfred Crick, and Crick would cut out his tongue before betraying Miss Georgiana.

Nope. It didn't make sense.

Unless . . .

Unless he'd missed something. Unless there was some detail that he hadn't thought of. Unless there was some possibility, however remote, that he had failed to take into consideration.

Unless the police had their own reasons for keeping the facts of the case under wraps.

Shit.

Coleman Worth knew in his gut that the men in the dark suits were the same men who had been in the black sedan following them earlier tonight.

It might be wise to disappear deeper into the safety and anonymity of the crowd, Cole decided, steering Georgiana toward a shadowy corner of the room.

The band finished playing one slow dance and immediately went into another. The words of the classic Drifters' song "Save the Last Dance for Me" filled the night.

Georgiana finally raised her head, leaned back in his arms and looked up at him from beneath the unfamiliar brim of a hat. "Which raises another subject, Coleman Worth."

He played dumb. "It does?"

"Yes. It does."

"What subject might that be?"

"It's about calling me 'darlin' ' and 'sugar,' and telling that sweet young couple that we're on our honeymoon." Green eyes stared into his. "I would like an explanation."

Ten

This had better be good, Georgiana thought, waiting for his explanation.

Cole took his own sweet time before he said, "I'm not a frivolous man."

She didn't know him well, of course, but Georgiana agreed with his self-assessment so far.

He made another claim. "I don't play games."

Georgiana arched one eyebrow in a knowing fashion, but before she could say anything, Cole quickly rescinded his statement. "All right, I admit I do play games. But not the kind that hurt anyone else or embarrass them or put them at risk."

Her interest was genuinely piqued. "What kind of games do you play, then?"

Cole stared over her head for ten or fifteen seconds, then gazed down at her. "I create diversions for myself."

That wasn't what she'd expected him to say. "Diversions?"

His expression darkened. His mouth tightened. His tone was one of exasperation. "I don't think this is the time or place to go into all of that, Georgiana.''

She didn't agree. ''I think it is the time *and* the place. What do you mean by diversions?''

The man drew a deep breath and blew it out slowly. ''I'll give you an example.''

''An example would be good.''

''I once had a pilot drop me off in the middle of the Canadian wilderness with just the clothes I was wearing and a small backpack of supplies.''

She was intrigued. ''Why?''

Cole seemed reluctant to say any more than he already had on the subject. It was almost as if he was afraid his answer would reveal too much about him. ''To test myself, I suppose.''

''Did it?''

''Yes.''

''What did you do?''

''I walked to the nearest town.''

Georgiana stared up at him in amazement. ''How long did it take you?''

''A week.''

''How old were you this time?''

Fierce blue eyes regarded her. ''What do you mean *this* time?'' he asked, his voice roughening.

She would not allow Coleman Worth to intimidate her. ''You told me this afternoon that you had once driven to California by yourself when you were only fifteen.''

He shuffled his feet and walked her through the motions, but they both knew they weren't really dancing. ''What does one have to do with the other?''

''You mentioned last night in your suite that you took off for parts unknown every now and then.'' He hadn't revealed the frequency. ''You don't see a possible connection?''

"Maybe," Cole allowed.

Wearing a hat was an unfamiliar experience for her. Georgiana adjusted the brim for comfort and pushed it back a little off her face. "So how old were you when you had the pilot drop you in the middle of nowhere?"

This time he gave her an answer. "I was thirty-six."

Nothing ventured, nothing gained. "And may I ask how old you are now?"

Cole gave it about thirty seconds of thought before responding, "I'm thirty-seven years old. The trip to the Northwest Territories was last summer."

"I see."

"Maybe you do, Ms. Burne-Jones, and maybe you don't," he countered.

"Which brings us back to the explanation you were going to give me," she reminded him.

Coleman Worth sure knew how to beat around the bush. He kept glancing over her shoulder as if he were looking for something . . . or someone.

It was some time before he began with, "I'm an average man from an average one-horse town in Texas."

Georgiana couldn't help it; she laughed out loud. "I'll admit that I don't know the first thing about one-horse towns in Texas, or anywhere else, for that matter. But you're hardly an average man, Cole."

"Thank you." He paused for a split second. "I think." Then he continued with his rationalization. "The 'darlin'' and the 'sugar' just kind of popped out naturally."

Georgiana supposed they had.

"As for the other matter . . ."

"Yes?"

"We both know the police, and anyone else on your trail, will be searching for a single woman. Since we're traveling together, I figured it was a convincing disguise for us to pose as a couple.''

''I can see the logic. I may even have agreed with you and consented to the charade. I just wish you'd consulted me first.''

He had an answer for everything. ''There really wasn't time to have a conference about it, Georgiana.''

She regarded him with a thoughtful expression on her face. ''You're used to being the boss, making the decisions, handing down the edicts, aren't you?''

Dark, enigmatic eyes were barely visible beneath the brim of his Stetson. ''I almost never hand down edicts. It's not the way successful companies are run these days.''

Georgiana was willing to bet that every last employee at Worth Industries knew who was boss.

She still wanted to know what purpose his tall tale had served tonight. ''Why did you lie to Sally and Jacob Meyers? Why introduce us as husband and wife?''

A muscle in Cole's otherwise granite jaw started to twitch. ''Under the circumstances, would you have preferred that I introduce you as Georgiana Burne-Jones?''

He had a point.

Maybe her name was out there as a fugitive from justice and maybe it wasn't. But she didn't intend to take any chances and, wisely, neither did Cole.

''It was simpler all around to allow Sally and Jacob to believe we're a married couple. It saved unwanted questions on their part and possibly awkward explanations on ours.'' Cole was dead serious. ''As I started to explain to you, Georgiana, I'm not a frivolous man. If I ever tell you to do something—or *not* to do something— you can be guaranteed it's for a damned good reason.''

''What would you consider a good reason?'' She honestly wanted to know.

"Your safety. Or mine. Or both of ours." He followed that statement with a warning. "We could find ourselves in some dangerous situations on this trip."

Georgiana decided she was already in a dangerous situation: she was being held in Coleman Worth's arms. She was firmly, unyieldingly, intimately pressed against the most attractive male body she'd ever laid eyes on, a male body that she had seen a great deal of—too much of—last night.

After all, she wasn't blind. She wasn't immune. She was a normal woman with normal urges, normal needs and normal desires. Despite what men might have said about her in the past, she wasn't frigid. She wasn't a snob with her aristocratic nose in the air or an ice princess who considered herself above others. She wasn't a nun, either. She hadn't taken a vow of chastity.

In fact, chastity, Georgiana realized, much to her chagrin, was the last thing on her mind.

It was the Coors Light.

It had to be.

This wasn't like her. She did not find herself attracted to strange men.

To strangers.

To Coleman Worth.

That wasn't quite the truth. In fact, it was a lie. If she was honest with herself—and she always tried to be (she had seen firsthand what willful self-delusion could do to someone, how refusing to face reality could wreak havoc with someone's life)—she was attracted to Cole. She couldn't imagine there were very many females between eighteen and eighty on the planet who wouldn't be attracted to him.

Being attracted to someone and acting on that attraction were two entirely different things, however. She was a mature woman. She could and she would keep her mind on the business at hand.

What had they been discussing?

Danger.

That was it.

"There hasn't been any sign of trouble since the roadblock on Pima Road early this morning," she pointed out to Cole. "And we don't actually know that the roadblock had anything to do with us." She immediately correctly that to, "With me."

"I'm afraid that isn't exactly true," he said, his voice deep and his words slowly spaced.

"What do you mean, you're afraid it isn't exactly true?" she demanded.

Cole exerted pressure on her hand and pulled her closer. "I didn't want to have to tell you this, Georgiana, but I spotted a car following us today."

Her heart plummeted to her feet. "Are you sure?"

"I wasn't at first," he admitted.

"But you are now."

He nodded. "I caught a glimpse of a black sedan behind us on the drive into Prescott. Then I saw the same car in the parking lot at the store where we shopped."

"It could be a coincidence. There must be dozens of black sedans on the highways. There are at least three blue pickups identical to yours in the parking lot right outside."

She could always hope, couldn't she?

"The same car was tailing us tonight on the way here," Cole said, bursting her bubble.

"What else?" she asked with forced calmness.

"Not more than five minutes ago I saw three men in dark suits walk in the front entrance."

Georgiana closed her eyes for a moment. She could feel the color drain from her face. Her shoulders sagged.

She recalled the night of the so-called party in Mr. Isherwood's suite at the Sonoran. "Men in dark suits?" She swallowed hard. "Here?"

Cole said, abruptly and clearly, "Yes."

She fought the urge to turn around. "I doubt if a local customer would show up at Hal's in a suit."

"That's what I figured."

"The three men you noticed are probably strangers in the area."

"It's pretty likely."

"You suspect they were also in the black sedan."

"It fits."

Unfortunately it did.

Georgiana had to ask. "Are they still here?"

"They were a minute or two ago."

She reminded herself to breathe. "Is that why you waltzed me back into this corner?"

"Yes."

Her voice was thin and stretched as tight as a drum. "They could be anywhere."

"They could be anywhere."

Something else occurred to her. "Is that what you've been keeping an eye out for?"

"Yup."

Cole adjusted his hat over his forehead and turned to the side, apparently so he could scan the crowd and still maintain a degree of anonymity.

Georgiana realized his intense blue eyes seemed to be in a perpetual squint, as if he were always on watch, as if he were always scanning the horizon.

Suddenly Cole stiffened. He lowered his head and put his mouth next to her ear. "Do exactly as I tell you," he ordered. "Slowly move your right hand and pull your hat down over your eyes. Slowly, now. No sudden or jerky movements."

The gravity of the situation was conveyed to Georgiana. She did as he instructed, knowing that her hand was trembling, that her arm was trembling, that she was trembling.

Cole drew her closer—apparently he was using the combination of their hats as a shield—and brought his lips right up to hers. He whispered, ''Get ready to kiss me.''

Georgiana could feel the anticipatory tension in every bone and muscle of his taut body.

''Now,'' he commanded.

With her hands resting on his shoulders, she went up on her tiptoes, steadied herself against his solid physique—she swore the man was carved from stone—and kissed him.

In those first few moments—moments may have stretched into minutes, minutes into hours; Georgiana seemed to lose all perception of time—she was aware of every sound, every movement, every sensation around them. She found herself waiting for, listening for an authoritarian voice stating her name and placing her under arrest for the murder of Paul Isherwood.

Or worse, someone silently, forcibly taking her from this place and away from this man.

Whatever else happened, she could not, she would not, allow herself to be separated from Cole. Other than dear Crick—and perhaps, on a professional and more impersonal level, Mr. Regen—Georgiana realized that the only person she trusted, the only person she felt she could rely on, was Coleman Worth.

She moved deeper into the shelter of his embrace. She clung to him for dear life . . . for life was suddenly very dear and very precious to her. Holding her breath, she waited.

Nothing.

Nothing but Cole.

Nothing but Cole and her.

They were pretending to be a man and a woman locked in a passionate embrace, a man and woman who had stolen away for a kiss, a caress, a few private moments together.

It was only make-believe. It wasn't real. It didn't mean a thing. It couldn't mean anything.

Why should it? She wasn't familiar with the shape of this man's mouth. She didn't know whether his lips were large or small, thin or full. She couldn't recall if his skin was smooth or rough. She didn't recognize his smell or his taste or the feel of him beneath her hands.

Yet the unknown could quickly become the known when two people were thrown together in intimate circumstances, when all the senses were heightened, when adrenaline was pumping like a drug through the bloodstream.

Georgiana realized she was hot, yet she was shivering. She was calm and she was as excited as she ever remembered being in her entire twenty-nine years. It was an act, but her heart was pounding.

She inhaled a deep breath, and with it came the distinctive scent of Coleman Worth. He had a clean and decidedly masculine smell that clung to his hair and skin and clothes. It wasn't artificial. It wasn't man-made. It was real and natural and his alone. He smelled of well-worked leather and a hot desert sun burning into sand and stone and scorched earth.

His taste was a heady mixture of the outdoors and wide-open spaces, something faintly alcoholic—no doubt the one beer he'd drunk with his dinner—and something she couldn't quite put her finger on. Maybe it was the lingering flavor of shadows and the night.

Beneath her fingertips, his shoulders and arms and

chest were hard and muscular, broad and strong. There didn't seem to be a spare ounce of flesh on his body.

Georgiana suddenly saw the similarities between Cole and the desert she had come to love and respect. They were both hard, unyielding, sometimes unforgiving if a mistake was made, tough to the core, and untamed by man or, in Cole's case, woman.

This was a man who was as straightforward as his kiss. He was direct. He was honest. He was a man who gave his word and kept his word. Georgiana didn't believe that Cole would ever lie to a woman to get what he wanted. He'd have the guts—or the effrontery—to come right out and ask her.

All of this Georgiana understood in the space of a heartbeat, perhaps two. Then the truth hit her: she was enjoying, savoring, relishing, loving the experience of kissing Coleman Worth.

And why not?

He was a wonderful kisser—a great kisser—even when his attention was focused on something else.

Cole was one of those unique men who could convey passion, curiosity, desire, intensity and incredible sensuality with a touch of his lips, the caress of his hand, the suggestion of a sigh that said it wasn't entirely an act.

But he was acting.

And she couldn't afford to confuse fantasy and reality at this point in the game.

In fact, unlike Coleman Worth, she never played games or acted out her dreams.

Yet a niggling thought persisted in the back of Georgiana's mind: even a grown woman was allowed a daydream now and then.

She couldn't afford dreams, she reminded herself, day or night or anything in between. Her dreams had come to an abrupt end the night her mother and father had told her the truth. Her life as she had known it, her future as she had dreamed it, had been gone just like that, and seemingly with a capricious snap of someone's fingers.

Still, the niggling thought persisted. Surely one innocent daydream was allowed. Surely for a moment she could feel needed, wanted, desired, protected, loved.

Could Coleman Worth possibly be having the same daydreams about her?

No.

After all, Cole was using the kiss between them, and the embrace they were sharing, as the means to an end: to put the men in dark suits off the scent.

Georgiana felt the sweet heat of Cole's breath waft across her face like a desert wind fanning the palm trees.

It might be an innocent daydream, but there was nothing innocent in the way the man kissed.

Eleven

The threat had passed.

The immediate threat had passed, Cole thought to himself; another type of threat still remained. In fact, he was holding that threat—he wasn't sure which was the greater danger—in his arms.

He had ordered Georgiana Burne-Jones to kiss him because he'd suddenly spotted one of the men in dark suits several feet, maybe less, from where they were dancing. The thug had obviously been searching for someone.

Had he been looking for them?

Under the circumstances Cole hadn't been about to take any chances. He had concealed Georgiana and himself the best way he knew how: by creating the illusion of lovers.

It wouldn't be the first time, however, that the "best-laid schemes" of a man had started out as one thing and then, inadvertently, through no fault and no intention of his own, evolved into another.

The gorilla in the ill-fitting black suit had moved on,

rejoined his colleagues at the front entrance to Hal's and then, *en trois,* vanished into the night.

Here one minute, gone the next.

What remained was Georgiana. Georgiana, with skin like porcelain and hair like silk. Georgiana, with lips that tasted of honey. Georgiana, with a body—in truth, neither the masculine-cut tuxedo she'd been wearing last night nor the jeans she was dressed in now did her justice—that trembled in his arms.

Did the lady realize she was trembling?

The first kiss between them had been an act, a ruse, unreal. It became very real. Suddenly Cole was kissing her in earnest, not because he had to but, damn it, because he wanted to.

He raised his head for a moment and gazed down at the woman in his arms.

She opened her eyes. "Cole?"

His mouth moved lazily. "Georgiana."

He knew what she was asking just by the way she said his name. Her tone was low and husky. Her manner was breathless and a little reluctant.

Yup, the lady had not one question, but a number of questions on her mind. Why was he kissing her again? Was it a good idea? Was it wise? Did the danger still exist?

He answered her by kissing her wholly and absolutely, thoroughly and soundly, without hesitation, and to within an inch of their lives. Hers and his own.

It probably wasn't the smartest thing he had ever done, Cole recognized on some level. As a matter of fact, he'd managed to come up with any number of less than brilliant schemes since first encountering Ms. Burne-Jones twenty-four hours ago. But it was too late to change his mind now.

So this time he might as well kiss her for himself:

not because there was any imminent threat of danger, not because they were pretending to be a cozy couple, but simply because he was curious what she tasted like, what she smelled like, what she felt like.

Cole got his answers. Georgiana was cool and she was burning up in his arms. She was hesitant and she was impatient. She was surprisingly shy for a woman of twenty-nine and she was bold as brass. She seemed of two minds: she drew closer at the same time that she pulled away from him.

Hé knew something about women. Certainly as much as some men; maybe—probably—more than most. He could sense that she wanted to kiss him and yet she was taken aback, maybe even bewildered and embarrassed that she was doing just that.

Cole had to confess that he'd found himself in more than a few precarious situations in his thirty-seven years. There had even been times when there was no guarantee that he would get out alive. After all, he was a man who loved a challenge, a man who admitted to creating "diversions" for himself.

Yet he had never deliberately or voluntarily done something he sensed deep down in his gut was plain stupid. He had never gotten in over his head when he'd gone into a situation with his eyes wide open like his eyes were right now.

Evidently there was a first time for everything.

Logic told him that Georgiana Burne-Jones wasn't his type. His type knew exactly what she was letting herself in for. His type was sophisticated—at least when it came to men. His type had seen a little of the world—maybe more than a little—and it hadn't always been a pretty picture.

His type was *not* a lady like Ms. Burne-Jones. She undoubtedly had a pedigree a mile long, while he was

a bastard straight out of nowhere Texas. She was a
woman born and bred in the city. He was a man who
thrived in the country. She was definitely East Coast. He
was the wild and wide-open spaces of the West.

Despite her present attire, Georgiana was all pearls,
imported-leather pumps and expensive perfume. He was
definitely jeans and scuffed cowboy boots and his ever-
present Stetson.

The woman didn't even like beer, for crying out loud.

For the moment Cole didn't care how far apart their
worlds were as long as he could kiss her, as long as he
could have his hands on her, as long as she kissed him
back as she was doing right now with her lips parted,
her tongue intertwined with his, her breath sweet and
inviting and her hips wedged tightly between his thighs.

He knew one thing, and there was no doubt about it:
the lady was excited.

Hell, so was he.

He heard a low growl of objection—it took a few
seconds for it to register that the sound was emanating
from his own throat—when Georgiana drew back and
stared up at him.

"Has the danger passed?" she asked, her eyes very
large and green and dark.

"Danger?"

"You must have seen one of the men in dark suits."

"I did."

"And?"

"They've left."

"You saw them leave?"

He nodded his head.

"So the coast is clear."

"The coast is clear." Cole discovered that he wasn't
ready to let her go. "Let's keep dancing, anyway."

"Why?"

He leaned closer and whispered in her ear, "Because I like dancing in the dark."

As Georgiana stepped back into his arms, Cole filled his lungs with her scent. God, she smelled like moonlight.

He could feel the faint flutter of her pulse where his thumb skimmed her wrist. He could almost make out the telltale hint of blue veins—maybe that was where the term *blue blood* had originated—against porcelain skin on the sensitive underside. He slowly raised her hand to his mouth, turned it over and brushed his lips along that sensitive skin. He felt her sharp intake of air. He felt her pulse begin to race. He felt the rising heat in his own blood.

A tiny cry seemed to escape her before Georgiana could stop it. Then she whispered his name wistfully and with her heart pounding against his. "Cole . . ."

"I know, darlin', I know," he murmured, burying his face in her fragrant hair.

She was all woman, he thought as his hands glided down her spine and around the curve of her derriere. And it was all there in his grasp: the soft female body, the contrasting texture of her shirt and jeans with the promise of smooth, silky skin underneath.

Cole's imagination took off. She would be so sweet to love. Sweet and hot. Buried somewhere deep within her, there was passion waiting, smoldering, ready to burst into flames and burn white-hot if the right man loved her in the right way. He could sense it. He could feel it. He was certain of it. She would catch fire and consume a man, and he would gladly die in the heat of that passion.

Yet she was cool and reserved and one hundred percent lady on the outside.

How could she be so cool and yet so hot?

Cole had the crazy urge to tear off her clothes and his, to lose himself in her, to run his hands over every inch of her body, to bring her into the rising heat of his thighs, to relieve the tension building inside him, to feel the fullness of her breasts, their tips hard and aroused, as they pressed against his chest.

A groan rose from inside him and settled in his throat, nearly choking him with its urgency, with a desperate need to be voiced. "My God, Georgiana," he swore softly. Dancing with her was torture, such sweet torture.

Cole slipped one arm around her waist. He clasped her right hand in his left and held it chest-high between them. A light sheen of perspiration broke out on his forehead and upper lip, then evaporated in the air-conditioned room.

It was Georgiana who broke her hand free of his and raised it to his shoulder again. She slipped her arms around his neck and interlaced her fingers, entangling them in the hair at his nape.

Cole's hand remained between them. That was when he realized his palm was just above her breast. If he were to move it a fraction of an inch . . .

Georgiana must know how close he was to caressing her. She had to know, he told himself.

She did.

Her breath was like a summer's kiss, all honey and heat, when she raised herself up on her tiptoes and whispered into his mouth, "Touch me, Cole."

It was crazy.

It was insane.

He couldn't.

He shouldn't.

But he wanted to touch her. He even told himself that he *needed* to touch her. Jesus, he'd lived his whole life by one simple rule: he never lied to himself. He wasn't about to start.

Besides, this wasn't the right time or the right place. She wasn't the right woman and he sure as hell wasn't the right man. He was supposed to be helping the woman, not placing her in greater jeopardy.

Coleman Worth was no Boy Scout—he'd never lived in one place long enough to belong to anyone or anything—but even a bastard from Texas didn't take advantage of a lady when she'd obviously had one beer too many.

It simply wasn't done.

He slid his hand from between their bodies. "God knows, I'm tempted. You're an attractive woman, Georgiana. You smell and taste and feel better than any woman I've ever known."

"Any woman?" she said, tilting her head to one side.

"Bar none." It was the truth. "It's been a long day. You haven't had enough sleep. You've had too much to drink on an empty stomach." The few bites of barbecue she'd eaten didn't count as dinner in his book. "You've been through a hellish twenty-four hours. I think it's time we called it a night." Cole blew out his breath. "Besides, I've got some arrangements that need to be made."

Her words were slightly slurred from fatigue. "What kind of arrangements?"

"I have to go see a man about a horse."

Twelve

"What do you do for fun?"

Georgiana took another sip of her beer and pondered the question put forth by Sally Meyers. She held the cool liquid in her mouth for a moment—on a warm night in a warm room packed with warm bodies, beer didn't taste half bad, she decided—then swallowed, and repeated the question. "What do I do for fun?"

Sally giggled and cast her a meaningful glance. "Besides the obvious, of course."

"The obvious?" she echoed, her words nearly drowned out by the country western band, the crowd and the general noise level in Hal's House of Honky Tonk that seemed to get progressively louder as the evening wore on.

Under the table her companion gave Georgiana a playful nudge with her knee. "You know . . ."

Her brain didn't seem to be working properly; she was drawing a blank. "I know *what*?"

Sally laughed in a suggestive manner. "What you and Cole do together."

"Ah . . ." Georgiana was pretty sure that Sally Meyers didn't mean running away from the scene of a murder.

The younger woman was bursting at the seams with curiosity. "Have you been married before?"

"No."

"Any kids?"

"No children."

Sally made a disbelieving sound and then got the most incredible expression on her young face: eyebrows raised, eyes wide open, mouth agape. "You weren't a virgin, were you?"

Georgiana choked and barely managed to get out, "I beg your pardon."

Her less-than-subtle table companion forged ahead in her own inimitable way. "Do you mind if I ask how old you are?"

Compared to some of the questions Sally had been asking, this one was relatively inoffensive. "I'm twenty-nine."

"You weren't a virgin," the girl concluded.

Georgiana decided what she was or wasn't in that department was none of Sally Meyers's business. She also recognized that the girl meant no harm; she just didn't know any better.

The young mother-to-be heaved a huge sigh and fell forward onto her elbows. "He sure is a dreamboat."

"Who is?"

Brown eyes rolled. "Your husband, of course."

Georgiana hadn't realized that the word *dreamboat* was still in use. "Cole is a handsome man."

"It's more than good looks."

"Is it?"

Sally lowered her voice to a confidential level, as if she wanted to make certain no one overheard her. "Even though I'm a married woman now, and Cole is a little too old for me, I can still tell that he's a babe magnet.''

Georgiana smiled to herself. ''A babe magnet.''

Sally shrugged her shoulders. ''He's one of those men who just seems to attract women.''

Georgiana recalled part of the telephone conversation she had overheard last night between Coleman Worth and Martin Davis. Cole had mentioned that a woman had made a pass at him in a cactus garden. Occupational hazard, she presumed.

''Yup. Like bees to honey: that's women and Cole,'' she said to Sally.

Crooked teeth sank into red lips. ''Still, your husband doesn't strike me as the slam-bam-thank-you-ma'am type, either.''

Georgiana wasn't even going to ask for an explanation.

Sally Meyers added for good measure, and with an air of worldly wisdom for someone not yet out of her teens, ''You'll have to keep your eye on him.''

''Yes, I will.''

In fact, Georgiana would like to have her eye on Coleman Worth right now. After they had concluded their dance, if one could call it dancing—a flame of color rose to her cheeks when she thought about the intimacies they had shared in full view of the public— Cole had muttered something about a horse and then gone off with Jacob Meyers, leaving her with the young Mrs. Meyers.

''Of course, I can see why Cole fell for you hook, line and sinker,'' Sally spoke up.

Georgiana was curious. ''You can?''

A penciled eyebrow was arched in a knowing fashion. ''You're not just another pretty face or one more sexy body. You're more than that. You're like those waters.''

Georgiana was stumped. ''Waters?''

"What's the expression?" Pretty lips pouted in thought. Then fingers were snapped. "I've got it. 'Still waters run deep.' That's what I was trying to remember. There's a lot more to you, Georgiana, than meets the eye."

She was amazed. Apparently there was more to Sally Meyers than met the eye, too. "Thank you."

As it turned out, Georgiana never had the opportunity to answer Sally's question about what she did for fun. No doubt the girl would have found it odd that Georgiana couldn't recall the last time she'd done something, anything, purely for fun.

The two men reappeared with smug, self-satisfied expressions on their faces. They stood beside the table.

"Thanks, Cole," the younger man said as they shook hands.

"Thank you, Jacob. We'll be seeing you again as soon as we can. Or you'll be contacted by Martin Davis."

Jacob's thin, youthful face was suffused with pleasure. "I'm not worried. I know she's in good hands."

The authority in Cole's voice was convincing. "I'll take care of her. You can count on it."

"And you can count on me."

Cole turned, looked down at Georgiana and took her hand in his. "Time for us to head out, sugar."

"We're leaving?"

"Yes." His eyes narrowed. "You look beat."

"I am tired," Georgiana admitted.

She was past tired. She was past exhausted. She had always wondered if it was physically, humanly possible to sleep with one's eyes open. She had her answer.

They quickly said good-bye to the Meyerses and made their way through the crowd to the front door of Hal's.

That's when Georgiana remembered to ask him, "Did you find your horse?"

"In a manner of speaking," was Cole's reply.

"In what manner of speaking?" she repeated, tagging along behind him.

"Horsepower."

"Horsepower?"

"You'll see," he promised as he took her by the arm and steered her across the parking lot.

Cole stopped beside a pickup she'd never seen before and opened the passenger door. Georgiana stood there and stared at the truck in front of them.

It was a piece of junk.

It was beat-up. It had patched rust spots here and there. One fender was missing altogether. It was a nondescript color; possibly more than one nondescript color. In the pale yellow glow cast across the parking lot from two security lights high overhead, it appeared to be brown or gray. Or maybe it just needed washing. The bed of the truck—she had the correct terminology down cold—was topped off with a homemade makeshift covering.

Georgiana ventured to guess, not really knowing, but definitely having suspicions, "Where's your pickup truck?"

Cole gave a decisive nod of his head, his eyes never leaving the vehicle in front of them. "I traded it."

She made a small, strangled sound. "For what?"

He patted the tricolored hood. "Bessie."

She'd heard that name before. "Bessie?"

The expression he turned to her bore no trace of apology. "That's what young Jacob calls the souped-up truck he's been working on for the past couple of years."

Bessie obviously needed more work done on her.

Georgiana's tone was incredulous. "You traded our beautiful blue pickup truck for this piece of—"

Cole quickly interjected, "Watch what you say about Bessie. She could be sensitive about name-calling."

Georgiana could think of nothing more appropriate to say. "Have you lost your mind?"

Cole leaned against the sagging truck door. "I hope not. I usually need it."

She wouldn't laugh. She wouldn't even crack a smile. But Georgiana had to admit she was tempted. "I thought you were a shrewd businessman."

"I am," Cole said in his own defense.

"And I suppose you acquired Bessie in one of your shrewder business deals."

"Bet your cowboy boots I did," Cole assured her as he helped her into the cab.

Georgiana noted the pair of red foam dice and the gold tassel from a graduation cap dangling from the rearview mirror. In one corner of the dashboard was a deodorizer in the shape of a crown: no doubt that was where the faint smell of rotting oranges emanated from. The overhead light glowed red instead of the traditional white. The bench seat and the steering wheel were covered in matching sheepskin.

"I've never seen anything like this," she admitted, with an attempt at lightness.

The door creaked and groaned as Cole slammed it shut after her. "This is a Cadillac compared to my first pickup."

Georgiana opened her arms and let them fall in the classic gesture of defeat. After all, what was done was done. And it was Cole's right to do whatever he wanted to: it was—it had been—his truck.

Still, she wondered, "Where's our stuff?"

"Don't worry. It's all secured in the back of Bessie. Jacob helped me move everything."

"I'll bet he was glad to help."

"He was." Cole headed around the front of the vehicle, but she could hear him through the open windows. "I promised Jacob that we'd take good care of Bessie and return her unscathed."

She took a wild guess. "Meanwhile he's going to be driving around in a brand-new blue pickup truck."

Cole confirmed her suspicions. "That's about the size of it."

She had to know the reason. "Why?"

Cole's answer was a good one. "To get the men in the suits off our backs."

Georgiana's mouth formed a perfectly round O. "Of course." She should have thought of that. She could only blame her lack of insight on her lack of sleep.

Cole yanked open the stubborn door on the driver's side. "I didn't want Jacob and Sally to end up trading safe old Bessie for any kind of trouble, so we made a few cosmetic changes to the blue truck."

"Like what?"

"Well, for one thing we switched the license plates."

"Can you do that?"

"We did it."

"And for another?"

Cole climbed behind the wheel. "Jacob and I added a few artistic dents."

She studied him for a moment or two. "You deliberately defaced a brand-new vehicle."

Cole turned the key in the ignition and Bessie's engine instantly revved to life. His answer, when he finally gave it, was adamant and succinct. "Had to."

She didn't understand.

An explanation was forthcoming. "If the men in the

dark suits spot the truck now, they won't think it's the same one we were driving. That way they'll be sure to leave the Meyerses alone.''

"Meanwhile we make our getaway in this . . .''

"In Bessie." Cole patted the dash. "There's a lot more to Bessie than meets the eye.''

" 'Still waters run deep,' '' Georgiana murmured.

"Exactly." He turned and studied her. "Then you do understand.''

"I understand.''

"Bessie has several unique features I'll show you when we stop and make camp for the night,'' Cole went on to tell her.

Make camp?

As in camping?

Camping was definitely *not* Georgiana Burne-Jones's idea of fun.

They had traveled for an hour, perhaps even longer, through the dark Arizona night when Cole turned off onto a gravel road and stopped the vintage truck. ''Make yourself comfortable for a few minutes. I need to make a phone call to Martin Davis.''

Georgiana watched as he got out of the pickup with his cellular phone in hand. He punched in a series of numbers and held the device to his ear as he paced back and forth in Bessie's headlights.

Martin must have answered on the other end. She could faintly hear Cole's voice when he spoke. The night was downright chilly, as nights tended to be in this part of the country in the late spring, so the windows of the truck were rolled up. No fancy automatic windows for Bessie. Hers went up and down the old-fashioned way: with a crank handle and manual labor.

Georgiana put her head back against the seat and

gazed out the front windshield. The only light visible was the headlamps of the pickup and the stars in the sky.

She watched the man striding back and forth in front of the truck. Sally Meyers, despite her age and lack of sophistication, was right. Coleman Worth was a "babe magnet." It was more than his rugged good looks or the fact that he was a powerful and wealthy man. There was something about him that made a woman feel that she was special, cherished, appreciated.

It was more than that, too.

Cole was the sexiest man she had ever met. Yet he wasn't sexy in a deliberate or obvious way: that would have put her off and turned her off cold.

His was the kind of sexuality that came from being a real man: a man who was strong in mind, body and spirit. It wasn't as if Cole flaunted his sex appeal—although the man certainly had his fair share and more of self-confidence—but he didn't go around behaving as if he were God's gift to women.

Georgiana intensely disliked men who thought they were God's gift to women.

Cole's sexuality, on the other hand, came from a healthy place. He was a male of the species in the prime of life. He was strong and robust and virile. He was appreciative of the female without being overbearing about it.

Yup, Coleman Worth was the sexiest man she'd ever met.

Hard as she tried—and even with the subject of sex on her mind—Georgiana couldn't stay awake. Her eyes kept closing. She finally stopped fighting the fatigue that insisted on taking over her mind and body. She curled up on her side, snuggled down into the sheepskin seat cover and let herself go.

After all, in the past twenty-four hours the world had suddenly become a very large place and she had become a very small cog in its wheel.

Yet for tonight, at least, she was safe. Cole was awake and watching over her.

''The young man's name is Jacob Meyers, and I'd appreciate it if you would take care of the matter we talked about, Martin.''

''Consider it done, Cole.''

He kicked at the loose gravel on the road with the toe of his boot. ''We ran into some trouble.''

Martin's immediate concern was apparent in his voice. ''What kind of trouble?''

''There was a roadblock set up on Pima Road last night or very early this morning. I'd like you to check it out with the highway department and see if they'll tell you the reason it was there.''

Martin voiced what was on both their minds. ''You want to know if it had anything to do with Ms. Burne-Jones.''

''Exactly.'' The night was getting downright cold. Cole stuffed his hand into the front pocket of his jeans. ''There's another matter I need to discuss with you.''

''What other matter?''

''I'm pretty sure we're being followed.''

''Who?''

''Three goons in black suits.''

There was a moment or two of silence on the other end of the connection. ''How would they—how would anyone—know you're with Ms. Burne-Jones?''

''That's what inquiring minds want to know.''

''Any ideas?''

''I don't have a clue.''

''Did the goons give you any trouble?''

"Nothing I couldn't handle." Cole decided not go into details on just how he'd thrown them off the scent.

Despite the late hour, Martin Davis sounded alert. "You must have figured it was necessary to switch vehicles."

"I think they were following the blue truck."

"Christ, Cole, that could mean there was a leak on this end," Martin swore.

"It could." He'd already considered the possibility himself. "Or it could mean somebody who's very good—a consummate professional—was keeping an eye on the Sonoran."

Martin was dead quiet for a minute. "You know what you're talking about here, don't you?"

Cole exhaled wearily. "Yes."

His second-in-command at Worth Industries recited the facts all the same. "Professionals in dark suits. Murder. This is nothing to mess with, believe me."

He did believe Martin Davis. "She's innocent. I would stake my life on it."

There was a telling pause. Then the other man said, "I think you have."

Cole threaded his fingers through his hair. He spoke more rapidly now. "I want you to check up on a few people for me."

"Shoot." Martin must have reconsidered his choice of words. "Go ahead."

"Paul Isherwood. He was supposedly some kind of financier who was staying at the Sonoran."

"The victim, right?"

Cole's mouth curved humorlessly. "Let's just say he's the guy who's dead."

"Who else do you want a background check on?"

"William Regen, head butler at the Sonoran. Alfred Crick, ex-butler for the Burne-Jones family: he currently lives in Carefree. Detective Mallory, Homicide. And anything you can find out about the men who showed up at Isherwood's suite that night.'' Cole added, ''Be very careful where you poke your nose in on that last one.''

''Got it.'' There was a pause on the other end. ''Anyone else?''

He hated like hell doing it, but he knew it was the only wise course of action. ''Better check on Georgiana, too.''

''Georgiana Burne-Jones,'' Martin repeated.

''I didn't see her name in the newspapers or on television. In fact, there wasn't any coverage of the event up here. Do you still have connections inside the Wichita Falls police force?''

''I do.''

''Think a friend of a friend of a friend could quietly find out what's going on with an investigation in another city?''

''I'll try.''

''Thanks, Martin.''

''Hey, I owe you a few.'' There was silence. Then, ''More than a few.''

''All the same. Thanks.''

''Take care of yourself, Cole.''

''I am.''

''Stay in touch.''

''I will.'' Then he signed off with, ''Adios.''

When Cole returned to the cab of the truck, he found Georgiana half-sitting up, her head on her arm, her hat on the seat beside her.

She was sound asleep.

He'd let her doze for a few more minutes while he found a better place to park for the night and got their sleeping bags ready. Then he wouldn't have any choice. He'd have to wake her up.

Thirteen

"Georgiana."

Someone was shaking her shoulder.

"We're there."

Reluctantly she opened her eyes. She moved her mouth with difficulty. "Where's there?"

It was Coleman Worth's voice that answered her. "This is where we're spending the night."

Georgiana peered out through small slits in her eyelids. "I don't see any hotel."

"That's right," he said in a voice laced with what sounded like sarcasm. "You don't see any hotel."

With a great deal of effort—her arms felt like pincushions—she pushed herself up into a sitting position and tried again in a half-hopeful tone, "Is there a motel?"

"No motel."

Her mouth tasted like gym socks. Or what she imagined gym socks would taste like, anyway. "A bed and breakfast?"

"No bed and breakfast."

Her eyes opened wider. "I don't see anything but a few trees, a mountain and darkness."

Cole was the picture of patience. "That's right, Georgiana. This is the great outdoors where we're camping."

"Camping." The word was foreign on her tongue. "I've never been camping before."

"Somehow I'm not surprised," the man beside her muttered under his breath. Then he declared loud and clear, "Camping will be a whole new experience for you."

She didn't want a whole new experience. At least not the camping variety, Georgiana wanted to tell him. But beggars couldn't be choosers, and she was lucky to have gotten this far. She knew it was only with Cole's help that she had.

The alternative, she must never forget, would have been "camping" in jail.

She was wide awake now. "I suppose it's foolish of me to inquire where the facilities are?"

"Facilities?" Cole paused and gave her a sideways glance. "You mean the latrine?"

Georgiana had never cared for the word *latrine,* or its rather rustic implication. "I suppose I do."

He made an all-inclusive gesture with one arm. "Take your pick of bushes."

"Bushes?"

Cole had the nerve to laugh at her. "You might want to make plenty of noise on the way to your designated bush, Ms. Burne-Jones, so you don't surprise any critters who, in turn, may have an even bigger surprise in store for you."

She wasn't amused.

She told him so.

"There's a roll of toilet paper in the back of the truck," he said as an afterthought.

She could be as droll as the next person. "I see all the comforts of home are provided."

"You get what you pay for." Cole paused in what he was doing, which appeared to be fastening some kind of heavy tarp over the end of the pickup truck, reached into a canvas duffel bag at his elbow and held an oblong object out to her. "You'd better take a flashlight along with you, too."

"Thank you."

"You're welcome." Cole went back to his task. Then he said, without turning his head this time, "Don't take any longer than you have to."

"Believe me, I won't."

It was impossible to tell whether or not he spoke ironically when he admonished her, "We need to get bedded down for the night as soon as we can."

"Why?" she called over her shoulder.

The man always had an answer. "Daybreak comes early. We have to be up and on our way at first light."

"I won't be long," she promised and took off for the nearest bush that still afforded her some privacy.

Squatting behind a brittle brush in the middle of nowhere in the dead of night was not Georgiana Burne-Jones's notion of fun. Heaven knew what kind of creatures were out and about at this hour. She took care of business as quickly as possible, especially when she heard something scurry through the underbrush nearby.

"I only hope it's you, Mr. Jackrabbit, and *not* you, Mr. Snake," she mumbled under her breath.

She made a beeline for the truck.

"We'll be sleeping in the back of Bessie," Cole informed her when she returned. "There's enough room for two sleeping bags."

Georgiana peered into the rear of the pickup truck. "It looks very . . . cozy."

Too cozy.

She hadn't realized in what close proximity they would be for the night. The one saving grace, she concluded, was that they'd each be in their own sleeping bag.

It wasn't that she was afraid of anything Cole might do, but circumstances like these were bound to create a sense of intimacy that wouldn't be lost on either of them.

Well, dammit, she'd just have to keep a firm grip on herself, stay away from any alcoholic beverages and not do anything foolish as she had at Hal's House of Honky Tonk.

Even if the idea for the kiss between them had originated with Cole, even if it had been the result of a potential outside threat and nothing personal, Georgiana still couldn't believe that she had responded to the man with such wild abandon, and then practically begged him to touch her. After all, she was a mature, strong-minded woman, not some inexperienced, easily reduced-to-Jell-O girl.

There would not be a repeat performance. She would stay on her side of Bessie and Cole on his. That was all there was to it.

She hoped.

They stood together by the tailgate of the pickup. "Do you want the right or the left?" he asked.

Georgiana studied the sleeping bags arranged side by side and swallowed hard. "Do you have a preference?"

"Yes. But you wouldn't want to hear it," Cole said with what sounded suspiciously like a chuckle.

That shut her up.

"I assume we sleep in our clothes," she finally commented with what she hoped was a casual air.

"Unless you have a better idea," he drawled in that Texas accent of his.

He gave her a helping hand as she quickly climbed up into the back of the pickup. She chose the sleeping bag on the left and plopped down. "Now what?"

"Now you pull off your boots, turn them upside down—that's to keep the creepy-crawlies out—and zip yourself in for the night," Cole instructed. Then he demonstrated how the two-sided zipper worked.

Georgiana shivered. "It's cold in here."

"You won't be cold once your body heat warms the inside of your sleeping bag."

She watched as Cole pulled the tailgate up after him, arranged the tarp, took off his boots, carefully turned them over and slipped into the sleeping bag alongside hers.

"You've done this before, haven't you?"

"Yup."

"Often?"

"Often enough." He stretched out, arm pillowed behind his head, and stared up at the ceiling.

That's when Georgiana realized there was a window of sorts directly over their heads: it was a piece of hard, clear plastic nailed to the makeshift truck cover.

She found herself gazing up at the sky. The moon was a crescent of pure silver against a midnight-blue backdrop. There were countless stars, mere pinpoints of light. Were there always so many stars in the night sky? Or were they only more visible once you were away from the distracting lights of the city?

For some time neither of them spoke.

Then Georgiana whispered in a reverent tone, " 'The night has a thousand eyes . . .' " She swallowed a deep breath of cool air. "I don't remember how the rest of the poem goes."

His voice was soft and cold when he said, "It's something melodramatic and sappy about a whole life's light dying when love is over.''

Georgiana turned her head and stared searchingly at him. In the shadows she could make out his profile and little more. "Do you believe that's true?"

It was some time before Cole responded. "I don't believe in that kind of love."

"What kind is that?"

"The 'through thick and through thin' kind. The 'till death us do part' kind. The everlasting kind. The 'for this life and whatever comes after' kind."

Georgiana wanted to know. As a matter of fact, she *needed* to know. "Why not?"

The man stretched out beside her didn't answer her question. Instead, he asked one of his own. "Do you actually know anyone who has loved someone else that much?"

She gave it serious consideration. "I think Alfred Crick loved his Mildred more than life itself."

Even in the dark, she knew that his mouth drew into a tight line. "One person. Maybe."

"You're cynical when it comes to love."

"I'm cynical about a lot of things." At least the man was honest. "Have you ever been in love?"

Georgiana snuggled down into her sleeping bag. Cole was right about one thing: her own body heat was warming her nicely. "I was in love with Jimmy Jenkins in the fifth grade."

He seemed amused and interested. "Tell me more."

"I finally got up my nerve and declared my feelings for Jimmy in the usual way."

"The usual way?"

"I wrote him a love letter, fifth-grade style."

"What's a love letter, fifth-grade style?"

"It's written in pencil on wide-ruled notebook paper."

"So what happened?"

"After three agonizing days of waiting for his answer, he informed me that he liked Karen Rebisell better."

"Shame on Jimmy Jenkins." Cole turned his head toward her in the dark. "Anyone since the fifth grade?"

"I've had my share of crushes and thinking I was in love," she said guardedly.

She couldn't read his expression in the dark, but something in his tone made her glance at him when he asked, "Then you've never been truly, madly, deeply in love with a man?"

"I suppose not." After a heavy pause, Georgiana went on. "What about you, Cole? Have you ever been truly, madly, deeply in love with a woman?"

"Nope."

That was a quick response on Mr. Worth's part. Perhaps a little too quick.

Georgiana voiced her observation. "You seem very certain you've never been in love."

With a touch of sardonicism in his voice, Cole listed his reasons. "First I was too poor. Then I was working too hard, at least twenty hours a day. Now I'm too rich."

She stirred in her sleeping bag. "Ah . . ."

"Ah what?"

"It's the how-do-I-know-if-I'm-loved-only-for-myself-or-for-my-money syndrome."

Cole's voice was clipped. "Something like that."

She was more sympathetic to his predicament than he realized. "My family had money once."

"And?"

She told him the truth. "When we lost our money, we also lost most of our friends."

"Which only goes to prove my point."

She supposed it did.

Without preamble, Coleman Worth changed the subject. "Hey, I promised that Bessie had a surprise in store for us and I nearly forgot to show you what it is."

"That's right, you did promise," she agreed.

"Close your eyes and don't open them until I tell you to," Cole ordered as he reached out of his sleeping bag and fiddled with some kind of mechanism situated behind his head. "Are your eyes still closed?" he double-checked.

"Still closed."

"Don't open them until I give you the word," he said, repeating his orders.

"Yessir, Mr. Worth. I will wait for the official word from you," she promised.

Cole seemed immensely pleased with himself. Georgiana could clearly hear it in his voice when he finally said to her, "You can open your eyes now."

She opened her eyes.

For a moment it took her breath away. She blinked several times in rapid succession. Then she stared and stared until she felt the sting of tears in her throat and at the corners of her eyes.

"What do you think?"

"It's magic," was all she managed.

For strung along the sides and the top of the battered old pickup truck were dozens of small, sparkling colored Christmas lights: red and blue and green and white. Cole must have plugged an electric cord into some sort of portable battery.

"Christmas lights in the middle of goddamn nowhere," he declared. Then it was some little time before he went on to ask her, "Do you like them?"

"I"—she swallowed—"love them."

Cole raised his head slowly to stare at her. His tone was inquisitive. "Are you crying?"

"Not exactly," she answered in a slightly distorted voice.

"What is 'not exactly' supposed to mean?"

Since he insisted on knowing, she'd tell him. "It means I'm surprised. It means I'm choked up. It means I'm feeling very emotional. I have tears in my eyes. I may even be on the verge of crying. But it doesn't necessarily mean that I am crying at the moment."

"Women," Cole muttered.

Georgiana tried to keep the quiver out of her voice. "What is that supposed to mean?"

He shook his head and sighed. "It means I'll never understand women."

"Men never do."

"Who does?"

"Sometimes other women." Georgiana cleared her throat. "Bessie is special, isn't she?"

He grunted in the affirmative. "Jacob claimed that she might not look like much on the outside, but she was special under the hood where it counted."

"I think Bessie is special on the outside, too." Georgiana lay there and basked in the glow of the colored lights. "Think of that sweet young couple stringing Christmas lights around the outside of their pickup truck."

"Yup."

"Did you ever have Christmas as a child, Cole?" she inquired very carefully.

"Not really."

Georgiana didn't wish to pry into his personal life. But then again, maybe she did. She wanted to know more about Coleman Worth, and it wasn't merely idle curiosity. She had a genuine desire to understand the man, if that was possible. She had a feeling that he had more layers to him than an onion.

"What was it like?"

"What was *what* like?"

"Christmas . . . when you were a child?"

His voice had a rough edge to it. "It's not something I like to talk about."

Georgiana unzipped her sleeping bag just far enough to get her hand free. She reached out and nudged the arm behind Cole's head until he put his hand in hers. She took heart from that single, small response on his part.

Nothing ventured, nothing gained.

"Perhaps life is playing some kind of cruel joke on us, Cole," she began. "Or perhaps we've been given an opportunity that few people ever get."

She stopped and moistened her lips.

He waited.

She went on. "Through no fault or intention or design of our own, you and I have been thrown together in extraordinary circumstances. We're strangers and yet we're not really strangers. Not anymore. For the rest of our lives, no matter what else happens to either of us, we will always have had this time together."

"You know the old joke," he said softly.

"What old joke?"

"Ours is a strange and wonderful relationship."

Georgiana waited for the punch line.

Cole delivered it with perfect timing. "You're strange and I'm wonderful."

She laughed.

It felt good to laugh. In fact, it felt better than good. It felt wonderful

"Damn, it is different," he admitted.

"You can say that again," she agreed.

So he did. "It is different being with you." Then Cole blew out his breath and, to her amazement, began to talk. "For a kid like me, Christmas, and every other day in the year, was, in a word, lonely."

"Is that the only word?"

He shook his head. "Sometimes it was frightening. Sometimes, most times, it was uncertain. For a long time I wasn't sure anyone cared about me."

She walked on eggs. "Did that change?"

"Once in a while a teacher would take a special interest in me. To this day I have a great deal of respect for anyone in that profession. It was one of my teachers who finally persuaded me to finish high school and even try college. I never made it past the first semester, unfortunately." She wondered if Cole realized that his hand had tightened around hers. "I'm strictly a self-educated man, Georgiana."

"We both know graduating from college doesn't guarantee that someone is educated or that they'll be successful. You obviously had the desire and the determination to succeed. Look how far it's taken you," she said in earnest.

Cole was silent.

She went on. "My parents inherited their money. They were spoiled and frivolous and they took their good fortune for granted. In the end, they lost a fortune and so much more." But this wasn't about her or her family. It was about Cole. "You're a self-made man. Wherever you are, whatever you have, whoever you are in your heart of hearts, you know that you've earned it all for yourself."

Fourteen

Cole didn't like it.

Not one damned bit.

He was spilling his guts to a woman he barely knew. He never spilled his guts to anyone: man or woman, friend or foe. It wasn't like him. It wasn't his style. He didn't confide anything to anyone. That was the way he wanted it. That was the way he preferred it to be.

Cole knew what his reputation was in the business world. He was considered a loner and one tough but fair sonofabitch. His business associates were right: he was the son of a bitch.

He also realized that his past set him apart, made him different from other people, made him alone, made him a loner.

In addition to going off by himself at infrequent intervals over the years, a while back Cole had bought a ranch in the middle of Texas, away from civilization, his nearest neighbors at least fifty miles in any given direction.

There was a housekeeper, of course. She was married to the ranch foreman. She came in three days a week to cook and clean for Cole when he was in residence, but she didn't live on the premises. The couple had their own bungalow more than several miles from, and out of sight of, the main house.

Cole didn't even try to explain why he lived alone in the huge, sprawling ranch house that had come with the property, or why he never invited any of his business associates or his so-called friends to stay at the Circle W.

He figured he didn't owe anyone an explanation.

The truth was the Circle W—the brand was created from his own initials, a C encompassing a W—was his place of sanctuary. He didn't want other people there.

Ever.

It wasn't that he had been around too many people in his life. It was the people he'd been around and the world he'd lived in, a world most ordinary people were unaware existed.

It was the underbelly of society that no one liked to talk about. It was a world where a man—he had only been a boy when he'd struck out on his own and entered that hellhole of a world—acquired certain skills if he wanted to survive: skills that might involve knives and guns, and certainly fists.

It was a world where nothing was what it seemed to be and no one was who he appeared to be.

It was a world where a man learned to trust only one person—himself—where street smarts and gut instincts saved a man when nothing else could.

He'd always been alone, Cole recognized. He always would be.

Women.

Well, women were another matter altogether.

Cole ran his free hand—the one Georgiana Burne-

Jones wasn't clasping in hers at the moment—along his jawline and around to the back of his neck.

He remembered discussing women in a cursory fashion with Martin Davis on one rare occasion several years ago, when they'd both had a couple of beers too many.

"Women are more trouble than they're worth, Worth," Martin had claimed and then they had both laughed at what had passed, under the circumstances, for a witticism.

Martin Davis should know. He was the same age as Cole and he'd already been married and divorced three times.

When it came to women, a man was apparently damned if he did and damned if he didn't.

Cole blew out his breath and stared at the twinkling Christmas lights strung around Bessie's homemade framework.

For chrissakes, what was he thinking of? What was he doing in the back of a beat-up old pickup truck with a woman like Georgiana Burne-Jones?

She was the kind of woman who drove him crazy.

She exuded class and breeding, culture and a privileged education, from the top of her light brown silky hair right down to the tips of her toes.

Cole knew in his gut that she was one of those women who ordinarily would never allow her hair to get mussed up. He was willing to bet that she was never wrinkled, that she was never frazzled or raised her voice or lost her temper.

He'd give odds that Ms. Burne-Jones was always in control—unless confronted by the prospect of murder—that she always said and did the right thing.

She was the wrong kind of woman.

She was the kind of woman who could make a man feel like he was meeting himself coming and going. She was the kind of woman who could turn a man inside out while she twirled him around her little finger. She was the kind of woman who could get inside his head, inside his heart, and rip him to shreds.

And she was a lady.

That made her the worst kind of woman of all.

"Women: we can't live with them," Martin had complained bitterly the night they had been drinking and commiserating together. "And we can't live without them."

Well, he could.

Cole hadn't met a woman yet who wasn't more trouble than she was worth.

"What's that smell?" Georgiana inquired, interrupting his solitary thoughts.

Cole put his nose in the air. "Rain."

"Rain." She repeated the word as if there were some special meaning to it.

"One of the world's most unforgettable fragrances is the desert after a storm," Cole heard himself telling her as if nothing had changed in the last two or three minutes.

She interlaced her fingers with his and asked, "What does it smell like?"

He recalled the memory of the desert after a downpour. "Sort of sweet-spicy and sort of pungent. It's the aroma of rain-drenched sage and rain-slicked creosote."

"I was in Seville once a few years ago," Georgiana reminisced in a slightly husky voice. "I was wandering through a little plaza—I remember I could hear the sound of a guitar being played somewhere in the distance—and then down the narrow streets of Santa Cruz, breathing in the heady scent of a Spanish flower called Lady of the Night. I was told later that its aroma can only be detected after dark, and that in Spain the flower is synonymous with love.''

How did she always manage to get the conversation back to a subject he preferred to avoid?

Rather abruptly Cole said to her, ''It's going to rain. I'd better turn off the Christmas lights.''

He heard her sigh of contentment. ''It was a lovely surprise. Thank you, Cole.''

''You're welcome, Georgiana.''

The lights blinked off. The night went black. And the rain began to beat down on the plastic covering above their heads.

Cole knew from the rhythm of her breathing that Georgiana wasn't asleep.

Then, out of the darkness, her voice came to him softly, a little hesitantly, he thought. ''Have you ever tried to discover anything about your parents?''

From the frying pan into the fire.

Maybe it was time to bring up the ghost of Christmas past again. Cole sure didn't like the direction their conversation was taking at the moment.

He decided to tell her just enough to satisfy her curiosity and hopefully get her off his back. ''Once. Years ago.''

He should have guessed that she wouldn't drop the subject. ''Do you mind if I ask what you found out?''

Of course he minded.

Cole recognized that his tone was approaching hostility when he informed her, ''I'm a nobody from nowhere.''

''We're all someone from somewhere,'' she finally said.

''Not the way you are.''

''I don't understand,'' she admitted.

Then he'd have to help her understand. "Who are your parents?" he asked.

"Their names are Maud and Jeremy Burne-Jones," Georgiana answered.

Cole continued his interrogation. "I mean, who are your parents in terms of their backgrounds?"

There was something different in her voice—perhaps she was feeling slightly on the defensive—when she said, "Well, my mother was originally from England."

He stopped her right there. "What's your mother's family history?"

She hemmed and hawed. "I don't believe we have the time to go into all of that."

He wasn't about to let her off the hook. "Why not?"

After several moments, Georgiana said, "Well, for one thing, I don't know that much about my mother's side of the family, and for another, the Burnes go back a few years."

He was like a bulldog. "How far back can the Burnes trace their ancestry?"

"To before the Conqueror."

He had her now. "I take it the Conqueror you're referring to is William the Conqueror, who arrived on Britain's hallowed ground and fought and won the Battle of Hastings in 1066."

Georgiana's voice was small but clear. "That's the one."

The cross-examination continued. "Tell me about Jeremy Burne-Jones."

He could almost see her nervously moistening her lips. "My father is a poet."

Cole managed *not* to blurt out the first thing that popped into his head. In this instance it had been a slightly snide comment like, *Now, there's a useful occupation for a grown man.*

Instead he remarked, "I've never actually known anyone who was a poet."

Georgiana wasn't apologetic. "Well, my father is."

Cole was curious. "Is he any good?"

"Some say that he is."

He made every effort to keep his tone of voice non-judgmental. "He's an American, right?"

She nodded. "He was born and raised in Boston."

His next question was, "When did your father's ancestors arrive in this country?"

There was a slight pause. "They came over on the Mayflower."

Why wasn't Cole surprised? "So your pedigree"—as he had suspected all along—"is a mile long."

"In this day and age, and in this country, we tend to think of dogs having pedigrees, rather than people."

"That is a matter of opinion."

To her credit—and somewhat to Cole's surprise—Georgiana Burne-Jones turned out *not* to be a snob. "I don't see what this has to do with anything."

Cole was determined to enlighten her. "I am in possession of the bare, if somewhat sordid facts about my own parentage . . . or at least the maternal half."

"You don't have to tell me this, Cole, unless you want to," she quickly assured him.

He was driven by a cold, cold anger, and he recognized the fact, but he didn't care. "My sixteen-year-old mother, alone and afraid and unwed, apparently had hitched a ride with a truck driver heading south out of Fort Worth, Texas. She made it as far as Coleman County before going into labor and giving birth to a son at the local hospital. The ink had barely dried on that son's birth certificate before the girl, who had given her name as Gloria Worth and who had refused to identify the father, hightailed it out of town, leaving her baby behind.''

''Oh, Cole,'' she whispered, trying to reach for his hand again. This time he did not cooperate.

''I was abandoned twelve hours after entering this world, Georgiana. It's not something that I have a problem with, but it is something I've never forgotten. I have no idea who my parents are, and frankly, at this point in my life, I don't give a damn.''

He was lying.

He did give a damn.

He did care.

And it explained so much, Georgiana reflected as she lay beside him in the back of the pickup truck.

She had suspected that Coleman Worth was a self-made man, but she'd had no idea just how right she was. Cole had created himself from scratch. He was even more amazing than she had thought.

There was an old saying: a pedigree and a quarter would get you a cup of coffee. Of course, that was years ago when a cup of coffee still cost a quarter.

Cole was right.

And Cole was wrong.

She had learned some time ago that who you were only mattered here, now, in the present. What you had been had no significance, was of no consequence.

Georgiana suddenly felt a warm hand against her cheek.

''It's getting late and we have to be up early and on our way,'' Cole reminded her.

''Where are we headed?''

''North.''

''What's north?''

''Utah.''

Fifteen

"The boss was really p.o.'d when I told him," Gruber said as he slid into the booth across from Samuelson and Ford.

"Whadya expect?" Ford mumbled over the rim of his coffee mug. "We screwed up."

"It wasn't our fault," Gruber whined. "We were given bad information."

"Not bad information." Samuelson found his voice. He rested his elbows on the speckled Formica tabletop, leaned forward slightly from the waist and carefully enunciated each syllable. "In-com-plete in-for-ma-tion."

Gruber snorted and reached for one of the plastic-coated menus wedged between the salt and pepper shakers and a red squeeze bottle with the word KETCHUP printed across the front. "Easy for you to say. You weren't the one who had to call the boss and tell him that we lost their trail."

Ford took another swallow of piping-hot, diner-strength coffee before he ventured, "There was no way we could have known they'd make a run for it last night.''

Samuelson contributed his two-cents' worth. ''Their actions were illogical.''

''Illogical or not, the pair of them have bolted,'' Gruber grumbled, studying the breakfast menu.

Ford continued to do his thinking out loud. ''They had no reason to suspect we were following them.''

It was Samuelson who finally speculated, ''I wonder what it was that gave us away.''

Over the top of the oversize menu Gruber offered his opinion. ''Maybe Worth is just one suspicious sonofabitch.''

Samuelson, always the best dressed of the three, said, ''Maybe he is and maybe he isn't, but I told you we shouldn't have gone into that country western bar dressed in suits.''

For once Gruber agreed with him. ''Suits were definitely out of place at Harold's.''

''Hal's,'' Ford automatically corrected him. ''And thank you both for your sartorial input.''

''It's all water under the bridge now,'' Samuelson pointed out, always the philosopher of the trio.

Ford was not a happy man. And that was before he downed his coffee, burning his tongue in the process. ''So much for handling this whole business with a certain amount of finesse, so much for taking care of matters in a discreet fashion, so much for goddamned subtlety.'' He wasn't finished. ''Right under our collective noses, Worth and the woman somehow manage to switch vehicles and apparently license plates, too.'' He shook his head in disgust. ''We don't even know in what direction they're headed.''

Gruber proposed, ''In other words, we're right back where we started.''

"We aren't that lucky. If our information is even partly accurate, we're up shit creek. Supposedly Coleman Worth knows this entire region of the country from Texas to California, from Arizona to the Canadian border, like the back of his hand."

Samuelson observed, "The man gets around."

"Why shouldn't he? He's a fucking millionaire or something," Gruber grumbled.

"Multimillionaire," Ford corrected.

"Whatever." Gruber rubbed his hand back and forth over his rounded belly. "I'm hungry. I'm gonna order some breakfast."

"We might as well all eat a leisurely breakfast," Ford said as he gazed out the front window of Maggie's Diner. "It doesn't look like there's much else to do in this one-horse town."

Gruber had his mouth full of eggs and sausage before he remembered to tell his cohorts, "The boss wants us to sit tight until new information comes in on their probable location."

For a change, it was Ford who complained. "In other words, we get to sit around a lousy, two-bit motel room and wait for the telephone to ring."

Gruber stuffed more eggs and sausage between lips already shiny with grease. "Something like that."

Samuelson had the last word. "You each still owe me fifty dollars from our last 'outing.' We'll pass the time by playing a few hands of gin rummy."

They were inept fools.

All three of them.

He wondered who could have hired them and why. They certainly weren't professionals.

At least not by his standards.

At first he had been upset—and rightly so—that they

were even involved in this affair. But then he had quickly seen that they could serve a purpose, that they could be useful to him.

They were stupid.

They lacked both style and subtlety.

Under other circumstances, certainly under most circumstances, their incompetence could prove to be dangerous. As it was, they had unknowingly made his job easier.

They had provided a distraction.

And a distraction, he realized, was just what he had been looking for.

Sixteen

It was a desolate, yet beautiful landscape.

It was red earth, blue sky and yellow sun.

It was towering buttes and juniper-studded mesas, sandstone pinnacles and tortured hobgoblins of stone, all of varied and ever-changing hue.

Often referred to as the "Eighth Wonder of the World," according to Cole, it was Monument Valley and the other rugged, sandstone canyons and formations straddling the Arizona-Utah border.

"This is one of the most remote regions in the U.S.," he said to Georgiana as they bumped along the narrow, unpaved road.

She wondered briefly if that was the reason Cole seemed to be enjoying himself so much.

Her guide went on. "Not only are the roads unpaved, but in wet weather they're often impassable. This is also rattlesnake and scorpion country, so you don't walk where you can't look first. Even worse are clouds of 'no-see-ums' that invade the area for about two weeks at this time of the year. And, of course, there's always the danger of flash floods and rockfalls."

"You make it all sound so irresistible," Georgiana said tongue-in-cheek, as she hung on to the hand strap over the passenger door.

"It is in its own way." Cole kept both hands on the steering wheel and both eyes on the stretch of rock-strewn and potholed road ahead. "It's one of the most beautiful desert landscapes on earth."

And, apparently, one of the most uninhabited. She hadn't spotted another human being since they had stopped at the park headquarters and been given official permission to enter the region.

They had driven a number of miles before she observed, "There aren't any people."

"A few hundred Navajo families reside here, but they're spread out over nearly two thousand square miles. The original inhabitants left centuries ago."

Georgiana knew something of the region's history. "The original inhabitants would have been the cliff dwellers."

Cole became downright loquacious on the subject. "The Southwest is home to a number of strange phenomena, not the least of which are thousands of ancient and now long-abandoned cliff dwellings. Nearly every ridge or canyon slope will show some sign of having once been occupied. The more famous and accessible of the ruins were rediscovered at the end of the last century by ranch cowboys. The remote sites probably haven't been visited by a human being since they were deserted nearly seven hundred years ago."

Georgiana took a pair of sunglasses, courtesy of Martin Davis and his impeccable planning, from her shirt pocket and slipped them on. "Isn't there some mystery as to what happened to those early cliff dwellers?"

Cole pulled his Stetson down over his eyes another

half-inch and nodded. "Some time around 1300 the Anasazi just up and left their settlements. No one knows why even today. There has been speculation among scholars and archaeologists that it was the result of changes in climate and the amount of rainfall in the area. Some people believe that the Anasazi were absorbed into the ancestral tribe that we know today as the Hopis."

"I remember reading about the Anasazi. Aren't they the people the Navajos call the Ancient Ones?"

"Yup. I met a Navajo once who claimed that he'd heard the voice of an Ancient One speaking to him. At the time I thought he was *habla a tontas y a locas*."

Georgiana was intrigued. "Do you still think he was crazy?"

"Nope." Cole rubbed the back of his neck as if the small hairs at his nape had unexpectedly stood on end, or as if he had felt a sudden chill despite the warmth of the morning sun.

She cast him a sideways glance. "What made you change your mind?"

The timbre of his voice altered. "I came here to Monument Valley. I saw the silent cities of the Anasazi for myself. I stood in the vacant rooms of their cliff palaces and I felt the dust of centuries beneath my feet." He laughed self-consciously.

"Is that why we're here?"

Cole gave another crack of laughter. "We're here because you can't drive a car on these roads."

She didn't get it. "We're in a pickup truck."

Cole's mouth curved up at the corners. "Yes, but the three men who were tailing us were in a car."

She got it. "So even if they figure out where we're headed, they can't follow us unless they change vehicles first."

"That's the general idea."

"It should slow them down."

"Considerably."

"It's brilliant."

"Thank you." Cole went on to ask her, "Have you ever seen a cliff dwelling?"

She shook her head.

"Would you like to?"

Georgiana would be the first to admit that up until very recently she'd never been known for her adventurous spirit. "Is it safe?"

Cole swerved around a bowling-ball-size boulder in the middle of the road. "As long as you're with someone who knows exactly what he's doing out here."

"Do you?"

"Yes."

"Then I would like very much to see a cliff dwelling."

Cole turned off the main road and headed down another: it appeared to consist of two faint ruts in the desert floor and led to an even more remote section of the canyon.

Georgiana blew out her breath and lifted her ponytail off her neck. "You act like this is your own backyard."

Cole measured out his words. "I spent some time here a few years ago."

"On one of your famous sabbaticals?"

His reply was ambiguous. "In a way."

Georgiana turned the tables on him and employed his own interrogation techniques. "In what way?"

"I guess I may as well come clean."

"I guess you may as well."

"How do you get me to tell you things that I've never told anyone else?" he asked.

"I don't know," she admitted. "But you manage to do the same thing to me."

An ironic smile touched his lips. "Ah, it must be our unique relationship, then."

"It must be."

Cole continued with his confession. "It was the summer I was seventeen. I got into some trouble with the law."

Georgiana waited and she listened. Over the past couple of days she had learned that technique from Cole as well.

"I took something that didn't belong to me. The man involved decided not to press charges if I would agree to come and work on the reservation for three months." Cole added in an aside, "It turned out that he was part Navajo."

Georgiana gazed out the window of the pickup at the forlorn landscape that seemed to extend in every direction as far as the eye could see. "So you spent the summer here?"

Cole moved his head. "It changed my life. As a matter of fact, it probably saved my life." He took off his hat and wiped the sweat from his brow with his shirt-sleeve. "At first I hated it. It was hotter than hell, the work was damned hard and I learned what it really meant to be lonely and alone."

Georgiana was surprised by the lack of bitterness in his voice. "And then?"

"And then this place, and the solitude, grew on me." Piercing blue eyes, seemingly in a perpetual squint, scanned the horizon. "I thought I was tough. I thought I was strong. I thought I knew how to survive." Cole shook his head at his own youthful foibles. "I found out soon enough that I was soft and weak and as vulnerable as the next cocky teenager. But I learned," he said with some sense of self-satisfaction. "The desert became my teacher."

Like tempered steel, Georgiana reflected, that's what the man was on the inside as well as the outside.

Cole's lips folded in an obstinate line. "If it doesn't kill you, the desert makes you strong."

The words came from her almost unconsciously. "You survived."

"I survived."

"And thrived."

There was a pause. "Eventually."

Her eyes focused on the rugged landscape again. "Where are you taking me?"

Cole made an emphatic gesture with one hand. "To a place with no name."

"It has no name?"

"Lots of places in Monument Valley are unnamed. I'm not sure anyone has even visited this particular site in the past few hundred years but me."

Georgiana's heart began to pick up speed. Cole was taking her to a place where he and he alone had been, a place that he considered special, a place that he had never shared with anyone else. But he intended to share it with her.

The significance of that was not lost on her.

"When we reach the canyon we need to follow a few simple rules," he said in preamble.

She was attentive. "What are they?"

"We move as quietly and as unobtrusively as possible. We carry out everything we carry in. We eat and drink only the food and water we take with us, and we leave no sign that we've been there." Cole apparently thought of one more cardinal rule. "We don't pick up any artifacts along the way, even if they're right in our path. Understood?"

"Understood," Georgiana said as he parked the pickup out of sight of the road.

They gathered up the few supplies they were taking with them, including their water canteens.

"We'll pick up the trail about fifty yards from where we're standing right now," Cole said.

Then they were on their way.

Georgiana could tell that Coleman Worth's basic instincts took over: he moved quietly, in long, easy strides, and spoke only when necessary. She had assumed the man was in his natural element in the boardroom, but, instead, it was in the outdoors.

The muscles of his back and shoulders were outlined in perfect detail as his denim shirt grew damp with sweat and clung to his upper body. The strength in his legs was evident as he tirelessly made his way along the trail in front of her.

It was a relatively cool and clear morning, yet they hadn't walked far before the perspiration started to run down Georgiana's back, as well. She didn't mind, somehow. The exercise felt good after riding in a pickup truck for two days.

Partway up a steep, rocky incline, Georgiana paused and untied the cotton scarf from around her neck. She took a minute to remove her hat and wipe the perspiration from her face. Then she retied the scarf, plunked the hat back down on her head and they continued.

A half-hour later, as they were approaching a small, level clearing, Cole said to her, "Why don't we stop for a few minutes? We could both use a drink of water and a short rest."

"I'm hot and I'm thirsty," Georgiana admitted to him as she sank down on a nearby ledge, first remembering to check that it wasn't already occupied.

Cole stood a short distance away and gazed out over a red rock canyon. Below them was a dry riverbed.

Above them was a boulder the size of a small mountain. There was a deep gash in the rock, worn smooth by the wind and weather. Veins of subtle colors ringed its surface.

After a few minutes, he turned and said, "It's time we were on our way."

Georgiana wasn't certain how long or how far they walked before the trail narrowed. It cut a path through an even steeper canyon that was no more than a dozen yards across. The canyon walls were dotted with desert vegetation and the odd scrub tree.

Just beyond the narrow ravine, they passed through a natural stone archway, no doubt carved out by ice and water eons ago. The shadow it cast gave welcome relief from the hot sun.

Small animals scurried in the underbrush, and the harsh, raucous call of a bird of prey overhead could be heard echoing through the ravine. The smell of dust, and something almost sweet, permeated the air.

Cole's pace picked up.

Georgiana began to walk faster and faster to keep up with him until she was running by the time she reached the end of the narrow trail.

She stopped and stood beside him.

For a moment the only sound was her own breathing. Then she detected a soft gasp. It was hers as well.

They were looking out over another sandstone canyon. Below, on the canyon floor, a small blue circle of water pooled in an oasis of disheveled loveliness: half-toppled trees, ancient rubble and fallen stones. On the far side of the canyon, rising two or three hundred feet or more, was a natural amphitheater.

It was there, set against the amphitheater's back wall,

bathed in the molten gold of morning light and seemingly carved from the very stone itself, that Georgiana saw the ancient city.

It was some time before she could speak. "You knew this was here, didn't you?"

Cole nodded.

There were no words to do it justice. Georgiana tried only one. "Magnificent."

"Yes, it is magnificent," he agreed. "I had forgotten how magnificent."

She was curious. "How far away is it?"

"Maybe a quarter of a mile. Maybe a little more."

She was eager. "Can we go closer?"

"If you'd like to."

"I would."

The stone amphitheater and the long-abandoned city weren't just larger than life, Georgiana decided as she and Cole made their way to the opposite side of the secluded canyon. The ancient ruins were somehow *other* than life. They were part of a dream that seemed to bridge time itself.

Georgiana could envision an Anasazi woman, her hair perhaps arranged into an intricate coiffure favored by the female members of her clan, balancing a large basket on one hip as she returned from visiting a nearby settlement.

She could imagine the joyous sense of homecoming the woman would have felt as she entered the canyon and beheld her people in the valley below, and in their homes high above. Perhaps the woman would be rejoining her family, her husband, her children, all that was of importance in her life.

They reached the bottom of the canyon and gazed up

at the city rising majestically before them. Cole paused briefly and looped one hand through his belt. That was when Georgiana noticed that his buckle was fashioned of hammered silver and inset with turquoise. Etched into its surface were Native American symbols.

"The Anasazi were known as the Basketmakers," he said. "They were intelligent and artistic, a peaceful society of farmers who displayed a knack for basket weaving and building."

"An ingenious knack for building," she observed as they drew nearer to the stone steps at the base of the ruins.

"I'm going to scout ahead and test the footing," Cole said. "You stay here."

"But—"

"No buts about it, Georgiana. Trust me. I know what I'm doing. Let me do it."

"All right, Cole. But be careful, please."

He gave an acknowledging nod of his head and started to climb the ancient stone stairway. Georgiana watched, her heart thudding in her chest.

She quickly developed a healthy respect for Coleman Worth's skills as a mountain climber. He was nimble, surprisingly graceful for a man his size and light on his feet.

Something else dawned on Georgiana as she watched him. Something about herself.

She was having fun.

Perhaps it was the excitement of a new experience, or the thrill of a new place. But this was exhilarating. It was enjoyable. It was fun. She'd even managed to temporarily forget the frightening set of circumstances that had created her unique partnership with Cole.

She grew impatient and finally called up to him. "Are the steps safe enough to use?"

"I think so. Before you come up I want to take a closer look at what's left of the buildings," he added. "These rocks are the perfect hiding place for rattlers." With that, Cole disappeared behind a fragment of stone wall.

Georgiana restlessly shifted her weight from one foot to the other. She took a drink of water from her canteen. She retied the scarf around her neck and began to pace back and forth.

At last Cole reappeared.

She said, "Well?"

"I don't think anything has changed since the last time I was here," he stated.

"When was that?"

"Twenty years ago." He shook his head. "The structures are still sound. It's amazing when you consider they're held together with mud that is hundreds of years old."

Georgiana sought reassurance from him. "What about rattlesnakes?"

"There's no sign of rattlesnakes on this side of the village," Cole said knowledgeably, pointing to his left. "There are a few sidewinder tracks north of that embankment. They're old, but I'd still stay clear of the area."

She would make a point of it. "May I come up now?"

"Yes. But only as far as this level," he admonished, holding out his hand to her. "The remaining walls and structures seem sound enough, but you don't want to take any unnecessary risks by leaning against them. It's possible that individual stones may have worked their way loose over the centuries."

Georgiana climbed the steps and stood beside him.

Cole shut his eyes and inhaled deeply. "You can almost smell it."

She took a breath. "Smell what?"

"Sagebrush. That's what the ancient cliff dwellers would have burned in their campfires." His voice dropped to a lower register. "Close your eyes, Georgiana. Picture a perfect spring night and a full moon on the rise. You can see countless small campfires dotting the city built into this great canyon wall. You can hear the rhythmic, almost hypnotic beat of the drums and the sound of the tribal chants."

Georgiana stood with her eyes closed. "There is something haunting about this place."

Cole's voice moved on, mesmerizing her. "The People believed, and some of their descendants still maintain the belief, that there will be eight fires. This is the time of the seventh fire."

"What is the time of the seventh fire?" Georgiana heard herself ask, her voice seemingly coming from far away.

"It is the time when Mother Earth must be renewed and replenished if she is to survive and flourish. It is the time when man must once again become one with the trees, the rocks, the birds in the sky, the fish in the sea and all of his fellow creatures. When this happens, it will mean the spiritual reunion of all living things. It will become the time of the eighth and final fire. . . ."

His voice trailed off.

When Georgiana finally opened her eyes, she was standing alone, looking out over the canyon floor.

Cole spoke from somewhere behind her. "I'm going to check out another pathway. You stay put. I promise I'll be back in fifteen minutes or less."

Georgiana selected a large, rectangular-shaped boulder and sat down. The warmth of the sun was on her face. The heat of the stone beneath her penetrated her jeans. A layer of dirt and sand dusted her hands and clothing where she touched the ancient sitting place. She put her head back and basked in the sunlight.

In ages past and long past, how many other women, each in her allotted span on earth, had sat in this very spot and gazed out over the landscape Georgiana was looking at?

Sitting here what had each of them been thinking? What had they been feeling?

Surely in ages yet to come countless other women would sit in this very place and ponder who had come before them. What would they be thinking and feeling?

Georgiana felt a strange chill course down her spine.

Perhaps this place of the Ancient Ones did create a bridge across time. But the men and women who had built this city out of the earth's stone and mud were long gone. They were dust unto dust, leaving behind only the ruins of their buildings, a shard of pottery, a crude drawing on a rock face, the remnant of a basket, an arrowhead, shaped like a leaf and perhaps still needle-sharp.

Things were all that remained.

The people had come and the people had gone, and who remembered their pain, their joy, their sorrow, how they loved, *who* they loved? Who recalled if they had been kind to their children? Forgiving of their parents? Generous with their friends?

Who knew the secrets of their hearts? Whether they had loved wisely and well?

As Georgiana sat there, her eyes closed and with warm sunlight on her face, she saw life more clearly than she ever had before.

Human life was painfully short. The past was done. The future was yet to be and it was promised to no one.

There was only today. That was all she had. That was all anyone had.

Georgiana Burne-Jones knew one thing for certain: when she left this place with no name, she would be a different woman than the one who had come here.

Seventeen

Coleman Worth faced the ancient Anasazi ruins and wondered then for one of the few times in his life, if he was a religious man.

He had to admit that he'd only said a prayer once or twice in his thirty-seven years.

Maybe that night when a knife had missed his throat by a hair's breadth during a free-for-all in Chinatown.

Or maybe when he'd lain in a back *callejón* of Tijuana, sick as a dog on bad tequila, and lacking the strength to drag himself out to the main thoroughfare. A seven-year-old kid had found him and had somehow convinced his frightened and understandably reluctant parents to help the *gringo*.

Or maybe when the man, the one who had first sent him here to Monument Valley and the Navajo reservation, had died five years ago. Maybe then Cole had said a prayer.

Without putting it into words, Coleman Worth knew one thing: he was thankful, grateful, to someone, some thing beyond himself, for bringing him back to this place.

He had almost forgotten.

Almost, but not quite.

This is where it had happened.

He went deeper and deeper into the stone alcove, picking his way, testing the footing as he went, until he was standing before the entrance to a concealed cavern: he had walked by it a dozen times that fateful day before he had finally spotted it.

It was still there, of course . . . as it had been for millennia.

Then he turned and gazed out over the deserted cliff dwellings and the canyon below. From here the trees looked like matchsticks and the small pool of water fed by an underground spring—it had provided life-giving water to the People who had once lived here—no more than a dot of blue.

This was big country. Big country had a way of making a man feel small, insignificant, inconsequential in the grand scheme of things. It wasn't the first time Cole had been aware of that essential truth, but he'd forgotten it along the way.

The mountains towering in the distance, the rugged landscape, the huge ravines and the desert beyond—they had been here for millions of years. They would be here for millions of years to come.

Three score and ten.

That was traditionally the span of a man's life on this earth. Yet it was no more than a split second in comparison to that of the life around him.

What was there for a man in those few brief moments he called his life?

Work that gave his years purpose and meaning. Dignity in the way he treated others and the way they treated him in return. Respect. Generosity. Charity. Sharing with those of his fellow men who had less, who had little, who, perhaps, had nothing.

But it wasn't enough: the work, the success, the respect, the admiration, the regard or the esteem. Not anymore. He was damned well missing out, Cole concluded.

What was he missing?

Love?

Love of family and friends?

He had no family, whether by birthright or by his own design. His friends—his so-called friends—were his business associates, his colleagues, the people who worked for him, the people he worked with, the executives he met in various boardrooms across the country and the world. The closest thing he had to a personal friend, he reflected with a twinge of regret, was Martin Davis.

Love of country?

He loved his country as much as the next man, maybe more. It was perhaps only in America that a man like himself could start from the bottom and end up on top.

Love of God?

He wasn't sure what form the Supreme Being took, and he didn't think it was necessary for him to know with certitude. It was enough to believe that there was something a whole lot bigger than himself in this universe.

Love of a good woman?

Cole blew out his breath. The truth was he didn't love anyone. And no one loved him. Maybe it was because he didn't trust women. Or maybe it was because he'd never met the right woman. Or maybe it was because there was no right woman for him.

Or maybe he was wrong.

As a young man of seventeen, headed for trouble and potentially a life of crime, he had learned the most valuable lessons of his life in this desolate and yet beautiful place. Perhaps he had been brought back to the desert to learn another lesson.

Because in some way, in some very important way, none of it mattered, Cole suddenly comprehended as he stood there, gazing out over the Anasazi ruins.

Not his business acumen.

Not his incredible financial success.

Not the vast empire he had built under the name of Worth Industries.

Not his charitable works, however discreetly performed or well-intentioned.

Not even this magnificent and ancient city preserved by the dry desert air.

None of it mattered, Cole realized, if he didn't *live* the life he had been given.

Georgiana went looking for Cole. When she found him he was standing on a natural rise overlooking the valley on one side and facing a wall of sheer rock on the other. There was an aloneness about him that made her want to wrap her arms around him and hold him close.

She climbed higher.

Cole had removed his sunglasses and his hat. They were at his feet, along with his water canteen. She could see the sweat running down his face.

She came closer.

She looked again and wondered if those could possibly be tears on his face.

She couldn't imagine Coleman Worth crying. She would be willing to bet that the last time he'd shed a tear he had been a very small and very lonely child.

Tentatively she approached him and touched his arm. "Are you all right, Cole?"

He didn't answer straight away. When he did, she

knew by the fullness in his voice that at least some of the moisture on his cheeks was, indeed, tears.

"I'm all right, Georgiana," he said, his eyes focusing on her face. "As a matter of fact, better than I've been in a long time." After a moment he added, "I'd forgotten what this place could do to a man."

"Or to a woman," she responded.

For a moment Cole hesitated. Then he seemed to make up his mind. "I'd like to share something with you."

She was encouraging. "You can tell me whatever you like."

"It's not something I want to tell you," he explained. "It's some place I'd like to show you."

She inquired, "Where?"

"Here," he stated, reaching down to retrieve his hat, sunglasses and canteen.

Georgiana wouldn't have dreamed of refusing his request. In fact, she was honored that Cole trusted her enough to share any part of himself with her.

She looked up at him with a cooperative air and a smile. "I'm ready when you are."

"I mentioned to you that I had been sent here to the Navajo reservation as a teenager because I got into trouble with the law," he said, in his Texas drawl.

"Yes, you mentioned it."

"I've always been grateful to the man who arranged that alternative to jail with the judge. Otherwise, I would have had to serve time. The older I got, the more I learned about misguided kids who end up in the juvenile detention system—a huge percentage end up incarcerated as adults, too—the more grateful I became."

Georgiana gave him a speculative glance. "You said that you hated it here at first."

"I did." The man beside her took in a deep breath

and then let it out again. "In the beginning I thought I was going through sheer hell." There was a self-deprecating laugh. "Today we'd call that approach to behavioral modification 'tough love.'"

It was the first time Georgiana had heard Cole use the word *love* in describing his relationship with anyone or anything.

"Anyway, one day I hiked into this remote canyon and I discovered the ancient cliff dwelling we just visited. But that wasn't all I found, Georgiana. I found a cavern as well."

For some inexplicable reason, her heart began to pick up speed and beat faster.

Cole rubbed his hand along the back of his neck in what Georgiana recognized as a habitual gesture. "I went into that cavern as one person and I came out as someone else."

His statement surprised her. But she had the sense—and patience—to wait and listen.

The man beside her held out his hand. "I'd like to share that experience with you."

Georgiana placed her hand in Cole's and allowed him to lead her to the wall of rock directly behind them.

He glanced up at the sky. "We'll have to go in now if we want to be in time."

Georgiana was inquisitive. "Does this place have a name?"

A very succinct, "Yes."

She almost laughed in reaction to his brusqueness. "Are you going to tell me what it is?"

Words were kept at a minimum. "Not yet."

She wanted to know. "Did you name this place?"

Cole nodded his head and then quickly shook his head. "No doubt I have been just one of many people over the past several millennia who have called this place by the same name.''

He was being very mysterious.

They squeezed between two enormous rock formations, made their way along a narrow corridor for some forty or fifty feet and eventually entered an irregularly shaped cavern.

The main chamber was fifteen to twenty feet across and slightly longer than it was wide. It was perhaps thirty feet in height, but that varied because of the jutting rocks and asymmetrical walls.

The walls were formed from variegated sandstone in shades of red and gold, and were worn smooth by a long-ago river that must have once flowed through the valley.

The cavern was surprisingly clean. It even appeared to have been swept, if only by Mother Nature herself. There were no footprints. No debris. Only the odd tumbleweed and dry white sand on the floor.

It took perhaps half a minute to register with Georgiana that it wasn't dark inside the rock-formed chamber due to an opening in the natural ceiling somewhere high overhead.

She and Cole stood there.

''What is it you want to show me?'' she finally asked.

''Patience, Georgiana. Good things come to those who wait,'' Cole promised her.

''Are you a patient man?''

His attention was momentarily focused elsewhere. ''I can be if I need to be.''

Georgiana wasn't sure that was an answer.

Cole stood in the center of the cavern, put his head back and studied the opening above them. Then he cautioned, ''We don't have much time. Do as I do.''

She agreed to.

Cole tossed his hat, sunglasses and canteen aside, and quickly stretched out on the sandy floor of the cavern.

Georgiana hesitated.

"Come on," he urged.

She supposed it was a little like playing snow angels without the snow.

Dropping to her knees, she had to ask. "Any bugs?"

"None to speak of," he assured her.

"Snakes?"

"Snakes never enter the cavern."

How did he know?

How *could* he know?

"Why not?" she posed.

Cole's determined chin jutted. "This is not a snake place."

Frankly Georgiana had been hoping for a more inclusive answer. She took the plunge, anyway. She removed her hat and sunglasses and piled them next to her water canteen. Then she lay down beside Cole, arms at her sides as his were, legs and back comfortable but stretched out straight, head relaxed, eyes open.

"Now what?" she whispered. Why had she felt it was necessary to whisper?

"Now we wait."

She wiggled her bottom in the sand to make it mold to her derriere. "What are we waiting for?"

"You'll see."

"When?"

"As soon as the sun is directly overhead."

"When will that be?"

"In a couple of minutes."

The sun appeared right on schedule. A minute or two later it was positioned directly over the opening in the roof of the cavern. Sunlight streamed in from above and suddenly the sandstone chamber was transformed.

It was alive.

It was aglow.

It was also unlike anything Georgiana had ever seen or experienced. She had no words to describe the way it looked or the way it made her feel. She was filled with . . . light.

They lay side by side.

They didn't move.

They didn't speak.

They scarcely breathed.

It was some time before Cole turned toward her. She looked at him. His eyes were staring straight into hers. "I call this place the Room of Light."

"The Room of Light," she repeated in a reverent tone.

Of course.

"This is also where I saw the light," he told her with a slightly wry smile.

She returned his smile.

Cole reached for her hand as he said her name. "Georgiana."

"Cole." She moved closer to him, the curves of her body fitting perfectly to his.

A frown momentarily appeared between his eyes. "Is this a good idea?"

She was honest with him. "I don't know." Then she asked, "Do you?"

Cole admitted, "I don't know, either."

Georgiana inhaled a tremulous breath. "I know I want you to kiss me."

"It's a place to begin," he said as he opened his arms and she moved into them.

Where would it lead?

Where would it end?

Those were the questions to which Georgiana had no answers.

Why wasn't she afraid? She should be afraid, she realized. She wasn't certain that this was the right time or the right place. She was even less sure that it was for the right reasons and with the right man.

No one was promised tomorrow.

No one was guaranteed a future.

There was no other time and there was no other place. This moment was her entire life.

And for this one moment, this one lifetime, Georgiana knew exactly what she wanted. Maybe not for the unpromised tomorrow, or even next week or next month or next year, but for right now, she knew.

What she wanted was Coleman Worth.

Eighteen

Why wasn't she afraid? Georgiana asked herself again as Cole lay beside her in the sunlight and the sand, and watched her with those blue eyes of his.

"Your shirt is damp with perspiration," he pointed out.

Georgiana glanced down. The cotton material of her blouse—it was one of those she had borrowed from Crick's charity jumbo—was clinging to her body, outlining her breasts, clearly showing her nipples.

It was odd. She should feel self-conscious. She was quite certain under any other circumstances or with any other man she would be. But she wasn't.

She wasn't afraid and she wasn't self-conscious when she said to him, "So it is."

"It's my fault," came a well-timed apology. But somehow Cole didn't sound sorry, and he didn't appear sorry to her, either. He appeared *interested.*

Georgiana gave him a long, questioning look. "How could it be your fault?"

An intense masculine gaze gave her the once-over. "I'd forgotten how far the hike was from the canyon to the ruins. Then I left you out in the heat of the day too long.''

"It doesn't matter." Georgiana wasn't just saying that. It really didn't matter to her.

When Cole spoke next, there was something different about his voice. The tone was deeper and his drawl was more pronounced. "I'll bet you're wet right down to your skin," he speculated.

"I am."

A muscle in his jaw twitched slightly. "Maybe you'd like to slip out of that damp shirt."

"Maybe I would," Georgiana murmured huskily.

She almost changed her mind.

Almost.

She wasn't a fool and she wasn't completely naive. She knew what Cole was asking her and she knew the answer she was giving him.

Georgiana sat up, unbuttoned her blouse, shrugged it off her shoulders and tossed it over a nearby tumbleweed to dry out. She fought the urge to cover with her hands what her skimpy bra left exposed.

Then it was her turn. "Your shirt is wet, too."

Cole didn't bother glancing down at his chest. "I know."

"It could be drying on the rock behind you."

He pushed himself up into a sitting position, undid the buttons down the front and yanked the denim shirt off. He gave it a toss in the general direction of the rock.

Blue eyes searched her face. "Are you afraid?"

Georgiana shook her head. "Not afraid, just a little nervous." She moistened her lips. "What about you?"

Cole's answer was a variation of her own. "I have to confess that I've got the . . ." He seemed to search for the right word; the best he could come up with was, "Jitters."

"I want you to know that I don't make a practice of this," she blurted out.

"Neither do I."

Her face was hot. "I'm not promiscuous."

"I never thought you were," he assured her. Then he added, "If it matters to you, neither am I."

It did matter.

"It's been a while for me," Cole went on to tell her.

"It has for me, too."

He rubbed the front of his bare chest with the flat of one hand. "As a matter of fact, I've been so wrapped up in the merger I realize it's been a hell of a long time."

She had literally been on call for her job twenty-four hours a day, Georgiana ruminated. "I've been staying at the Sonoran more often than my own apartment."

Cole arched a knowing brow. "A butler's work is never done."

"Something like that."

He attempted a faintly self-deprecating smile. "I hope I haven't forgotten how."

"I hear it's like riding a horse," she volunteered. "Once you learn how, you never forget."

"I thought that was riding a bicycle."

She frowned. "Is it?"

He nodded. "Horses or bicycles, we'll have to cut each other some slack."

In addition Georgiana suggested, "I'll give you the benefit of the doubt, if you'll do the same for me."

"It's a deal," Cole agreed.

She passed her tongue along the edges of her teeth and laughed nervously. "We're bound to make mistakes."

"We're bound to."

"We'll have to be patient."

"I'm a very patient man," Cole stated.

"I'm a very patient woman." In fact, patience was absolutely essential in her line of work. Georgiana heard herself admit to him, "I don't want to be a disappointment to you, Cole."

He reached out and gently cupped her chin in his hand. "Believe me, you won't be. You couldn't possibly be."

"You're not just saying that to make me feel better, are you?" she said, her lack of confidence showing for a moment.

He was dead serious. "No."

She wanted to believe him.

Cole assured her, "We'll take it real slow."

Georgiana swallowed hard. "Slow is good."

"Slow can be very good," he told her in a tone of voice that brought the color to her cheeks.

"Where do we go from here?" she finally asked.

"How about we start at the bottom and work our way to the top?" he proposed, reaching down to pull off his leather cowboy boots and the socks underneath.

Georgiana followed his lead. Her boots and socks were quickly in a heap on the sandy floor of the cavern.

"I'll go first." Cole stood, undid the silver and turquoise belt buckle, unbuttoned the waist of his blue jeans and carefully eased the zipper down past the most vulnerable part of a male's anatomy. In another few seconds he was shoving the jeans aside with his foot and was left standing there in a pair of dark cotton briefs.

The man was, in a word, magnificent.

Of course, she knew that from the other night, Georgiana reminded herself. The first time she had laid eyes on Coleman Worth he had been wearing only slightly more than he was now.

There was one difference, of course. One *big* difference. This time he was fully erect.

"Oh, my God," she muttered under her breath.

Cole's reaction told her that he had misunderstood her response. "What is it?" His handsome face was marred by a scowl. "Is something wrong?"

Georgiana moved her head: it wasn't yes and it wasn't no. "Nothing's wrong."

"Then why are you staring at me like that?"

"I've heard the wild assertions like everyone else, of course, but I have to admit that I didn't believe them until now," she said without really clarifying her statement.

"What wild assertions?"

"The kind that one always hears about Texas from nearly every passing Texan."

Masculine hands were firmly planted on masculine hips. "Would you care to explain that remark, darlin'?"

Georgiana wet her lips with her tongue and drew in a deep sustaining breath. "One is told . . . one hears . . . one is apprised that everything about Texas is bigger and better than anywhere else in this country," she said, trying not to stare at the one place on Coleman Worth's body that seemed to draw her eyes like a magnet. "I'd always assumed that the claims were exaggerated. I see I was wrong. I apologize."

He snorted softly. "You're apologizing to me?"

"Yes."

Cole seemed amused. "Are you trying to tell me that size does account for something?"

Not everything, perhaps, but certainly for something.

Georgiana found her lips were already dry again. "Yes. That's exactly what I'm telling you."

"I don't know whether to be embarrassed or flattered," the nearly naked man declared.

"I don't think you're either one," she countered.

"What makes you say that?"

"Your shrewd business sense."

He was obviously curious. "What does business have to do with this business?"

Cole had asked. So Georgiana told him. "Quality over quantity. Corporate downsizing. Customer satisfaction. JIT: Just in Time delivery. The ups and downs—"

Apparently he'd heard enough. The man raised his hands in the air in mock surrender. "All right. I give up. You win. I think you've made your point."

She couldn't resist adding, "I must say, Mr. Worth, I am impressed."

"And?"

Was he seeking compliments? This man with the impressively broad shoulders and narrow waist, muscular chest and strong, muscled arms and legs? It wasn't as if she had much basis for comparison, but anyone could see that this was no ordinary man.

"I'm impressed and . . ."

"Interested?" he supplied.

"Well, of course I'm interested."

"Curious?"

"Yes, I'm curious." That's what had gotten her into this situation in the first place.

Curiosity killed the cat. Satisfaction brought her back.

Georgiana only hoped the same was true for human beings.

"Perhaps even a little bewitched, bothered and bewildered?" Cole provided next.

Georgiana put her head back and laughed for the sheer pleasure of laughing. It felt good. As a matter of fact, it felt better than good: it felt wonderful. She would never have imagined there could be anything fun or even vaguely amusing about intimacy. In her limited experience, it had always been fraught with tension.

"This is fun," she told him.

Cole's mouth turned up at the corners. "Isn't having fun the whole point?"

She was serious. "Of sex?"

"Yes."

Georgiana gave it some thought. "I don't know."

There was the faintest hint of teasing in his tone. "Well, I do know. It's supposed to be about fun and pleasure and feeling good."

She returned to the immediate subject at hand. "Where do we go from here?"

Cole made a gesture. "I believe we were working our way up or down, as the case may be, to your jeans."

Georgiana unsnapped the waistline, wiggled the snug jeans over her hips and derriere, pulled them down her legs and finally gave them a nudge with her toe. Then she stood there in her bra and panties.

A hot, masculine stare caught and held her in its grip. "We're getting down to the bare essentials."

They certainly were.

Out of sheer bravado—and before she lost her nerve—Georgiana unfastened the front of her bra, tossed it beside her discarded blue jeans and quickly slipped off her panties. When she looked up again, Cole, too, was straightening, his briefs gone.

She looked her fill. "You're beautiful."

He gave a husky and pleased chuckle. "So are you."

Georgiana took a step toward Cole. She reached up and ran her fingers through his sun-streaked hair and made a discovery. "Your hair is so soft," she marveled. "I had no idea it would feel so soft. It's almost like silk."

He tugged at the elastic band holding hers in a ponytail. Her hair came tumbling down, cascading around her shoulders, covering his hands. He seemed to delight in burying his face in the thickness of it, in inhaling her scent, in tasting her skin.

"Silk," Cole repeated as his lips brushed along her neck and that sensitive spot just below the ear.

She traced a path from his mouth, up the side of his face to the temple, from the temple to his eyebrows—they were dark brown, emphatic, and yet nicely arched—across the bridge of his nose, around each well-shaped ear and finally back to his mouth.

"I like your mouth."

"And I like yours," he echoed.

Georgiana went up on her tiptoes and kissed his mouth, softly, a little tentatively at first. Then she grew bolder and began to tease him, torment him, with her tongue until Cole opened his mouth and devoured hers in a kiss that left her without breath in her lungs, without strength—her legs were trembling and threatening to give way on her—without a rational thought in her head.

"I—I—ah, can't seem to think straight," she confessed to him.

"Then it's time to stop thinking and start feeling," Cole suggested, his breath hot and sweet and insistent as he dragged his lips along her bare shoulder.

"It feels so good," she groaned.

"It's only going to get better," he promised her as he cupped the fullness of her breasts in his hands. He circled her nipples with his thumbs and she shivered from head to toe, despite the warmth of the sun above them.

Georgiana inadvertently brushed up against Cole's erection. His penis was smooth and hard, and it was nestled in a tangle of dark brown curls. She watched as it twitched and moved. It seemed to have a life, and a mind, of its own.

"That is fascinating," she murmured, reaching out and wrapping her fingers around him.

She squeezed him. She measured the length and breadth of him with her hand. She gently flicked at the small opening on the tip with her fingernail.

She heard a sharp inhalation of air. She noticed that there was a fine line of perspiration on Cole's upper lip and another across his forehead. He seemed to sway a little unsteadily on his feet.

"Are you all right?" Georgiana inquired, concerned.

"I—ah, I'm fine."

"Are you sure?"

"No. Yes." Then Cole tried to smile. But the simple act of smiling seemed beyond him at the moment.

When it seemed he couldn't stand it a second longer, he bent his head and touched her breast with the tip of his tongue, flicking it back and forth across her nipple. Then he took her into his mouth and suckled, drawing her deeper and deeper, nipping on her tender flesh, tugging at her, until her head fell back, her lips parted and a low moan of arousal issued forth.

"Cole, I'm losing control," she cried out softly.

"What's wrong with losing control?"

She laughed, but there was an edge to her laughter. "You, of all people, have to ask that."

He made a statement of the obvious. "Neither one of us likes to feel out of control."

She tried to nod her head. "Letting go, losing control, especially in a situation like this, means you have to trust the other person."

"Do you trust me, Georgiana?"

She stared up into his endless blue eyes. She moved her mouth painfully. "Yes."

Cole lowered his head again and took her nipple between his lips and drew her into his mouth until she could feel the erotic tug in every nerve cell of her body.

Georgiana buried her hands in his hair, grasping fistfuls of the silky stuff. "Do you trust me, Cole?"

"Shhh, now, darlin'," he urged as his mouth moved lower still, his tongue dampening already damp flesh.

He urged her legs apart. His fingers sought her, found her, caressed her, dipped into her, again and again.

Georgiana couldn't think. She couldn't speak. She couldn't breathe. She couldn't even stand.

Cole took her with him to the sandy floor of the cavern. He hovered over her, his strong arms on either side of her body. He whispered words, sounds, she knew not what, into her mouth, and then he probed, divided, separated and sank deeply into her body.

Then he was there inside her, stretching her to the limit, filling her utterly and completely. He thrust into her again and again, farther, stronger, harder, deeper. It went on and on and on. There was no beginning and, for a long time, there was no end.

"Georgiana, sweet, darlin' Georgiana," Cole murmured against her lips, his breath mingling with hers, his flesh inseparable from her flesh, two bodies moving, feeling, becoming one.

"Cole. Cole," was all she could say.

Then the moment was upon them, and Georgiana placed herself in his care, trusted him enough to lose control, to cry out her climax, to fly higher and farther than she had ever flown before.

The world looked different when she was soaring high above it. She could see it all so clearly: the mountain peaks, the vast desert, the dots of blue water, the clouds around her and the sun.

There was the dazzling sun: sun in her hair, sun in her eyes, sun in her heart and mind and soul.

It was like coming out of the darkness and into the light.

Nineteen

Why was he afraid?

He shouldn't be afraid, Coleman Worth told himself, but that didn't alter the fact that he was.

What was he afraid of? Or maybe the question was, *who* was he afraid of?

Georgiana?

Himself?

Neither of them? Both of them?

Maybe he was afraid because he didn't know if it was the right time, or the right place, for the right reasons, or with the right woman. Maybe he was afraid because he'd wanted, desired, needed Georgiana more than he had thought possible.

For that matter, he still wanted her, desired her, needed her, and the throes of his climax had barely subsided.

What in the hell could he have been thinking of?

That was the next question Cole asked himself as he gazed down at the lovely and disheveled young woman beneath him on the sandy floor of the cave.

That was the problem, of course. He hadn't been

thinking. He had acted *and* reacted like a kid half his age: impulsively, irrationally, even irresponsibly. Except he wasn't a kid. He was a full-grown man and he should have known better.

The trouble was he had dreamed of making love to Georgiana last night. Sometime around two A.M. he had awakened in a cold sweat, his body covered with a sheen of perspiration, his heart pounding in his chest, every muscle tensed, his erection rock-hard. In fact, painfully hard against the zipper of his jeans.

Right then and there he should have taken matters into his own hands. No pun intended. At least it would have taken the edge off and given him some semblance of sexual release, but, frankly, he had been reluctant to do that with Georgiana's sleeping bag, and her body, so close to his.

As a consequence, he had just broken more than one of his own cardinal rules: he'd had sex with a woman without discussing it ahead of time, without laying down the ground rules, without letting her know right up front that he wasn't the marrying kind, without taking the necessary and sensible precautions.

No doubt Georgiana was on the Pill—surely she would have said something to him otherwise—but he should have asked, he should have double-checked.

He was a fool.

He'd wanted to share this special place with her. The next thing he'd known he had been suggesting that she take off her damp blouse. She had sweetly complied. After that, one thing had led to another, and here they were.

He blew out his breath. It was too late now. What was done . . . was done.

Cole gently withdrew from her and rolled over onto his back. He lay there and stared up at the natural opening in the cavern as the sun passed overhead.

Earlier he'd admitted to Georgiana that making love with her gave him the jitters. The truth was it scared him shitless. It was the kind of situation he scrupulously tried to avoid. He'd had women before—after all, he had the sexual drive and needs of any normal thirty-seven-year-old man—but he had never gotten involved with a lady.

At least Georgiana had been right about one thing: it was like riding a horse or a bicycle. Despite his recent and somewhat prolonged celibacy, he hadn't forgotten how. He had apparently forgotten just how good great sex could feel, and it—*she*—was the best he'd ever had.

And that scared Cole as well.

Georgiana turned her head. He could feel her watching him. It was another minute, perhaps longer before she said his name rather tentatively. "Cole?"

He knew what she was asking. Had she been a disappointment to him? Had it been a mistake? Did he have any regrets? Was he sorry they'd made love?

He turned and met her questioning gaze. He heard the words form on his own lips. "Are you sorry?"

She shook her head.

"Any regrets?"

She shook her head again. Her voice was low and husky when she inquired, "What about you?"

He chose not to answer her directly. "I can't believe that I want you again so soon," he admitted with a somewhat self-deprecating laugh as he came up on one elbow and bent over to kiss her mouth, her eyes, the tip of her nose. "You were wonderful. You are wonderful."

Pleased, Georgiana laughed softly. It was a lovely sound that came from the back of her throat.

Cole pulled her into his arms as he rolled over onto his back in the warm sand. She was splayed across his body; long, slender legs on either side of his. He settled

her astride his hips. He knew she could feel his erection—hell, he'd climaxed and yet he was still as hard
as ever—wedged between her thighs.

Full, pale, perfect breasts grazed his chest. He lifted
his head, opened his mouth and caught her nipple between his serrated teeth. He nipped and licked and rolled
his tongue around the sensitive tip. He caressed her,
pinched her with his thumb and forefinger, suckled
her until she threw her head back, the graceful line of
her throat enticing, the arch of her back thrusting her
ever deeper into his mouth. He tugged on her nipples,
each in turn, and she cried out in arousal.

Instinctively Georgiana began to move against him,
her mouth fulfilling his every unspoken request while
making equal demands of its own. She ran her tongue,
pink and moist, across his lips and down his neck to his
shoulder, as if she were savoring the taste of his skin,
as though she wanted to take in the very essence of him.

She pressed her lips into the palm of his hand and
flicked her tongue back and forth until goose bumps
were raised on every inch of his body. He shuddered.

She ran her fingertips along the solid wall of bone,
muscle and flesh that comprised his chest and abdomen,
then strayed lower to explore the vulnerable male flesh
caught between her thighs.

"Sweet Jesus . . ." Cole groaned aloud.

He brought his hips up off the ground, seized the two
rounded halves of her derriere in his hands, separated
her flesh with his thumbs and proceeded to nudge, to
prod, to probe and finally to pierce that moist and
sweetly erotic aperture with his own hot, demanding
flesh.

She was impaled on him.

Georgiana sat there for a moment, eyes half-closed,
lips slightly parted, breathing erratic as she appeared to

be absorbing the fact that their bodies were once again joined.

She leaned forward and touched her mouth to his, her tongue making swift little forays between his lips, teasing him, baiting him, distracting him, driving him to distraction. Then she straightened and began to move, slowly at first, her inner muscles gripping him, squeezing him, bringing forth another moan from somewhere deep inside him.

Georgiana did drive him crazy, and he never wanted her to stop. That was Cole's last rational thought.

For now there was only the two of them, this time and this place. Everything and everyone else could wait. There would be time enough later for regrets.

Cole finally stirred.

He had no idea how much time had passed since they'd entered the cavern until he glanced down at the watch on his wrist.

Two hours.

Georgiana's head was resting on his shoulder. Her arms were wrapped about his neck as she held him close. She slipped off his sweat-slick torso and stretched out in the sand beside him, eyes closed, body relaxed, unself-consciously naked, the only movement her breasts rising and falling as she softly breathed in and out.

Her eyes blinked opened.

She gazed up at the sky above and the passing sun. Then without turning her head she said to him, "What happened to you the last time you were in this cavern?"

Cole lay there, satiated in mind, body and spirit, not really wanting to think, to speak, to do anything for the present. Somewhat reluctantly he answered her. "I saw the light."

"The same light we just saw together?"

"Yes."

Georgiana waited.

He went on. "You have to remember that I was seventeen at the time."

"And headed for trouble," she supplied.

He moved his head and lazily brushed the sand from his chest. "I'd been working on the reservation for about two months when I accidentally stumbled onto this cavern."

"Are you one of those people who believe in accidents?" Georgiana interjected.

"As opposed to what?"

She licked her lips. "Fate. Providence. Kismet."

That brought a smile to his mouth. "Karma?"

"Something like that."

"Meaning I was destined to find this cavern."

"There are those who would believe so."

"Your question is, am I one of them?"

Georgiana shrugged and pushed her damp hair back off her face. "I guess that's my question."

Cole was honest with her. "I don't know. But I do know this much. When I lay in this exact place at the age of seventeen and watched the sunlight fill the cavern, I was somehow . . . changed." He almost said *transformed*.

"You wouldn't have known about the sunlight. You weren't expecting it," Georgiana concluded.

"I wasn't expecting it."

"So you just happened to be in the right place at the right time," she observed.

"Yup."

"A few minutes earlier or later and you would never have known," she went on.

"I guess so."

He knew so.

She was persistent. "So what happened to you the last time you were in this cavern, Cole?"

He might as well tell her. He only hoped it didn't sound sophomoric. "It became clear to me that my life—my destiny, if you will—was in my own hands. What I was, what I did, what I became, was entirely up to me. It didn't matter what had come before."

Georgiana made a small sound that seemed to be in agreement with what he was saying.

Cole continued in the same vein. "Nobody can change their past. The past is always the past. Once the moment is over and done with, it no longer matters. And since no one is guaranteed a future, the only thing we have is the present." He slowly breathed in and out. "*That* was the great truth that came to me in this place."

Georgiana was forced to face a few truths of her own as she brushed off the sand sticking to her body, reached for her clothes and got dressed again.

Her sexual encounter with Coleman Worth hadn't even been a one-night stand. It had been a one-afternoon stand.

His words echoed in her mind: *Once the moment is over and done with, it no longer matters.*

Easier said than done.

Because there were other self-evident truths she knew about herself: She wasn't the one-night or one-afternoon stand type of woman. She took sex seriously. She wasn't casual, offhanded or blasé about physical intimacy. It had meaning for her. It meant love and commitment, family and home, even marriage.

She was an old-fashioned kind of woman in a modern world, Georgiana recognized. She supposed that made her an anachronism.

Still, she had no one to blame but herself for this

afternoon. She had gone into the situation with her eyes
wide open. She had even convinced herself that the only
thing that mattered was the present, the here and now.
She'd believed it, too.

At the time.

It certainly wasn't Cole's fault. He had made no
promises and no commitments. Great sex did not make
for a great relationship, or any kind of relationship.

That was the truth.

There were no guarantees; he was dead right about
that, too. Whatever the future consequences of her actions, she would have to take responsibility for them
herself. It had always been true for women when it came
to men, when it came to sex. Especially when it came
to the consequences of unprotected sex.

She was a fool.

But she'd do it again in an instant if Cole turned to
her now, if he looked at her with those endless blue eyes
of his, if he held out his arms to her.

She was worse than a fool, Georgiana Burne-Jones
realized as she settled her hat on her head and followed
Coleman Worth out of the cavern, down through the
ancient Anasazi ruins, through the narrow canyon path
and back to the concealed pickup truck.

It was the wrong time and the wrong place. She was
the wrong woman and Cole was definitely the wrong
man.

And she was falling in love with him.

Georgiana suddenly realized that the greatest danger
to her wasn't the men she was running *from*, but the
man she was running *with*.

Twenty

Cole wasn't sure which was the greater danger: the storm brewing ahead of them in the dark, foreboding, early evening sky or the four-wheel-drive SUV he suspected was following them.

What made him nervous was the fact that he'd caught a glimpse of only one man in the vehicle: a driver behind the wheel wearing a black suit and a pair of metallic, mirrorlike sunglasses. There weren't any passengers visible.

So where were the other two men in dark suits?

Maybe he was getting paranoid, Cole decided as he steered the vintage pickup truck along the narrow two-lane road leading into the small Idaho town. He didn't have a shred of evidence to support the notion that anyone was still on their tail.

He certainly had no intention of sharing his suspicions with Georgiana. Since leaving Monument Valley a couple of days before, she had been quiet and withdrawn, riding beside him, eyes straight ahead, posture rigid, speaking only when spoken to.

Frankly he didn't know what to make of the woman.

She was a damned mystery to him. She was also illogical, unreasonable and unpredictable, in his opinion. His entire existence had become a crapshoot since the minute she'd burst into the presidential suite at the Sonoran five nights ago.

He couldn't have his cake and eat it, too.

He had been bemoaning the fact that his life had become predictable and even downright boring. Ms. Burne-Jones had nicely taken care of that problem. Unfortunately, she had created another in its place: Cole couldn't stop thinking about the afternoon they had spent together in the Room of Light.

He wasn't sure what he had expected her reaction to be after their lovemaking, but she'd been as icy cold as a January wind blowing down from Canada. She had stayed on her side of the pickup truck—day *and* night— and he had stayed on his.

Their present situation gave a whole new meaning to the term the "Great Divide."

Cole had to admit that he'd never worked at a relationship with a woman before.

Hell, he'd never even tried.

His idea of a long-term alliance was a sexual affair between two mature and consenting adults that might last a few months. The women he dated—when he had the time to date—were successful in their own right, independent and even less interested in commitment and marriage than he was.

It had been the perfect arrangement.

Until the fateful moment when Ms. Burne-Jones had entered his life, without an invitation, written or otherwise, and had turned his world upside down. Cole wasn't sure he liked it. But it had been his choice. He could always have turned her over to the police that first night.

Then it occurred to him. Maybe all Georgiana needed was a home-cooked meal, a hot shower and a decent bed to sleep in: one with a dry blanket and clean, sweet-smelling sheets. They'd put in two long, hard days on the road, barely stopping long enough to eat or sleep. Now they weren't more than a few miles from the ranch and the couple that Crick had mentioned would help them.

First things first, however.

The first item on the agenda was to fill Bessie's gas tank, plus the spare in the back of the truck. The second was to check in with Martin Davis. Then they would look up Crick's friends.

Cole opened his mouth. "Do you have the address that Crick gave you handy?"

Georgiana's answer was efficient and succinct. "Yes."

Cole nudged the Stetson back on his forehead, leaned forward slightly and glanced out the window of the pickup. "Looks like a storm's blowing in."

Sunglasses came off. Green eyes gazed in the same direction he was looking. "Yes, it does."

Cole pulled up alongside one of the two ancient gas pumps in front of an all-purpose general store. The neon sign out front alternately flashed, GAS. EATS. GAS. EATS.

"I spotted the ladies' rest room around to the right side of the building if you want to use the facilities."

Georgiana was excruciatingly polite. "Thank you."

Cole didn't crack a smile. "You're welcome." Then he went on to tell her, "Once Bessie has been taken care of, I'll see if the proprietor of this establishment can give me directions."

She dug around in her handbag and produced the piece of paper from Alfred Crick.

"Would you like a cold drink or a cup of coffee or anything?" he asked.

Georgiana shook her head and handed over the note. "I'll use the facilities and then wait for you in the truck."

Cole was suddenly a little apprehensive about letting her out of his sight. "I won't be long," he called after her as she disappeared around the corner.

Georgiana had used the facilities and was washing her hands in the sink when the small, nearly infinitesimal hairs on the back of her neck suddenly stood on end. She started to get a funny feeling. It was almost as if she were being watched.

She turned around, ponytail swinging.

No one was there.

The rest room was empty except, of course, for herself. The door was locked and the only window had long ago been whitewashed over for privacy.

Then she noticed there was another window—a small, rectangular one—above the door. It was cranked open an inch or two.

No one, short of a giant, would be tall enough to see into the rest room through a window that high off the ground. Unless they had a ladder handy, and under the circumstances that seemed extremely unlikely.

She must be imagining things.

Or maybe she was simply tired, Georgiana acknowledged. Tired of running. Tired of looking over her shoulder. Tired of keeping her distance from Cole.

Not that she had any choice.

Or did she?

She could always march outside to the public telephone booth, pick up the receiver, dial the police, offer to surrender to Detective Mallory and take her chances.

What were her chances?

Lousy.

Worse than lousy.

Nothing had changed since that fateful night at the Sonoran. She was still in big trouble. She was still the prime suspect in Paul Isherwood's murder. Her fingerprints were still on the steak knife.

She had set her course the minute she'd decided to throw her lot in with Coleman Worth and make a run for it. She had no choice now but to see this business through to the end.

Georgiana drew a hairbrush through her ponytail and dabbed on another layer of bright red lipstick before unlocking the door. That was when she spotted a folded newspaper stuffed in a trash receptacle outside the ladies' rest room. She hadn't noticed it on her way in, but she'd had her mind on other matters.

Something about the newspaper caught her eye now. Georgiana picked it up and there on the back page, down in the far left-hand corner, wedged between an advertisement for a close-out sale on furniture and the world's largest tomato-producing plants, was a small headline that read, WOMAN'S DISAPPEARANCE REMAINS UNSOLVED.

Her heart began to pick up speed.

The newspaper, she noted, was dated yesterday. Quickly scanning the article, she obtained the few facts that were available: a young woman had been reported missing from an unnamed luxury resort in the Phoenix area. Unfortunately that was all the information Georgiana could ascertain. The remainder of the article was missing, the corner torn from the newspaper.

Could she be the missing woman?

Was it merely a coincidence?

What was the likelihood that two young women

would be reported missing under similar circumstances, in less than a week?

Then it suddenly occurred to Georgiana: by now her parents must have been informed of her disappearance. They would be worried sick. They might even be assuming the worst.

Her mother and father weren't getting any younger. Neither of them had been in the best of health for the past year. She couldn't allow them to needlessly suffer.

She knew what she had to do.

Georgiana opened her handbag and dug out the few coins she had. She wouldn't be able to talk long, but at least she could reassure her parents that she was alive and relatively well.

She made a beeline for the telephone booth, picked up the receiver, dropped in the necessary coins and punched in the numbers for their home in Tucson.

After the second ring, she heard the familiar and cultured tones of her mother's voice announcing, ''The Burne-Jones residence.''

She wasted no time. She had none to waste. ''Hello, Mother. It's Georgiana.''

Maud Burne-Jones promptly—and uncharacteristically—burst into tears.

''Please don't cry, Mother. I'm fine, but I don't have long to talk.'' The handful of coins weren't going to buy her much time.

There was a muffled response on the other end.

The next voice she heard was her father's. ''Georgiana?''

''Hello, Dad.''

He sounded older than the last time they had talked. How long ago had that been?

''Are you all right?'' inquired an obviously distressed Jeremy Burne-Jones.

"I'm fine, Dad."

"Men were here looking for you."

Her heart began to beat in double-time. She had been afraid for herself. She hadn't realized she might also need to be afraid for her parents. "What men?"

"Policemen. Homicide detectives. Agents from the federal government."

Georgiana was actually relieved to learn her parents' visitors had been the authorities. She supposed she shouldn't have been surprised. "Then you know that there's been a bit of trouble at the Sonoran, Dad. I want you to know that I didn't do anything wrong."

"Your mother and I never believed for an instant that you had," he assured her. "We've only been concerned for your safety."

"I'm safe." For the moment. "I didn't want you to worry. That's why I called."

"Can't you come home?" Her father's voice quavered slightly.

Georgiana's throat tightened. "Not yet, but soon." She dropped the last of her coins into the appropriate slots. "I'm almost out of change, Dad."

He hastened to tell her, "Just a minute, Georgiana, your mother is picking up the extension."

"Are you both there?" she inquired, suddenly fighting back tears.

"Yes," they answered in unison.

"I just want to say that I miss you." Georgiana took a deep sustaining breath. "And I love you both."

"We love you," came the emotional response from the other end of the line.

"I've got to go now. Try not to worry. I'll call again when I can," she promised.

She was out of money.

The line went dead.

Georgiana hung up the receiver, rummaged in her purse—it was an inexpensive fake leather handbag that she'd bought that afternoon several days ago in Prescott—and came up with a tissue.

Regrets.

She had a few.

She had more than a few when it came to her parents. But she wasn't sorry she had called her mother and father. She'd wanted to hear their voices. And she had needed to say that she loved them.

"Sorry, Cole, that's all I could find out for you."

Cole spoke into the cellular telephone. "Hey, Martin, even you can't move mountains every time."

"At least you can put your mind at rest about the list of names you gave me," his second-in-command reported. "But my sources within the police department are really keeping a tight lid on this case. I couldn't find out a damned thing about the Isherwood investigation. I couldn't even find out if there is an official investigation."

Cole leaned back against an ironwood tree outside the gas station cum general store. "Doesn't that seem a little odd to you?"

"Yes. It does."

"Do you have any idea why there's no information available on Isherwood?"

There was a humorless chuckle on the other end of the secured line. "You're assuming, of course, that Paul Isherwood was the victim's real name."

Cole slapped his forehead with the palm of his free hand. "An alias. I should have thought of that possibility."

There was a soft snort. "I believe you've had your mind on a few dozen other things." Martin Davis went on to tell him, "You were dead right about the men who visited Isherwood in his suite that night. There isn't any record of them. Not so much as a single physical description or a license plate number. Zip. Nothing. Nada."

"You know what that means, don't you?" Cole said, suddenly straightening.

"Yup."

"Whoever is behind this will assume that she's the only one who can give the police a firsthand account or any kind of description of that evening."

"Which makes your Ms. Burne-Jones target numero uno."

"Shit."

"She's in it right up to her neck, buddy."

"I know."

"Keep alert, Cole."

He began to pace back and forth. "I will."

Martin was concerned and worried. Cole could hear it in his friend's voice. "You've always claimed to have eyes in the back of your head. This would be a damned good time to use them."

"I am."

"Do you want me to join you?"

"Thanks for the offer, Martin, but you're more help to me where you are."

There was a pause. "Keep in touch, Cole."

"I will."

"*Vaya con Dios,* pal."

"*Hasta más ver.*"

Till we meet again . . .

Twenty-One

"Goddamned frigging things," Gruber swore under his breath as he posed in front of the full-length mirror hanging on the back of the bathroom door. Then he reached down and attempted to adjust the crotch of his recently purchased blue jeans. "I don't see how anybody can stand to wear them."

"New jeans need washing," Ford spoke up from the other room, where he was cleaning the dirt out from under his fingernails with a Swiss army knife. "Breaks them in. Takes out the stiffness."

Gruber leered at his own reflection. "There are some things a man wants nice and stiff."

Ford didn't crack a smile. "Jeans aren't one of them," he said, stating the obvious.

Gruber finally emerged from the bathroom in a perfectly pressed denim shirt, stiff new jeans and, from the way he was limping, cowboy boots that pinched his feet. "Do you actually think we're going to . . . what was the phrase you used, Samuelson?"

Samuelson glanced up from the coffee-stained table where he was playing a game of solitaire. "Blend in."

Gruber nodded his head. "Blend in with the locals wearing these clothes?"

"Probably not," Ford admitted.

"I feel like a fucking fool."

Samuelson seemed only too willing to offer his unsolicited sartorial opinion. "You look like one, too."

Gruber glared at him. "Who asked you?"

As always Samuelson remained unruffled. In fact, in all the years Ford had known the man he had never seen Samuelson lose his cool. Gruber, on the other hand, had a very short fuse.

Samuelson proposed a hypothetical situation. "Wouldn't you want someone to tell you if you had a piece of spinach caught between your front teeth?"

The glare on Gruber's features turned to puzzlement. "What does spinach or teeth have to do with this?"

Samuelson flipped over another card and meticulously placed a red ten on a black jack. "Even without the suit and tie, you stick out like a sore thumb."

"Well, excuse me."

Gruber wasn't in the best humor. In fact, he showed signs of being downright testy. It was probably the snug fit through the crotch of his jeans, Ford mused with a certain amount of satisfaction.

Gruber never knew when to give up. "Just what do you suggest I do about it?"

Samuelson always had an answer. "Take your jeans to the Laundromat around the corner. Run them through the wash cycle half a dozen times. Use plenty of fabric softener in the rinse, by the way. Then dry them on permanent press or they'll shrink two sizes and you'll never get them back on."

"Well, aren't we the knowledgeable little homemaker." Gruber's Neanderthal forehead wrinkled into a frown. "How come you didn't have to do that with the jeans you bought this morning?"

Samuelson played the queen of hearts on the king of spades. "I was smart enough to buy prewashed and preshrunk jeans."

"You always have to have the last word, don't you?" Gruber said accusingly.

Samuelson responded, "Nope."

Gruber jumped at the chance to answer the telephone when it rang later that afternoon. No doubt because he'd lost another fifty bucks to Samuelson playing gin rummy. It would have been cheaper to watch TV, but Gruber had complained that he couldn't find any reruns of *The Brady Bunch*. The cheap motel they were staying in only carried four channels and three of those were either the news or weather.

"Gruber here," he stated. Then he stood a little straighter. "Hello, boss."

Ford listened. The man on the other end spoke for a minute or two. Gruber paid attention.

"Of course I understand. I'll repeat it word for word to Ford and Samuelson. We'll get right on it, boss." There was another pause while Gruber grabbed a pen and a piece of paper from the cheap particleboard desk. He scribbled down a word or two. "Got it. Consider it done, Uncle Johnny."

The familial relationship between Gruber and "Uncle Johnny" explained why the least talented and the least intelligent of the three of them was supposedly in charge. Ford and Samuelson played along with the ruse, but when push came to shove, they all knew who the real leader of the pack was.

"That was the boss," Gruber announced unnecessarily after he'd hung up the receiver.

"What's the latest?" Samuelson inquired as he nonchalantly and expertly shuffled the deck of cards.

"We have the location of Worth and the woman."

Ford was a man of few words. "Where are they?"

"Idaho."

"They've made good time," Samuelson observed.

"Where in Idaho?" Ford asked.

"I wrote it all down, including the name of the nearest town." Gruber shook his head in bewilderment. "I wonder how Uncle Johnny gets his information."

Ford figured it was none of his business. "The boss has his ways."

Gruber pondered the possibilities. "Inside sources. Payoffs. Blackmail."

" 'Ours is not to wonder why,' " Samuelson quoted, slipping the deck of cards into his pocket.

Even Gruber seemed to catch on. "In other words, it's none of our beeswax."

"That's right," Ford agreed, getting to his feet. "Our business is to find Worth and the woman and have a friendly little chat with them."

"Time to pack up our gear and hit the trail," Gruber added in a phony western accent, followed by his distinctive, and what the other two considered irritating, laugh.

"I'll drive," Ford informed the other two men. He didn't trust either of them behind the wheel of the powerful four-wheel-drive vehicle he'd rented the day before yesterday. "Samuelson, you take the rear and keep an eye on our backs."

Gruber started to whine. He nearly always did. "What do I get to do?"

Ford gave him a feral grin. "You get to sit up front with me and ride shotgun."

* * *

Flopsy, Mopsy and Cottontail.

That was what he had taken to calling them.

After all, he reflected with a self-acknowledged superior smile, it was supposedly a bunny-eat-bunny world.

The only "bunny" he'd ever had any personal respect for was the killer rabbit in an old Monty Python movie that he had once watched on late-night television.

It was about time they caught up with him. If it hadn't been for him, the three men would still be sitting in that dingy motel room back in Prescott, twiddling their thumbs.

He had placed the pieces on the chessboard and maneuvered them like the master gamester that he was, of course. He'd made it easy for them. Indeed, he had practically erected signs: This way to Worth and the woman.

Unlike Flopsy, Mopsy and Cottontail, he was a consummate professional, *the* consummate professional. He did his job well. In fact, nobody did it better. He took pride in his work. He was neat and tidy and utterly reliable. He had never failed to complete an assignment. After all, he had a reputation—a stellar reputation at that—to uphold.

He was also very well paid.

Not that he did it for the money. In many ways, he saw himself as an artist.

Nevertheless, there was ample compensation given for his services. Consequently, there was also an account in a Swiss bank, another in the Grand Caymans and a third in Hong Kong. He could have retired several years ago, but his work gave meaning and purpose to his life. He saw no reason to give it up at this point in the game.

It was all a game to him.

And being the master gamester, it was a game that he always won.

Twenty-Two

Georgiana usually liked storms.

Storms were a natural and inherent reminder that there was a power in the world that man had not tamed, a force that man could not control, that there was something bigger, stronger, greater than any man or woman, than mankind itself.

Storms were larger than life and a constant reminder that life was filled with the unexpected. They could be beautiful, breathtaking, wondrous and awe-inspiring.

Storms didn't give Georgiana a feeling of helplessness, but of hopefulness.

But she had to admit that she didn't like this storm.

Within minutes blue skies darkened to an ominous, angry, roiling sea of black. There was a distant rumble of thunder and a portentous flash of lightning, followed by rain: just a few sprinkles at first, then a steady downpour and finally a blinding curtain of precipitation that obliterated the road in front of them.

It quickly became a deluge.

The windshield wipers were working furiously,

swishing back and forth in an attempt to keep the front window clear.

It was futile.

"How can you see where you're going?" Georgiana finally asked Cole, pitching her voice to be heard above the din.

"I can't," he informed her, lips thinned, mouth grim, eyes squinted, gaze glued to the headlights that illuminated the narrow country road only a foot or two in front of the pickup truck.

"I don't like it," she added a minute later.

"I'm not too thrilled with the situation myself," Cole said, both hands gripping the steering wheel.

Just when Georgiana assumed conditions couldn't get any worse, it began to hail chunks of ice the size of golf balls. The clatter on the metal roof was deafening. It went on and on and on until she wanted to scream or cover her ears.

She chose the latter over the former.

"I'm going to pull over," Cole suddenly announced as he applied the brakes.

The pickup truck came to a stop. The hail slackened off, but the downpour continued.

Georgiana huddled on her side of the bench-style seat, arms wrapped around herself, shivering. "Are we far enough off the road?" she inquired, anxious.

Cole peered out the rain-slicked driver's window. "I don't know for sure. I do know I don't want to end up in a drainage ditch when there's a danger of flash floods."

She licked her lips nervously. "What if another car or truck comes along?"

There was a definite edge to his voice. "Then we hope and pray they see our taillights before they ram into us."

It was small comfort.

Cole finally turned and looked at her, his blue eyes nearly as dark and stormy as the sky. "Are you cold?"

"A little," Georgiana admitted.

Mostly she was tired. She hadn't been sleeping well the past several nights. If she was honest with herself, she had scarcely slept at all since the episode in the Room of Light.

Episode?

What a mundane, ordinary, ridiculous, polite word for the passion and intimacy that she and Cole had shared on the sandy floor of the cavern that afternoon.

Episode?

It had been an epiphany. Georgiana had discovered more about herself in those two hours than she had ever dreamed possible. She had thought of herself as poised, discreet and unflappable; proper and perhaps occasionally even a little prim in her manner.

She had always regarded herself as a woman of delicate sensibilities, as someone with discerning tastes and a marked preference for the subtleties of life's experiences.

In short, she had been born and bred a lady.

It was all a lie.

She was a wild thing, a creature of the senses, a woman of strong passions and insatiable appetites. She was capable of giving as good as she got when it came to the raw, primitive, erotic exchanges between a male and a female.

She was not the modest and chaste young woman she had assumed herself to be.

She had been unself-conscious about her nudity, shameless in her effrontery, bold and daring in what she had taken from Cole and what she had given back to him.

When she recalled what she had done with her hands and her mouth and her lips, even her teeth; when she relived the intimacies she had granted Cole—granted? he had wanted, taken, demanded them of her—Georgiana felt her nipples harden and the awareness, the tingling, the arousal begin all over again.

She had been putty in his hands. (Oh, Lord, what he could do to her with those hands!) She hadn't stopped him then. She couldn't stop herself now.

A shiver shook Georgiana from head to toe.

Cole saw her tremble. There was very little that Cole didn't see. "You're cold." He motioned with one hand and urged her in a surprisingly soft voice, "Come here."

She shook her head. They both recognized that it was a token refusal.

"My body heat will warm you up," he told her, as if an explanation was called for.

She looked at him.

"It's nothing personal," he assured her.

She slid across the seat and into his waiting arms.

He was warm and he smelled good. He was gentle and strong. He cradled her, encompassed her, surrounded her with himself. She felt safe. She was no longer afraid. She quickly grew warm, then almost hot.

"Better?" Cole asked.

"Much better," Georgiana replied. Some time passed before she said to him, "May I ask you a question?"

She sensed a hesitancy in the man before he answered her with a studied nonchalance. "Sure."

"Why aren't the police after us . . . after me?"

He thought about it. "I don't know."

"But they aren't, are they?"

"I don't think so."

Georgiana craned her neck and looked up as far as the chiseled line of Cole's jaw. "We agree that the three men in the dark suits probably aren't the authorities.''

His lips disappeared. ''They aren't the authorities.''
He left her in no doubt on that count.

She found that she needed to talk about it. ''Someone
else sent them, even if we aren't sure who.''

''They were sent by someone,'' he agreed.

Her next question was an impossible one for Cole to
answer, but he must have known that she was simply
seeking reassurance. ''Will the men catch up with us
again?''

''Not if I can help it.''

''Do you think they've changed vehicles by now?''

He was honest with her. ''Yes.''

''So they can travel wherever we travel.''

''Pretty much.''

''I wish they would simply go away and leave us
alone,'' she said wistfully.

Cole breathed in and out. ''It doesn't work like that
in the real world, Georgiana.''

''I know,'' she responded in a small voice, leaning
her head back against his chest and listening to the
strong, regular, rhythmic beat of his heart.

''You have one huge advantage, of course,'' he declared as he stretched out his long legs in front of him.

Georgiana was curious. ''Which is?''

She could almost feel the smile that appeared on his
face. ''You've got me,'' Cole pointed out.

''Just how is that a huge advantage?'' she inquired,
going along with him.

''I'm from Texas.''

''That goes without saying.''

''For another thing, I know this part of the country
like my own backyard,'' he claimed.

''So where are we?''

Cole made a production of looking out at the rain as

if he could actually see something, anything, in the downpour. "We're in the middle of nowhere."

"I guess you do know what you're talking about," she acknowledged. "We are in the middle of nowhere."

"Another thing in our favor: I have our final destination in mind," he pointed out logically.

"You're the only one who does." She knew generally, if not specifically, where they were headed.

Cole went on listing what he considered their advantages. "We're driving Bessie."

"Actually you're driving Bessie. I'm riding in Bessie." A fine, but necessary, distinction.

"It's an advantage either way."

"Why?"

"Horsepower."

She repeated what he'd said to her that night in Hal's House of Honky Tonk. "As in 'I'm going to see a man about a horse' horsepower, I presume."

"You presume correctly." Cole reached out and patted the dashboard with one palm. "Bessie has an engine that would be the envy of any pickup truck."

"Please put that in layman's terms."

"Bessie's fast."

"Very fast?"

Cole's chin moved against the top of her head. "Deceptively fast." He added with all due respect, "I'll bet she can easily accelerate from zero to ninety in ten seconds."

"Meaning?"

"She has get-up-and-go."

"In other words, Bessie is a Ferrari at heart," Georgiana said, interpreting his words.

"Something like that."

"I find that very reassuring," she told him.

"I thought you might."

Georgiana settled deeper into his chest and rested her hands on his forearms. "What other advantages do we have?"

"I've been in tight spots before."

She put her own slant on this latest statement of his. "You're not afraid."

"I didn't say that."

No. He hadn't.

Cole was deadly serious when he related, "There's a difference between fear that keeps a man sharp, alert, on his toes, and fear that makes him freeze up."

"Fear keeps you on your toes," she deduced.

"It always has before."

Georgiana found that especially reassuring. It wasn't that she hadn't known fear in her life. She had in many guises. But she'd never had to face the threat of physical violence before. And she'd never seen violent death up close until that night in Isherwood's suite.

"Tell me more," she urged.

It was a minute before Cole responded by saying, "I know my way around weapons."

"Weapons?" A crease formed between her eyes. "Would you care to elaborate?"

Cole apparently decided to dispense with modesty. "I'm a crack shot. I know how to fight the old-fashioned way with my fists. And I can handle most types of knives."

Georgiana swallowed hard. "And that's supposed to make me feel better?"

"Under the circumstances, it should." The man exhaled slowly. "We aren't going up against a troop of Boy Scouts, honey."

Georgiana fell silent.

"Are you all right?" Cole inquired after she failed to respond.

She nodded.

"I didn't say that to frighten you."

"I know you didn't," she replied in a voice that was scarcely above a whisper.

Cole had misunderstood. He hadn't frightened her by mentioning the men in dark suits who were in pursuit. It was the fact that he'd unconsciously and unintentionally called her honey. They had both kept their distance since that afternoon in Monument Valley. His slip of the tongue only served to remind her that, at least for a short while, this man had been her lover.

Almost as if he could read her mind, Cole allowed his voice to sink to a caress. "What are you thinking about?"

You.

Me.

Us.

The way we were together.

Georgiana was very tempted, but she mentioned none of these things to him.

"You don't have to answer that question if you don't want to," Cole finally said, giving her a way out.

"I know."

He waited.

She'd forgotten how good he was at waiting.

Georgiana took in a deep breath and released it. "You called me honey."

"Yes. I did."

"Was it a slip of the tongue?"

"No. It wasn't." There was silence for a count of five. "Why do you ask?"

"I'm a little surprised, that's all," she admitted with a degree of circumspection.

Cole, on the other hand, came right out and laid his cards on the table. "You're surprised because we've kept each other at arm's length since the afternoon we made love in the Room of Light.''

"Was it making love?" she blurted out.

Georgiana felt his body stiffen, heard the change in his tone of voice. "As opposed to what?"

She dared herself to say it. "Having sex."

"Is that what it was for you?"

Among many other wonderful things, yes.

Georgiana didn't answer his question. Instead, she asked one of her own. "What was it for you?"

"Great," came out in a rush. Obviously he hadn't had to stop and think about it.

"It was great for me, as well," she conceded.

"Anything else?"

Georgiana wetted her lips with the tip of her tongue. "Wonderful."

Cole repeated. "Wonderful."

She racked her brain and came up with, "Sandy."

That got his attention. "Sandy?"

She quickly went on to confess, "I've never made love before in the sand."

"Ah . . ."

Georgiana could have recited an endless list of adjectives describing what the experience of making love with Cole had been like for her: intense, earthshaking, profound, exquisite, heart-stopping, beautiful, mind-boggling, soul-shattering.

But words had a power all of their own. Words were power. If she divulged the words to this man, she would be giving him incredible power over her.

She wasn't ready for that.

Georgiana suddenly noticed the rain was letting up. The road was visible for twenty or thirty feet ahead of the pickup truck.

She glanced up at Cole and inquired, "Where do you see us going from here?"

Was this one of those trick questions women always liked to ask men?

Cole cleared his throat and racked his brain. Where did he see them going from here?

Hell, he didn't know. He did know one thing. He wasn't the marrying kind, and any relationship with him was temporary. He had always made that clear to his women right up front.

Was Georgiana his woman?

If so, why hadn't he told her?

Cole decided that he'd have to think about that one. But this wasn't the time or the place.

He paraphrased her question. "Where are we headed?"

Georgiana turned in his arms. Huge dark green eyes gazed expectantly into his.

Muscles in his back tightened, but Cole knew he had to say something. "I don't know."

She frowned. "You don't know?"

He swallowed. He'd been in some tight and down-right uncomfortable positions in his thirty-seven years, but this ranked as one of the most uncomfortable. "I'm not certain."

Georgiana listened intently and made a small sound in the back of her throat.

She had a beautiful throat, and a long, graceful, beautiful neck, for that matter. Her features were patrician: delicate ears, delicate nose, delicate chin, riveting green eyes. Her complexion was pale ivory in color and flawless. Her shoulders were slender without being bony. And her breasts . . . well, in a word, her breasts were perfect.

Cole almost blurted out that she had perfect breasts, but somehow he didn't think that was the answer Georgiana was looking for.

He flexed his tensed shoulders, quietly blew out his breath and offered to her, "It's too early to tell."

Georgiana glanced down at the watch on her wrist and made a small sound in the back of her throat again. He couldn't tell if she was agreeing or disagreeing with him.

Cole consciously tried to relax his shoulders. "I think we need to give ourselves some time under more normal circumstances and see where it takes us."

A finely arched eyebrow was raised and lowered. "In other words, you don't know where the road leads."

Cole shook his head. "Not metaphorically speaking."

Georgiana frowned.

Had he missed something? Had he said the wrong thing? Cole took a moment and thought hard. Maybe it had been his choice of words.

A delicate and feminine forehead wrinkled in puzzlement. "Metaphorically speaking?"

He nodded.

Georgiana gestured toward the front window of the pickup. "The rain is letting up." She glanced down at her watch again and lightly tapped the face with her fingernail. "It's nearly seven o'clock. I meant where do we go from here."

Cole exhaled. He knew the answer, after all. "Bison Bill's," he stated.

Twenty-Three

The Dwigginses' Cattle and Guest Ranch consisted of eighty-seven thousand acres in the heart of the Idaho countryside. The owners, Bill Dwiggins and his wife, Amelia Earhart Dwiggins (she was in charge of the adjoining airfield for those visitors who preferred to fly in rather than make the long drive from Boise), were known throughout the region as colorful personalities. Amelia was most often described as "all-get-up-and-go," and Bill as "sit-down-and-whoa."

Guests—limited to an even dozen at any one time— were welcome year-round to the Dwigginses' hands-on cattle operation. Its 1940s log cabin buildings were nestled in a pine-filled valley near the Idaho and Washington state lines. There were two miles of private trout stream, campouts, cookouts under the stars and wilderness pack trips.

Well-trained horses and a large herd of bison were the trademarks of the Dwigginses' working ranch. The brochure they occasionally mailed out to travel agents and the like—although most of their guests had learned about the place through word of mouth—made it clear what could be expected by warning, "It helps to be in shape and have had a little time in the saddle. Have your butt broke in."

Georgiana's butt was currently and comfortably settled in a rocking chair on the front porch of the main log cabin, otherwise known as the "lodge."

Bison Bill himself was clearing up a misunderstanding as he explained to Georgiana and Cole, "*Buffalo* is the common name for any of five species of wild cattle native to Africa and Asia. The term is also commonly, but mistakenly, applied to the American bison." The surprisingly spry septuagenarian pointed to the large herd of shaggy-maned animals that could be seen in the fading daylight. "Those are bison. That's why I'm called Bison Bill."

The elegant woman rocking alongside Georgiana laughed and remarked to her husband and their two newest guests, "Besides, there already was a Buffalo Bill."

Bison Bill eased himself out of his rocking chair. "He was misnamed. Just like the cattle." The older man motioned to Cole. "We'll leave the women to their chit-chat. I'd like to show you the latest additions to my herd."

As the two men shuffled off the wraparound front porch and in the direction of the nearest barn, Georgiana heard Cole say to their host with genuine respect, "It's amazing what ranchers like yourself have accomplished, Bill. It wasn't that long ago that the American bison was in danger of becoming extinct."

"That would have been a tragedy. We would have lost more than just another species of cattle," Bill Dwiggins claimed as they ambled along. "The bison has always been symbolic somehow of the American West." Then the older man went on to inquire, "What do you raise on your ranch, Cole?"

Cole kicked at a stone with the tip of his well-worn boot. "A few longhorns."

"Maybe I could get you started with a pair of bison if you're interested."

"I might be, Bill," Cole replied as the men disappeared around the corner of the barn.

"By the time those two return from the calving barn, Coleman Worth is going to know a lot more about bison than he probably ever needed or wanted to know," Amelia speculated, but it wasn't meant as an unkind remark.

Georgiana was content to sit quietly and rock. "It seems so peaceful here," she said at last. "And you've been so kind to us. I wouldn't want to bring our troubles down on you or this place."

Amelia would have none of that. "Friends share the good times and the bad times."

"But you've only known Cole and myself for a few short hours," she pointed out.

As a matter of fact, they had showed up unannounced, dripping wet from the rain and ravenously hungry. They had been made to feel welcome. They had been given the best rooms in the house, and they had been fed, generously and well.

"Any friend of Alfred Crick's is a friend of ours. Besides, Bill and I can take care of ourselves."

Georgiana's throat tightened. "The men following us could be dangerous."

"Life is fraught with danger." Amelia Dwiggins gazed out at the tranquil landscape and the glorious colors of the setting sun as it slipped below the horizon. "That was one of the first lessons I learned when I came here."

Georgiana was curious. She only hoped she wasn't

being impolite, as well. "Where were you from originally?"

"New York City."

She couldn't hide her surprise. "How in the world
did you end up in Idaho?"

Amelia Earhart Dwiggins laughed with genuine self-
amusement. "I came out here on a dare. My brother had
met Bill during a long trip he made after the war." The
woman paused and decided she'd better explain which
one. "That was World War Two, by the way," she said
dryly. "Anyway, I flew cross-country in my own plane,
intending to stop over in Idaho for a few nights."

"And?"

"I've been here ever since."

Georgiana was astonished. She opened and then
closed her mouth, then opened it a second time. "You
just gave it all up and moved out here to the middle
of . . ."

"Nowhere," supplied her hostess. "That's about the
long and short of it."

Georgiana didn't wish to sound rude, but she was
afraid that was the way it came out. "Why?"

"For the usual reason." The still-attractive older
woman heaved a sigh. "I fell in love."

"With Bison Bill?"

"He wasn't called Bison Bill back then, of course.
He was just plain Bill Dwiggins in those days. But he
was the handsomest son-of-a-gun I'd ever met and the
only man to ever make my heart sing." Amelia ceased
rocking for ten or fifteen seconds. "It may sound corny,
but the old saying is true."

"Which old saying is that?"

"Opposites attract." Amelia Earhart Dwiggins elaborated, "I was a city girl. I was the epitome of the modern, postwar woman with a career, and a mind, of her

own. I was going places and I wasn't going to let anyone stop me.''

''Bill stopped you.''

''To the contrary. He figured we had even less chance of making it work than I did,'' the woman stated.

Not failing to see the similarities to her own situation, Georgiana had to know. ''What happened?''

Amelia began to rock back and forth again. ''As they said during the war, no guts, no glory.''

Georgiana brought her teeth together. ''Meaning?''

Intelligent, dark brown eyes nailed her to the spot. ''Life's very short. If you want something, you'd better have the guts to go after it.''

''You wanted Bill.''

''I wanted Bill.''

''You went after him.''

''And I got him.''

Georgiana couldn't prevent the wistful sigh that escaped from between her lips. ''I wish it were that simple today.''

''It is.''

Georgiana's brows drew together in a frown. ''Maybe for some people.''

Amelia Earhart Dwiggins, onetime New Yorker, sometime aviatrix, occasional philosopher and full-time rancher, summed up her opinion in a few words. ''Now you're making excuses.''

''I beg your pardon,'' she murmured.

Amelia reached out and patted Georgiana's arm affectionately. ''Don't go getting your dander up, girl. I'm a plainspoken and an outspoken woman. And I'm too old to pussyfoot around.'' She placed her hands on the arms of her chair; it was the first time that Georgiana had noticed the age spots on the thinning skin or the gnarled, arthritic knuckles. ''Besides, I figure age has its privileges. It's part of the compensation for growing older.''

She wondered how old Amelia was.

''I'm seventy-eight,'' the woman informed her.

''I wasn't asking.''

''But you were wondering.''

Georgiana smiled at her companion a little ruefully. ''All right, I admit I was wondering.''

Amelia's next statement caught her by surprise. ''Don't be afraid to make a fool of yourself.''

''I don't understand,'' she quickly claimed.

''I think you do.''

Georgiana swallowed. ''You mean over Cole?''

The gray head nodded. ''If you let your pride get in the way, if you don't tell him how you feel, you'll always wonder what might have been. You'll always have regrets.''

Georgiana's stomach flipped over. Her mouth was suddenly dry. ''I can't.''

Shrewd eyes, wise eyes, observed her. ''You're in love with the man, aren't you?''

''Yes.''

''You haven't told him.''

''I haven't told him.''

Curiosity of a sympathetic kind was clearly written across the aged yet somehow ageless features. ''Why not?''

Georgiana admitted it out loud for the first time. ''It wouldn't go anywhere.''

There was no subtlety to Amelia's style of interrogation. ''How do you know that?''

''Cole isn't the marrying kind.''

There was a soft, feminine snicker. ''Of course he is.'' Some allowance was made. ''He just doesn't know it.''

"I don't think he ever will," Georgiana said with no small measure of regret.

Amelia reached for the glass of homemade lemonade at her elbow. She took a sip and returned the glass to the wooden outdoor table. "The man has a lot of hurt inside him."

Georgiana sighed. "He does."

"Are you the cause?"

"No."

Amelia Earhart Dwiggins leaned back in her rocking chair. "Do you know about it?"

"I know something, a little, about it."

It was the voice of experience that said to her, "All Coleman Worth needs is the love of a good woman, the love of the right woman. Are you that woman?"

Georgiana didn't rush to answer the question. She took her time and she thought about it. "I don't know," she finally admitted.

Amelia Dwiggins gave a decisive nod of her head, her eyes never leaving her companion's. "Well, that's the first thing you have to figure out."

"What's the second thing?"

"What does he need?"

"And the third?"

"Can you give it to him?"

Georgiana had never thought of herself as a selfish person, but she needed to know one more thing. "What about me?"

"That's the last thing you need to determine . . . and maybe the most important."

"What is it?"

"Is Coleman Worth the right man for you?"

If only it weren't so complicated. If only there was some way of knowing for certain. If only a bright neon sign would flash on over the man's head and announce,

THIS IS THE RIGHT ONE FOR YOU, GEORGIANA BURNE-JONES.

They were all wrong for one another, she and Cole. They couldn't be right for each other. They were like night and day, apples and oranges, left and right.

"We're so different."

Georgiana hadn't realized she had expressed the thought aloud until the woman sitting beside her responded.

Her sideways glance was disconcertingly shrewd. "It's been that way since time began. Men and women are different. Don't let any fool tell you otherwise."

Georgiana heard herself laughing softly in the twilight. "Do you mind if I ask how you got to be so wise?"

"I don't mind in the least."

Georgiana felt compelled to point out to her newfound friend, "Because we both know that wisdom doesn't necessarily come with age or experience."

Something flickered behind deep, dark brown eyes. "I'm seventy-eight years old. I've been married to Bill Dwiggins for over fifty of those years. I've found out a thing or two about my man and about men in general in that time," Amelia stated without coyness. "There is only one important thing."

"What is it?"

"Each woman has to learn the best way to love her man."

"It must be different for each man," Georgiana surmised.

The only light was the pale glow cast from a lamp inside the lodge. Georgiana sensed rather than saw Amelia move her head. "It's different . . . and it's the same."

Georgiana wasn't certain she understood completely. Her hostess concluded their conversation by saying,

"I put you and Cole off by yourselves. You have two separate bedrooms, but there is an adjoining door. It's up to you, Georgiana, whether that door is left open or closed."

Twenty-Four

No guts, no glory.

Georgiana chanted the phrase to herself over and over again like a mantra as she lay in her bed at the Dwigginses' ranch that night, thinking about Cole in the next room: the room just on the other side of the connecting door.

Easier said than done.

That was another familiar saying that kept running through her head. Amelia Earhart Dwiggins had given her a good deal of advice tonight as the two women had sat on the front porch, rocking. But she had failed to tell Georgiana where she could find the courage to accept rejection, if rejection was what she encountered.

"No guts, no glory," Georgiana repeated aloud as she threw back the covers, sat up on the edge of the mattress and touched her bare feet to the hardwood floor.

What were her intentions?

To march into Cole's bedroom in the middle of the night and inform the man that she was falling in love with him, that she might already be in love with him, that she loved him?

To slip into bed beside him, wrap her arms and body around his, kiss him, caress him, arouse him, make love to him?

A woman must learn the best way to love her man, according to the wise Amelia. Sex was only one part—although an important part—of that equation.

Georgiana had once read somewhere that *falling* in love was easy; *being* in love was difficult.

What did she know about being in love?

Very little.

Next to nothing.

Nil.

When it came to love between a man and a woman, it was all on-the-job training. At least she was willing to learn. And there was no better time to start than right now . . . before she lost her nerve.

She tiptoed across the cool hardwood floor, grasped the doorknob in her hand and quietly, noiselessly, opened the door between the two guest rooms.

Cole's room was dark, but not so dark that she couldn't make out the pine dresser against the far wall, the antique oval mirror, the desk in the corner, the oversize bed in front of her and the outstretched form of a man's body.

Georgiana took three steps into the room.

From the soft, regular rise and fall of his chest it was obvious that Cole was sound asleep. Little wonder. He had driven at least eighteen hours out of every twenty-four for the past several days. Even a man with his stamina would be tired.

Georgiana stood there in her nightgown—actually she was wearing a man's oversize T-shirt with a pair of panties underneath—and debated whether to return to her own bed or crawl in beside Cole. In the end, her heart overruled her head: she made her way around to the other side of the bed and slipped in between the sheets.

Cole never moved.

The rhythm of his inhaling and exhaling didn't alter. He seemed oblivious to her presence.

Georgiana gave a sigh.

His bed was warmer than hers had been; she could feel the heat radiating from his body. The sound of his breathing was somehow comforting and reassuring. She could feel herself relaxing.

She had one last thought before she drifted off to sleep: she wasn't alone anymore.

Cole found her at dawn's first light, curled up in his embrace, her arms wrapped around his waist, her face buried in his chest. She was warm and sweet-smelling. Her breath softly wafted across his skin, raising goose bumps on every inch of his flesh.

He felt his body starting to respond to her nearness. He was half-tempted—more than half-tempted, if the truth be known—to kiss her awake and make love to her.

But what a man was tempted to do and what a man did were two entirely different things.

The initial encounter between them in the cavern had been wild and wonderful, crazy and spontaneous. It had also been irresponsible. To make love again, without discussing it rationally ahead of time, without making certain that the necessary precautions were taken, would be stupid and unforgivable.

Cole liked to think he wasn't a stupid man.

Of course, there were always ways—very satisfying ways—for a man and woman to make love, to enjoy physical intimacy, to give pleasure to and receive pleasure from each other, that ensured there were no risks involved.

In the case of Georgiana Burne-Jones, however, there were also emotional risks at stake.

Coleman Worth reminded himself that he was a patient man. He could wait. He was good at waiting.

Good things come to those who wait.

Cole took in and let out a shallow breath of air—he was trying not to disturb the young woman asleep in his arms—and wondered if this time it would be true for him.

He gently rested his chin on the top of Georgiana's head—her hair was fine and silky and smelled faintly of lilacs—and pondered the predicament in which he found himself.

In a few short days—hell, in a few brief moments—Georgiana Burne-Jones had entirely changed his life. Before she had burst into the presidential suite at the Sonoran that night, his ducks had been neatly lined up in a row, his business empire had been under control, he had been in command of his world.

He had been a satisfied man.

True, he had *not* often thought about personal happiness, but he'd always believed that happiness was fleeting at best and undoubtedly highly overrated, anyway.

He had *not* dreamed, planned or taken into account the prospect of having a home or a wife and children. He already owned a sizable ranch in the middle of Texas, a penthouse apartment in Wichita Falls and a cabin in the wilderness of upstate Washington.

A real home.

A loving wife.

Children.

These things were not for Coleman Worth.

He had made his peace with that a long time ago. He had also accepted the fact that he'd made his own bed and he would have to sleep in it. He simply hadn't realized, until the past few days, how lonely that bed, and his life, had been.

Cole faced the truth straight on: he was a lonely man.

He had assumed he always would be until the woman in his arms, the woman snuggled up against his body, her arm flung with abandon across his chest, had stumbled into his life and shown him possibilities that he had never imagined existed.

He didn't have to be lonely.

It was not cast in stone.

It was not his destiny.

When Georgiana was with him—which had been pretty much night and day for nearly a week now—Cole found himself thinking of her, caring for her, watching out for her, watching over her, needing desperately to keep her safe.

Sometimes the lady seemed so strong, and at other times she appeared so vulnerable.

Suddenly Cole realized that he not only wanted Georgiana Burne-Jones in all the ways a man wants a woman he finds sexually attractive, but he wanted to protect her: from the men in the dark suits who were pursuing her, from the ravages of a thunderstorm, from the "slings and arrows of life's misfortunes," from hurt, from threats, from fear, from harm's way.

It was a revelation.

He wanted to keep her safe.

He longed to make her happy.

He needed to see her smile and hear her laugh.

Coleman Worth reflected on his life before and after the arrival of Georgiana, and he made an amazing discovery: maybe he didn't have to be lonely anymore.

*   *   *

"Cole!"

The urgency in the voice speaking next to his ear and the vigorous shake of his shoulder brought Cole out of a sound sleep. His eyes flew open. Amelia Dwiggins was standing beside the bed, waiting for him to awaken.

He immediately glanced down at the young woman still asleep in his arms.

"It can't be helped," the older woman told him, although she spoke low. "Georgiana will have to wake up in a minute, too."

Cole returned the brown-eyed gaze unflinchingly. "What is it?"

Amelia Dwiggins gave it to him straight. "One of our ranch hands just rode in on horseback with the news that three men in a four-wheel-drive vehicle are headed in this direction."

Cole silently bit off an expletive. Aloud, he said, "Then they've found us."

"It looks that way," Amelia acknowledged. Then she added, "Bill's on the lookout with a pair of high-powered binoculars. He'll spot anything that moves before it gets within miles of the lodge."

Cole's expression was as somber as his thoughts. "We'll have to hightail it," he announced.

Their hostess didn't agree with him. "You don't have to leave. You're both welcome to stay here. This is a big ranch. We've got places we can hide you."

He made a dismissing gesture with his free hand. "We appreciate the offer, Amelia, but this isn't your fight and it's not going to become your fight. If Georgiana and I stay, it won't be fair to you or to Bill or to your paying guests."

She was a stubborn woman. She was also fearless. "Bill and I aren't strangers to danger."

"Maybe not. But I know a place where Georgiana and I can hide where no one will find us. I don't know your ranch. I do know the place where we're headed."

Amelia Earhart Dwiggins gave an emphatic nod of her head. "Gives you the upper hand."

"Yes, it does."

She was a no-nonsense, practical kind of woman. "I'll go downstairs and fill a thermos with strong black coffee and pack some supplies for you to eat on the road."

Cole was appreciative. "Thanks."

"No thanks are necessary." The woman dressed in well-worn jeans and a plaid flannel shirt paused in the doorway. "Promise me one thing, though, Coleman Worth."

He pushed himself up in the big, comfortable bed. "And what's that?"

Amelia Dwiggins gazed down at Georgiana with affection and concern. "Take good care of her."

"I will." He added solemnly, "I promise."

Once Amelia was gone again, Cole reached down and placed his face next to Georgiana's and softly nuzzled her cheek. She stirred. Then she snuggled closer to his warmth.

"Georgiana."

"Hmmm."

He repeated her name a little louder. "Georgiana."

Green eyes slowly, reluctantly opened. A smile touched her mouth as she said his name. "Cole."

He brought his teeth together. "I'm sorry, honey."

She frowned. "About what?"

There was no time to lose. "We've got to get up, quickly get dressed, grab our gear and be on our way."

Georgiana turned her head and looked out the window at the gray light. "It's not morning yet."

"No. It isn't."

Some of his agitation and urgency must have conveyed itself to her. Georgiana pushed herself up into a sitting position. "What is it?"

"Amelia just woke me up."

"Why?"

Cole knew his expression and his tone of voice were equally grim. "Trouble."

"Trouble?"

"One of the cowhands reported seeing three strangers driving onto the outskirts of the ranch."

Georgiana's face sank. He knew her heart sank as well. "Three men in dark suits?"

"No. But we have to assume that they exchanged their suits for something more practical."

"They've found us."

Cole wished like hell that he could tell her otherwise. "It looks that way."

She sat up on the edge of the mattress and looked back at him over her shoulder. "How?"

"I don't know," he admitted, reaching for the jeans and denim shirt he'd casually tossed over the back of a nearby chair last night.

Georgiana was suddenly all business. "How long do I have to get dressed and packed?"

Cole grabbed his boots and pulled them on. "Can you be ready in fifteen minutes?"

"I can be ready in ten," she stated.

"Even better. We need to get a move on."

They expressed their thanks and said their good-byes to Bill and Amelia Dwiggins. They promised to return one day, on a happier day. Then they took off in a cloud of dust.

They were on the run again.

Twenty-Five

"Are they behind us?" she asked Cole for the tenth time in as many minutes.

He glanced in the rearview mirror. "No."

Georgiana clasped her hands tightly together in her lap. "You mean you can't see them."

"That's what I mean."

"But they're probably somewhere back there on the road following us," she nitpicked.

"Yes."

"It's not like there are all that many roads in this remote area of the country," she chattered nervously.

"That's true."

She gave a mirthless laugh. "You'd think I would be used to this by now."

"Used to what?"

"Being on the run. Being chased. Being hounded." Feeling frightened, Georgiana added to herself.

"I doubt if anyone gets used to something like that," Cole said, his eyes constantly going back and forth between the rearview mirror and the highway ahead.

"I wonder how those men knew where to find us, or

even what direction we were traveling in,'' Georgiana speculated after a few minutes of tense silence.

Cole shook his hatless head; he'd tossed his Stetson into the cramped space behind them when he had climbed into the pickup that morning. ''I've been wondering the same thing,'' he admitted. ''Maybe someone spotted us and blabbed.''

An idea began to formulate in her mind. ''What about your cellular phone?''

Without explaining the specifics, Cole assured her, ''It's a special secured number. No one can trace where I'm calling from or where I'm calling to.''

Georgiana grew very still. ''That isn't true, however, for a regular telephone line, is it?''

''No.''

She grew even more still. ''Can a call be traced back to a telephone booth?''

Cole apparently knew the answer to her question. ''Yes. If the right equipment is already in place on the other end.''

Georgiana swallowed hard and said in a slightly husky voice, ''Like a legal wiretap.''

''Or an illegal one.''

She'd have to confess. She took in and let out a deep breath before she said to her partner-in-crime, ''It's all my fault.''

Cole gave her a quick sidelong glance. ''What's all your fault?''

A huge sigh, followed by, ''It's because of me that those three men discovered where we were.''

''How do you figure that?''

Georgiana moistened her lips before going on. ''I called my mother and father.''

That surprised him. ''When?''

''When we stopped at the general store and gas station for directions to the Dwigginses' ranch.''

"You didn't mention it to me at the time."

"No. I didn't." Georgiana felt she owed Cole an explanation. "I was walking out of the ladies' rest room when I spotted a newspaper in the trash receptacle. There was a headline about a woman disappearing from a luxury resort in the valley. A corner of the newspaper had been torn away, so most of the article was missing, but I thought it might have been about me." She paused and took another deep breath. "I suddenly realized that my parents would be worried. So I telephoned to reassure them that I was all right."

Blue eyes turned glacial. "What did your parents say?"

Georgiana gnawed on her bottom lip. "They said policemen had been there looking for me."

"Anyone else?"

The words stuck in her throat. "Police detectives."

"Mallory, for one, no doubt," Cole said as though he wasn't in the least bit surprised by that piece of information.

Georgiana clasped and unclasped her hands in her lap. Then she decided she might as well tell Cole everything. "And apparently federal agents."

The man's forehead wrinkled into a studied frown. "Federal agents, as in the FBI?"

She didn't know. She hadn't thought to ask. "My father didn't say specifically."

" 'Hail, hail, the gang's all here,' " Coleman Worth muttered under his breath. "Makes a person wonder if there is anyone who *isn't* looking for you."

"But none of those people appear to be following us," Georgiana pointed out. "The only ones after me are the men in the dark suits." She immediately corrected herself. "The men who were dressed in dark suits the last time you saw them, anyway."

Cole shook his head. "Curiouser and curiouser."

Georgiana's voice was stretched taut. "That's exactly what I said to you about that night," she reminded him.

"Which night?"

She was anything but nonchalant when she answered, "The night of Mr. Isherwood's party."

Apparently Cole recalled the details, as well. "Isherwood instructed you to be like those wise monkeys."

She moved her head up and down. " 'Hear no evil. See no evil. Speak no evil.' "

Cole frowned in thought. "That was just before the men in business suits showed up at the door of his suite for the so-called party."

Hers was the understatement of the year. "It wasn't much of a party."

Cole's laugh was cold. "I don't think it was a party at all."

"What do you mean?"

"I'm not sure." One hand left the steering wheel long enough to stroke his chin. "Twelve men. An even dozen," he muttered under his breath.

That's when it occurred to Georgiana. "Twelve men, as in a jury of his peers?"

"Maybe." Cole gave the matter another thirty seconds of thought. "Or in the case of the late Mr. Isherwood, maybe judge, jury and executioner."

Georgiana shuddered despite the promised warmth of the morning sun. "I don't like to think about that night or about finding poor Mr. Isherwood with a knife. . . ." Her voice trailed off.

Cole changed the subject. "If it's any comfort to you, I doubt if the telephone call you made to your parents tipped the three goons off as to our present location."

Tears threatened. She blinked several times in rapid succession and stared straight ahead.

"Hey, you made the call late yesterday afternoon or early evening. Unless they hired a private plane, managed to rent a vehicle from God knows who and then drove like bats out of hell, there's no way they could have caught up to us so soon."

Georgiana took a swipe at her damp cheek with the back of her hand. "You aren't just saying that to make me feel better, are you?"

There was a momentary flash of white teeth. "Maybe a little. But it's probably true as well."

She sat up straighter. "Which means we still don't know how they found us."

"No. We don't."

She offered a possible explanation. "Of course, they are professionals."

Cole snorted with disdain. "That is a matter of opinion." He took a minute to clarify the reason for his skepticism. "If they're professionals, then they aren't very good at their jobs."

"What makes you say that?"

"I spotted them a mile away."

"But you know as well as I do the average person probably wouldn't have noticed them," Georgiana ventured. "You see things most of us don't, Cole."

Yup, he was one observant sonofabitch, Coleman Worth thought to himself as he made a run for the border.

Or in this case, the Washington state line.

The more he deliberated about the three men in the dark suits—the three clowns, as he was beginning to think of them—the angrier he got. There was just so much a man was willing to take. There was only so far or so often that a man could run.

The truth was, if it hadn't been for Georgiana, he would have stopped, picked his time and place and confronted the three by now. But Georgiana was at the center of the problem and her safety was his main concern.

Cole knew one thing for certain. He wasn't going to take any chances and lead the pursuing trio of thugs to his cabin. If they didn't make their move pretty darn soon, he'd be forced to take matters into his own hands.

Maybe that was where he had been making his mistake, Cole ruminated as he reached down between the seat and his leather boot to make sure the loaded revolver was still where he had stashed it that morning.

He had been *reacting,* instead of *acting*.

It wasn't natural for him to sit back and let someone else set the pace, establish the rules of the game, determine the stakes, choose the field of play. He was used to being in charge. He was the one who gave the orders. He ran the show.

Maybe it was time he took command.

Fear.

For perhaps the third or fourth time in her life—most of those times in the past week—Georgiana understood on a primitive, gut level what fear felt like.

As a young woman—she'd been a teenager at the time—she had truly been afraid the night her tearful and terrified parents had informed her that the Burne-Jones money was gone: the family was reduced to abject poverty.

At fourteen she had envisioned the worst. No food. No clothing. No roof over their heads. She had assumed they would be destitute, homeless, friendless, even hungry.

That had not been the case, of course.

True, there had been no more fancy houses, fancy

cars or fancy yachts, no more servants at their beck and call, no gardeners to tend the yew topiaries trimmed into the serendipitous shapes of birds and squirrels and even the occasional pachyderm.

The Burne-Joneses no longer possessed an indoor swimming pool, or an outdoor swimming pool. There were no more tennis courts, lighted or otherwise, and they could no longer stroll in the dead of winter through an orangery that boasted thirty types of palm trees and nearly as many varieties of orchids.

Within a week Georgiana was no longer enrolled in the very private and very exclusive girls' school that she had attended since the age of four. There were no more piano lessons, dance classes, language tutors or trips to the Louvre for art appreciation.

Overnight her world had changed.

In the days and weeks, the months and even in the years that had followed that traumatic period in her life, Georgiana discovered something about herself: she was a survivor.

A survivor and a fighter.

It had held her in good stead time and time again. It would hold her in good stead tonight.

"What do you think of my plan?" Cole asked her as he leaned forward, arms resting on his knees, fingers loosely interlaced, eagerness written all over his handsome features.

Georgiana sat on the edge of the sagging motel bed. "You're the expert."

"I'm not an expert."

"But you are compared to most people. You are compared to me," she stated, and they both knew she spoke the truth. "Do you think it will work?"

"I do." Cole pushed himself out of the chair, paced back and forth across the cramped budget motel room, halted, drove his hands into the front pockets of his jeans and then rocked back and forth on the heels of his cowboy boots. "But there are never any guarantees. There are always factors that are overlooked, possibilities that are missed and should have been taken into consideration."

"Very few things in life come with a one hundred percent guarantee," Georgiana pointed out.

"We agree the plan is viable, then," he said, stopping in front of her. "The question is, do we dare take the risk?"

"I think we have to."

"We don't *have* to do anything."

Georgiana reached out and brushed her fingers across his. "I'm tired of running. I'm tired of looking over my shoulder. I'm tired of being afraid. I'm just plain tired."

Cole cupped her chin in his hand. "I know you are. I am, too. That's one reason I think we need to take a stand here and now, before we lose our advantage."

"Our advantage?"

He spelled it out for her. "The element of surprise."

Her mouth formed a round O.

"They won't be expecting us to take the offensive."

There was an expression on his face that surprised her, but it shouldn't have: it was cunning.

After all, Coleman Worth, the multimillionaire CEO, must have a healthy dose of shrewdness in his personality to have succeeded in the world of big business.

He finally went on. "Trust me, the last thing these men will suspect is a trap."

"What makes you so sure?"

"Because all we've done is run and hide from the minute we left the Sonoran. We've never given the slightest indication that we're even aware of their existence."

Georgiana knew her eyes grew larger in the dim lamplight. "They don't know that we know."

Cole grinned at her. "That's it in a nutshell."

It was during a more detailed discussion of their plans that Georgiana asked the question uppermost in her mind. "Do you think the three men will be armed?"

"We have to go on the assumption that they are."

"I'm not very good with guns," she admitted.

"You don't have to be," he assured her.

"You'd better tell me again exactly what you want me to do," Georgiana admonished.

"Don't worry. We'll go over it until it's second nature to you," he told her.

"Then what?"

"Then we'll set up a warning system, get a little shut-eye and wait for the rats to take the bait."

Twenty-Six

"There's their pickup truck," Gruber pointed out unnecessarily to the other two men as they cruised through the parking lot of the only motel in town. "It's a piece of junk," he added.

Samuelson spoke up from the backseat of the vehicle. "Appearances can be deceptive."

"You can say that again," Ford muttered under his breath as he slowly circled the block around the budget motel in an effort to get an overview of the "lay of the land."

Gruber snickered with a superior kind of intonation in his usually nasal tenor. "You'd think a frigging millionaire like Worth could afford something better."

"I'm sure Coleman Worth can afford whatever kind of vehicle he wants," Samuelson observed dryly.

Gruber seemed baffled. "Then why would he choose to trade in that brand-new pickup for this old heap?"

The deep baritone from behind him offered, "The man must have his reasons."

He could think of several excellent reasons right off the top of his head, Ford deliberated as he pulled up alongside a row of semi-trailer trucks parked for the night at the north end of the lot. This far out from the motel—the neon vacancy sign above the office door blinked on and off VAC-N-Y, VAC-N-Y—the parking was on gravel rather than blacktop.

There were any number of logical explanations for why Worth would be traveling in an old pickup truck.

Like camouflage, for one.

Like a very clever disguise, for another.

Not that a man like Gruber would or could appreciate anything as subtle as cleverness.

Ford began his usual routine. On the surface it appeared that his remarks were addressed to both of the men under his command, but he and Samuelson understood that the warning was for Gruber. "We aren't going to do anything stupid."

"Right." Gruber snapped his gum and repeated, as if he needed to remind himself, "Nothing stupid."

"You can start by losing the gum," Ford snapped.

Gruber was sloppy, undisciplined and unprofessional. He was a bad joke. For two cents, Ford would be only too happy to somehow lose the loser.

Gruber punched the button on the passenger door and the automatic window lowered. He put his lips together, puckered up and blew. A wad of chewing gum went flying through the air and struck the window of the vehicle next to them. The small, pink glob hung there against the tinted glass.

He grinned and patted himself on the back. "Pretty damn good shot, huh?"

There were times when Ford wondered if he was getting paid enough to put up with the adolescent antics of Gruber . . . Uncle Johnny or no Uncle Johnny.

"Listen up, men," Ford softly barked in his best ex-military command voice.

It was a tone of voice that had always worked back when there were real wars to be fought. When he had been a leader of real men, instead of a glorified errand boy.

Maybe when he got back to Texas after completing this mission, he would look into doing some independent contract work south of the border or in Asia. The trouble was, Ford acknowledged somewhat begrudgingly to himself, he wasn't getting any younger and fighting wars was a young man's profession.

Gruber crossed one leg over the other—the stiff material of his new blue jeans made a strangely abrasive sound when one knee rubbed against the other—and toyed with the toothpick that had suddenly appeared between the gap in his front teeth.

Ford's instructions were explicit. "We're going to do this by the book."

Gruber had the nerve to ask, "Which book?"

Ford ignored the crack. "Once we approach our destination, there will be no talking."

"Yeah, yeah, no talking," Gruber repeated.

Ford managed to keep his cool and his composure. It took more than a moron like Gruber to get under his skin. "If you must communicate, use hand signals."

"I'll give you a hand signal," the man beside him tittered as he raised a euphemistic middle finger.

Ford gave a rundown of their position. "As far as we know, Worth and the woman are unaware of our existence."

Vacant eyes opened wider. "You mean they don't know we're out here?"

"I mean they have no idea that we've been following them, period," he explained, enunciating each syllable carefully.

The moron made an observation. "I thought you said Worth was smart."

"He is." Ford opened his window, inhaled a measure of cool night air, held it for a moment in his lungs and then exhaled.

"The man's had a lot on his mind," Samuelson finally spoke up from his position behind them.

"Like a woman," Gruber stated. "Not that she's my type. Too skinny. Besides, I prefer blondes."

Ford resumed control of the conversation. "As I was saying, it's more than likely the couple are unaware of our existence. But there is a slight possibility that I'm wrong."

A fleshy hand flew to cover a fleshy mouth, forgetting the toothpick stuck between the front teeth. "You wrong?" Followed by, "Ouch! Dammit."

Ford hated repeating himself, but it seemed necessary. "So, we'll go by the book. We skirt the perimeter first. I'm pretty certain there aren't any back doors to these units, so once the area has been secured, Samuelson will take care of opening the front door of their room. I'll see to the lights."

Gruber gave a petulant scowl. "What do I get to do?"

Ford had already thought of an answer. "You get to say, 'Room service.' "

It *almost* went according to Ford's plans.

The motel was half-deserted and the premises were relatively quiet. There was a raucous bar right next door that boasted ALL NUDE WOMEN ALL THE TIME, and TO-NIGHT ONLY: SPECIAL APPEARANCE BY MISS NUDE AMER-ICA. The noise from the roadside establishment would conveniently cover any sounds the three of them unintentionally made.

As Ford had surmised, there was only one way in and one way out of the motel units, not counting a minuscule window in the bathrooms. The rooms must be downright claustrophobic.

Samuelson wasn't only agile and mobile with a deck of cards; he could do anything with his hands. Maybe it was because his fingers were unusually long and slender. Or maybe it was simply because Samuelson was one smart son of a gun.

He took a thin piece of wire from the pocket of his prewashed, preshrunk jeans and inserted it into the lock. Within seconds there was a soft click.

They held their collective breaths.

Ford put his ear to the cardboard-thin door and listened.

Nothing.

He gave a thumbs-up to the other two men. The door would open *into* the room on his left. That meant the light switch would be on the right-hand side.

Ford moved quickly and quietly. He turned the door-knob and stepped into the motel room. Samuelson and Gruber followed him. He located the light switch and gave it a flick.

Nothing.

Nada.

Then bright lights suddenly blinded him, blinded all three of the men.

From somewhere behind the bright lights came a voice that sent chills down even Ford's experienced spine. "The first man that moves, dies. Now drop your weapons!"

"Jeez," Gruber whimpered, "Uncle Johnny is really going to be p.o.'d at us this time."

For once Ford had to agree with him.

Twenty-Seven

"What do you mean, you aren't carrying any weapons?"

Georgiana heard the disbelief in Cole's voice. She could almost read his mind as well. The three men had easily and neatly fallen into his trap. Perhaps too easily and too neatly.

She had switched the lights back on in the motel room and turned off the powerful, oversize flashlights just as Cole had instructed her to do. The three goons were presently down on their knees, ankles crossed, hands on top of their heads, fingers interlocked.

It was deliberately a helpless, powerless, impotent and awkward position.

One of the men—he was a little older than the other two—seemed to be in charge. He looked up at Cole without any subservience or defiance in his manner, but with a certain degree of respect. "We aren't armed, Worth."

The only thing that appeared to move was Cole's lips. "You know who I am."

There was a flicker of acknowledgment in the intelligent, if snake-cold eyes. "I know who you are."

"Then you must also know what I'm capable of."

The other man looked away first. "I have a pretty good idea," he conceded.

Cole was frightening when he stated, "I don't suffer fools, and I sure as hell don't suffer liars."

The man raised his eyes again. "I'm not lying to you, Worth. We aren't carrying any weapons."

"I told you that was a mistake," whined the youngest and the softest of the three thugs. Even Georgiana could see that he was soft and weak and inept.

"Shut up, Gruber."

Gruber refused to shut up. "What's he going to do with us?" He carried on in a whimper. "Is he going to shoot us? I don't want to die. I'm too young to die."

The quiet one of the trio finally inquired, "What are you going to do with us?"

Nonchalantly Cole remarked to nobody in particular, "You mean after I frisk you?"

There was a nod of several heads.

"I was thinking of dealing with you one by one," Cole responded with characteristic aplomb. He motioned to Georgiana and handed her the revolver just as they had rehearsed earlier that evening. "If necessary, you're to shoot to kill."

She had quickly understood the importance and the necessity of bluffing. Her gaze never faltered. "Yessir."

Cole made a quick yet thorough job of checking the three men for weapons.

"Did you learn that technique in the military?" the older man asked as Cole completed his search and came up empty-handed.

Cole's answer was brusque. "Mexico."

He took the revolver back from her, stuck out the toe of his boot and snared the only chair—it was straight-backed and sturdy—in the room by one of its legs. Then he slowly turned the chair around, straddled the seat and sat down, facing the men on their knees. His revolver was pointed directly at them.

Something wasn't right here.

Indeed, something was very wrong.

Georgiana found that she was more perplexed than frightened by the situation in which she found herself.

It was Cole.

How could the man be so damned blasé, so nonchalant, so cavalier in his attitude?

"They're clean," he finally tossed over his shoulder at her.

Now Georgiana was even more perplexed. "Why aren't they armed?" she demanded as if it were her right to know.

The leader kept his gaze fixed on Cole. "Because we're here to talk to you, and that's all."

Georgiana spoke up again. "I don't understand."

"Look, miss," the man began politely but firmly, "this doesn't concern you. It's between a certain party we represent and Mr. Coleman Worth."

Cole's brain scrambled to absorb the information he had just been given. He made certain that surprise neither registered on his features nor was conveyed in any way by his body language. He took his time. He straightened his back, relaxed his shoulders and spread his legs another inch or two.

"So you're here to talk," he finally drawled in a voice filled with indifference.

"That's right."

Cole knew his smile was more than faintly predatory. "Well, then, you talk, and I'll see if I want to listen."

"Tell the man, Ford," beseeched the weak one, the

one called Gruber. "Tell him, for chrissakes."

So the leader's name was Ford.

Cole leaned forward just enough to appear interested. "Why don't you tell me?"

There was no immediate response from Ford.

Behind him, Georgiana opened her mouth. "You're not here about Isherwood?"

There was a scowl on the older man's craggy and weatherbeaten features. "Who?"

"Isherwood," she repeated a little louder, as if he were hard of hearing.

"Never heard of Isherwood," the thug claimed.

Cole was tired of playing games. It was time to get down to business.

He leaned forward an inch or two and made his position crystal clear. "I want to know what this is all about and I want to know right now." His tone of voice had no leeway in it. "I ask the questions. You give the answers."

There was a reluctant, but defeated nod.

Cole began at the beginning. "Why have you been following us for the past week?"

Gruber glared at the man kneeling beside him. "You said he didn't know."

"I said it was unlikely that he knew," came the immediate correction. Weary eyes met and held Cole's. "We were instructed by a certain party—"

"Ordered by the boss," interjected Gruber.

"Uncle Johnny," supplied Cole with a sly grin.

"Oh, shit," muttered Gruber, apparently realizing that he had been the one to blab the name.

Ford was more circumspect. "We work for a certain prominent gentleman. We were sent to the Sonoran to speak with you about a matter of importance to this gentleman. We were keeping an eye on the resort when we spotted you and this lady sneaking away in the middle of the night." Despite the current contortions of his body, Ford managed to shrug his shoulders. "It was our job to talk to you. Period. *Where* didn't matter. *When* did. So we followed you."

Cole's expression spoke for itself.

"I know it sounds crazy," Ford maintained.

Cole agreed. "It does."

"It happens to be the truth."

He was more than a little skeptical, and with good reason. "Why should I believe you?"

"Because I have no reason to lie to you," the man stated.

For some strange reason Cole believed him.

"You're talking in generalities," he pointed out after giving it some thought. "I want specifics."

Ford wetted his lips as if all the talking had left him dry. "This is a delicate matter."

Cole snorted and shook his head from side to side. "Are you trying to tell me that your boss sent the three of you blundering after me to discuss a delicate matter?"

"Yes," was the answer.

" 'Discretion is the better part of valor,' " the quiet man quoted, more or less accurately.

They weren't armed.

They weren't after Georgiana.

They obviously knew nothing about the incident that had taken place at the Sonoran.

One of them was ex-military. One was as dumb as a rock. One quoted Shakespeare.

"You can put your hands down now," Cole finally ordered. "But keep them where I can see them."

From behind him Georgiana offered her two cents' worth. "They look uncomfortable kneeling like that, Cole."

"All right. You can sit on the floor." That was as far as he would go, however. It wasn't his intention to treat these three intruders like welcome guests.

Ford stretched out his legs and rubbed his knees. Then he looked up at Cole and started talking again. "A few years back you did some research into your personal background."

Cole heard Georgiana's breath as it caught in her throat.

He didn't move a muscle.

The leader of the threesome went on. "It was done discreetly, but it was noticed."

He didn't say a word.

Ford continued. "There is a sealed envelope in my shirt pocket. There is a piece of paper in that envelope, and on that piece of paper is written a name."

Cole feigned indifference. "So?"

"There is a certain person who is interested in your intentions," was the next comment.

"My intentions are no one's business but my own."

"That may be true."

Cole was unyielding. "It *is* true."

"I have been instructed to give the envelope to you," Ford informed him. "With your permission I will raise my hand slowly and take it from my shirt pocket."

Cole nodded his head.

Ford removed the envelope and held it out toward him.

"You can carefully toss it here," he said, not trusting the man even yet.

The man called Ford said, as if he were reciting from memory, "The two men with me know nothing about what you and I are speaking of. Even I don't know whose name is in the envelope. I was charged to say this much: Have Coleman Worth open the envelope and read the name to himself without anyone else seeing the information.''

Cole's hands were full. He wasn't about to take his eyes off these men or put down his revolver.

He motioned to Georgiana. ''I want you to pick up the envelope and open it for me.''

Ford repeated. ''No one else is to see the name.''

''The lady is with me. If I say so, she can see anything I want her to.''

Georgiana quickly picked up the envelope as he'd asked and tore it open. Inside was a single piece of expensive, pale ivory vellum. There was a name clearly written in a feminine hand, a name that Georgiana instantly recognized.

''Please hold the piece of paper where I can see it,'' Cole requested.

Georgiana positioned the paper in his line of vision. She noticed that her hand was shaking slightly as she did so.

She wasn't certain what this was all about, but something began to niggle at the back of her mind. She had some inkling that it was important; she just wasn't sure how it related to Cole.

''I've read the name,'' he said to Ford.

''Then I have been instructed to repeat the question: What are your intentions?''

When Cole spoke, his voice was as cold and as hard as Georgiana had ever heard it. ''I have no intentions when it comes to the person whose name is written on this piece of paper.'' He said in an aside to Georgiana, ''Burn it.''

''Burn it?''

''Burn the piece of paper right here and now.''

She lit a match and touched it to the expensive paper,

then dropped it into an ashtray on the table in front of
them and watched as the flames consumed it.

Once it was nothing more than ashes, Cole said,
"You can go back to your boss, to Uncle Johnny, and
you can tell him this: I don't know the person whose
name was written on the paper. I have never met this
person. I have no interest in *ever* meeting this person.
In fact, you may make it clear that that is the last person
I would ever be interested in meeting or knowing. Is that
clear?"

"Not to me," Gruber mumbled. "I didn't understand
a damned thing you said."

"You don't have to understand," Ford told him.
"Someone will and that's all that matters."

Cole wasn't finished. "You may tell your boss that
he has my word on it."

Gruber sniggered. "That and a dollar will get you a
lousy cup of coffee."

"Shut up, Gruber," Ford commanded. "You
wouldn't recognize an honorable man if your life de-
pended on it."

"You're free to go now," Cole informed the men.
"In fact, if I were you three I'd hightail it out of this
room, out of this town and out of this state just as fast
as I could."

It was Gruber again. "Why?"

"Because I just might change my mind about shooting you," Cole said in deadly earnest.

"That's it?" Gruber was saying to Ford as they
scrambled to their feet. "We came all this way and went
through all of this shit to deliver a goddamned mes-
sage?"

"That's right."

"That was our job?"

"That was our job."

"And you're going to take Worth's word for it."

"Coleman Worth's word is good enough for any man who has half a brain."

Gruber glared at the older man. "Are you telling me that I don't have half a brain?"

"I didn't say that, Junior."

"Junior?" Gruber's voice rose half an octave. "I hate it when people call me Junior.

The men disappeared from sight and Georgiana turned back to Cole. "Well, that, as they say, is that."

He was strangely quiet.

There were a dozen questions on the tip of her tongue, naturally. The most important one being, what was his relationship with the well-known and prominent socialite whose name had been written on the piece of paper?

It was none of her business, Georgiana reminded herself.

Cole had made it her business.

Cole had asked her to open the envelope. He had requested that she take out the piece of paper. He had known that she could read the name as clearly as he could.

He finally said to her, "I'll talk about it this once, Georgiana, and then the subject will never be raised, discussed or talked about ever again. Is that agreed?"

"Agreed." She sat down on the edge of the sagging mattress. "Don't you think you can put the gun away now?"

Cole stared down at the revolver in his hand. Apparently he'd forgotten he was still holding it. He got to his feet, sat down beside her on the mattress and placed the gun on the bedside table within easy reach, she noted.

He took in a deep breath and blew it out. "I told you once that I was a nobody from nowhere."

She slipped her hand into his. "And I told you that we're all someone from somewhere."

Cole almost smiled. "So you did." Then he went on, "I claimed to be in possession of the bare, if somewhat sordid, facts concerning my so-called parentage."

Georgiana sat and waited as she had learned so well from this man.

"You recognized the name written on the piece of paper," he speculated.

It was a name nearly everyone would have recognized, she wanted to say. "Yes."

"That woman," he said, "is my mother."

Twenty-Eight

"For a long time all I had in my possession were a few facts and even fewer recollections that I had garnered from an old nurse at the hospital where I was born. She apparently remembered my mother because she was so young and so beautiful and so afraid, and because her eyes were such an unusual shade of blue," he recounted.

Georgiana recalled every word that Cole had told her before about his background, but she listened now with renewed interest.

"A few years ago I had the resources and the means to make discreet inquiries. Apparently the girl was from a socially prominent family who threatened to disown her if she married the father of her unborn child. He was no one of importance, in their opinion, and wasn't considered good enough for her." Cole paused. "To this day I have no idea who my biological father was. I never will."

None of it mattered to Georgiana, if it didn't matter, if it wasn't important, to Cole.

"At the last minute my mother decided to run away from the facility where her family had placed her for the last few months of her pregnancy. No one may ever know the reasons beyond the fact that she was sixteen, alone, afraid and unwed. Anyway, she hitched a ride with a truck driver heading south out of Fort Worth, Texas.''

Georgiana sat and listened.

"She made it as far as Coleman County before going into labor and giving birth at the local hospital. She gave the fictitious name of Gloria Worth on my birth certificate, refused to identify the father and disappeared sometime during the night, leaving me behind.''

She could have recited from memory every word he had said to her the night they had lain side by side in the back of Bessie: *I was abandoned twelve hours after entering this world, Georgiana. It's not something that I have a problem with, but it is something I've never forgotten. I have no idea who my parents are, and frankly, at this point in my life, I don't give a damn.*

She had somehow sensed then that Cole wasn't telling her the whole truth. He had given a damn and he had cared. And he had known his mother's real identity.

But it had also been his right and his privilege not to share that information with anyone else. Georgiana was only surprised that he trusted her enough to confide in her now.

"After I found out the basic facts, I dropped the inquiry.''

"Why?''

Broad shoulders were raised and then lowered again. "It didn't make sense to pursue a course of action that could have no satisfactory conclusion.''

She was curious and assumed her question wasn't too personal, under the circumstances. "What about the three men?''

"To tell you the truth, I never connected them with

the past. Like you, I assumed they had to do with the incident at the Sonoran.''

"Who sent the men after you?"

"The woman whose name you saw written on that piece of paper is a widow. Her first husband was a wealthy and well-known businessman. They were married for more than two decades. Anyway, he died several years ago, and she is about to remarry—very advantageously, I might add—for a second time.''

"To Uncle Johnny."

"To Uncle Johnny." Cole stared off into space for a few moments. "Apparently the gentleman who is about to make her his wife wanted to be certain that I didn't intend to cause any trouble for her or embarrass her. She is the chairwoman of any number of well-known charities, including one for unwed mothers."

The irony didn't escape either of them.

"It was so different back in her day," Georgiana murmured with some degree of understanding and perhaps even sympathy.

"Maybe," was all Cole said.

"Can you just walk away?"

"She did." The man sitting beside her took in a deep breath and let it out again. "When I was making my inquiries, I didn't find a single shred of evidence that the girl who'd called herself Gloria Worth had ever tried to locate her child, find out what had happened to him or even wondered if he was dead or alive.''

Georgiana didn't know what to say. Perhaps there was nothing for her to say.

Cole set his jaw. "The woman obviously wants her past to stay in the past. Sometimes it's best to leave it there. I've finally made my peace with that.''

Georgiana had to know. "So you honestly believe you can put the past behind you and not look back?"

"I can."

Curiosity overrode good manners. "How?"

"Because I have to. Because all of my life I've done whatever I had to do to survive." Cole gave her a long, penetrating sideways glance with those unusual and incredible blue eyes of his. "Hasn't the same been true for you?"

Georgiana nodded her head. "It has."

"We're both survivors," he concluded.

"Yes, we are."

"There are questions in all of our lives to which we'll never learn the answers. That's just the way life is."

He was absolutely right.

Then Cole suddenly grew restless. "This may sound like a strange request, but would you mind if we packed up and left these lovely"—he was being sarcastic— "accommodations tonight?"

"Right now?"

"Right now."

"Not in the least," Georgiana responded. "I wasn't looking forward to trying out the bed, anyway."

That brought a raised eyebrow from Cole and a flush to her own cheeks.

"I meant because of the sagging mattress and the questionable cleanliness of the sheets and blankets," she hastened to tell him.

"I know what you meant."

"Where are we headed?" Georgiana inquired as she quickly threw her few belongings into the small valise that Crick had supplied her with last week.

"North."

"To your cabin?"

Cole said with a certain eagerness, "It's not far now. We'll be there by sunrise."

*   *   *

Georgiana couldn't recall ever standing in such a breath-taking spot before. She was looking out at the myriad of islands known collectively as the San Juans. She could feel the warmth of the sun at her back as it climbed into the morning sky, its rays hitting the surface of the channel with such radiance that the reflection hurt her eyes.

She had never been in such a wild and secluded place. There was the steep hillside behind her. The deep, dense forest on either side and the seemingly endless blue waters of the Pacific straight ahead.

She inhaled deeply. Her nostrils filled with the smell of clean water and pine needles, wild azaleas and the moldering dankness of the forest floor and the thick, lush underbrush.

Gazing at the single, rutted, unpaved road that had led them to the log cabin in the small clearing, she dropped her voice to a whisper and said to Cole, "No one knows it's here but you."

"You know," he pointed out.

"That makes only the two of us."

"There were three."

"Who was the third?"

"The old man who sold me the place five years ago. But I think he died not long after."

"The deed must be officially recorded somewhere."

"It is. But so far no one has shown any interest in going to the courthouse and looking it up. I doubt if anyone is aware that there's a log cabin in the middle of the acreage."

Georgiana removed her hat, tugged on the rubber band securing her ponytail, let her hair fall down around her shoulders and gave her head a shake. "How many acres do you have here?"

"Two hundred."

She was impressed. "That's a lot."

Cole laughed with amusement. "My ranch in Texas is over one hundred thousand acres."

Her mouth dropped open. "You're kidding."

"I'm not."

"That's huge."

He was still laughing at her. "I told you everything was bigger in Texas."

She joined him. "Yes, you did."

"It's good to hear you laugh," Cole told her as they stood and basked in the sunlight.

"It feels good, too."

"It would also feel good to get some sleep," he said. "Just be forewarned that the accommodations aren't fancy."

"I don't mind," Georgiana replied.

And she didn't mind. Cole's secluded if primitive log cabin was far superior to the run-down motel room they had vacated several hours ago.

"I'll move our sleeping bags from the pickup truck into the cabin. I think we should sleep first and then wake up in time to enjoy the sunset," he proposed.

"It sounds good to me," Georgiana confessed as she stifled an errant yawn.

She was suddenly tired and ready to sleep the day away.

It was late afternoon when Cole awakened and gazed across the one-room cabin at the sleeping woman in the next bunk. She opened her eyes and looked straight into his.

"You're awake," he said.

"I'm awake."

"Hungry?"

"Starved."

"Me, too." He rubbed his stomach with his hand. "What would you like for dinner?"

"What do you have on the menu?"

They'd made a brief stop at a small grocery on their way through the nearest town. "I think I can manage scrambled eggs and toast made over an open fire."

"My favorites."

Cole suddenly realized that there were so many small, ordinary, even mundane things that he didn't know about this woman. "What are your favorite foods?"

"At the moment, anything you happen to be cooking," Georgiana declared.

He pushed himself up on one elbow. "Can you cook?"

She pretended to be offended by his skepticism. "Of course I can cook. I can do any number of things well. Any butler worth his or her salt has to be a jack of all trades."

Cole's mouth turned up suggestively at the corners. "What else can you do well?"

Georgiana listed a few of her accomplishments. "I play a decent game of both tennis and golf. I'm quite good at bridge, poker, baccarat and Monopoly."

One brow arched. "Monopoly?"

"Sometimes my duties include keeping a guest's children entertained and amused."

"Go on," he urged.

"In a pinch I can sew on a button, fix a torn hem, steam the wrinkles from a designer evening gown, mix a perfect martini or provide a personal review of the latest movies playing in town."

Cole rolled over onto his back, his head turned toward her, and said, "This is fascinating. Please go on."

Georgiana thought for a minute. "I can obtain front-row seats for sold-out plays and concerts. I know the best shops in the valley for everything from orchids to diamonds to Grand Crus.'' She seemed to be on a roll. ''I can recommend books to read, restaurants to eat in and the best roller coasters to ride.''

''You are an amazing woman,'' he declared.

''I am,'' she agreed without her usual modesty.

''It's all related to your work.''

''It is.''

''What do you do for fun?''

There was silence.

Georgiana changed the subject. She pointed over their heads to a woven circle with several feathers dangling from the rim and asked, ''That's a dream catcher, isn't it?''

Cole nodded. ''The old man who sold me this place made me promise to always keep it as part of the cabin.''

''I wonder why.''

''He claimed that his mother, who was a Native American, had suspended it over his cradleboard so that only good dreams would enter him as he slept.''

''What a lovely notion.''

''The People believed that good dreams were to be treasured as the source of all wisdom. As children were put to bed at night they were told to try to dream and remember what they dreamed.''

He watched as Georgiana put a hand against her lips. Her voice was different somehow, kind of trembly, when she finally asked him, ''What were your dreams, Cole?''

''To never be cold or hungry again. To have a roof over my head and clothes on my back. To be someone.''

''Your dreams have come true, then.''

''Yes.'' Cole turned slowly, staring into her eyes. ''What about you? What were your dreams?''

She wet her lips with her tongue and drew in a deep breath. ''I don't know.''

"Sure you do." He asked her again, "What are your dreams, Georgiana?"

She began to speak in a wistful tone. "To one day have my own home and my own family. To love one man for the rest of my life and have him love me in return." She suddenly laughed and said in a lighter mood, "And to eat the scrambled eggs and toast you promised to cook me a half hour ago."

"Delicious," Georgiana pronounced as she shoveled the last bite of food into her mouth. "I didn't think eggs and toast"—she graciously did not mention that the toast was slightly burned on one side—"could taste so good."

"It's because you were hungry."

"It's because I was starved," she corrected. "And since you did the cooking, Mr. Worth, the least I can do is the cleaning up." She rose from the stump that she had been using as a seat and looked around the small clearing. "How does one clean up in the middle of no-where?"

"Well, first you have to haul water from a stream about fifty yards in that direction." He pointed to the north. "Then the water has to be heated over the camp-fire to a roiling boil. Next, you pour the boiling water over the dirty dishes and finally dry them off with a clean towel."

Tongue-in-cheek, Georgiana observed, "Is that all there is to it?"

"Yup." Cole got to his feet. "I'll help by fetching the first bucket of water."

"The *first* bucket," she muttered.

Cole suddenly stopped dead in his tracks and cocked his head to one side.

Apparently Georgiana didn't fail to notice. "What is it?" she asked him.

He raised a finger to his lips. After a minute, he lowered his hand and said in a quiet voice, "Did you hear anything just now?"

"No."

"See anything?"

She answered no again. "Did you?"

"I don't know." He knew he was making her uneasy, but something wasn't right.

In fact, something was definitely wrong.

He heard a sharp inhalation. "I see something now," she said, her eyes fixed on a point behind him.

"What is it?"

"Not what." Georgiana swallowed hard. "Who."

"Who is it?"

The color instantly drained from her face. Her skin was blanched white. Her eyes were huge. In fact, she looked like she'd just seen a ghost.

Georgiana opened her mouth and said in a hoarse tone, "Mr. Isherwood."

Twenty-Nine

"Sonofabitch," Cole muttered under his breath.

"Turn around slowly, Mr. Worth," cautioned a cold and high-pitched yet definitely masculine voice directly behind him.

Somehow he should have suspected. Somehow he should have known. But there was no way he could have known: *Isherwood wasn't dead.*

Cole realized in an instant that he had to buy himself some time. Time to think. Time to act. Maybe even time to save Georgiana's life and his.

He slowly rotated on the heel of his cowboy boot. "What the . . . ?"

"Be very careful, Worth." The man was of medium height, slender in build and nondescript in appearance, but there was something snakelike and deadly in his eyes. "I have my gun pointed directly at Ms. Burne-Jones's heart."

Cole hated feeling helpless, impotent. Bile rose in his throat. "So help me God, if I ever get my hands on you . . ."

"Speaking of hands"—there was no sign that the

man had any nerves—"place yours on top of your head where I will be able to see them at all times."

Adrenaline was shooting into Cole's bloodstream. Every one of his senses was on red alert: better late than never. But he understood the absolute necessity of keeping his wits about him and maintaining a poker face. He knew only too well the price he and Georgiana might pay if he didn't.

Hands on his head, fingers interlaced, Cole faced his greatest adversary.

"I've seen you somewhere before," he remarked, making certain that his expression and his tone gave nothing away. It was a technique he had used to his advantage often enough in business.

"Have you?"

Cole suddenly remembered where and when. "You were following us in an SUV."

The gunman's features were cold and calculating and almost *un*human. "So you did spot me . . . that one time."

Georgiana finally seemed to find her voice. "B-but I don't understand," she stammered.

"I know you don't, Ms. Burne-Jones," Isherwood said with just the slightest indulgence.

She stood there and stared at him. "You were dead."

"Was I?"

"I saw you with my own eyes." Those uncomprehending eyes blinked shut for a moment. "Your eyes were wide open and staring lifelessly at the ceiling. There was blood on your shirt and a knife in your chest." She shuddered at the recollection.

"A steak knife."

A reluctant, "Yes."

"With your fingerprints on it."

An even more reluctant admission. "Yes."

"Because you were so diligent in your duties when I ordered dinner served in my suite and then requested that you cut my filet mignon for me." His manner was appreciative. "The service provided by the butlers at the Sonoran is first-class."

"Yes. It is," Georgiana acknowledged, and then apparently felt foolish for having agreed with a man who was pointing a gun at her. "But if you're not dead, Mr. Isherwood, why would it matter if my fingerprints are on the steak knife?"

"Why do you think?"

Isherwood was playing games. Games that Cole didn't care for. Not one bit. Georgiana's was not a devious or a criminal mind. She wouldn't think along the same lines as someone like this cold-blooded killer. She was the innocent victim in a deadly charade.

"I don't know," she finally admitted.

The man glanced at Cole. "I would imagine that Mr. Worth has worked out the answer by now. Haven't you, Mr. Worth?"

He was walking a tightrope. He must play it very cool and very calm. Cole ventured, "A look-alike."

The responding smile was reptilian. "Very good."

Georgiana blinked in bewilderment. "You mean there *was* a dead body."

"Of course," Isherwood said.

"But it wasn't you."

"It wasn't me."

"But the man looked just like you," Georgiana blurted out. "Who was it?"

Isherwood took a menacing step closer to them. "Unfortunately my cousin Vinny."

"You killed your own cousin."

"Yes, Ms. Burne-Jones, I killed my own cousin."

Isherwood seemed amused by her, perhaps even

slightly diverted by her. Maybe it would help him when the time came to make his move, Cole reflected.

"Why?" Georgiana asked.

She was apparently curious, in spite of herself. Or maybe she was showing far greater presence of mind than Cole had been giving her credit for. Maybe she realized that as long as she kept Isherwood talking, he was unlikely to shoot them.

A small, mocking smile appeared on the man's lips. "Why? Because I needed to die."

She looked briefly disconcerted. Then she said, her distaste showing for an instant, "Does this have anything to do with those men who came to your party?"

"Didn't you like my guests?"

"It's not my place to like or dislike a Sonoran guest's choice of guests," she said, reverting to proper butler form.

"How very diplomatic you are, Ms. Burne-Jones." Isherwood added, "It might have held you in good stead if you had gone to prison."

"If I had gone to prison?" she echoed.

"That is highly unlikely now, of course," the gunman pointed out, without giving her a complete explanation.

Georgiana wasn't fooled by him. "If you're going to shoot me anyway, perhaps you will satisfy my curiosity and answer a question or two."

"Perhaps I will," he said, making no promises.

"Was there any significance to the fact that exactly twelve men were invited to your suite that night?"

"Ah, you picked up on that, did you?" Isherwood didn't bother looking at Cole. "Or was it Mr. Worth here?"

Cole shrugged and tried to appear noncalculating as he moved no more than an inch to the right.

"Not that it matters which of you was clever enough to figure it out. Yes, there was significance to the number twelve."

"A jury of your peers," Georgiana proposed.

"Something of the sort. Although not quite like a jury of peers in your world, Ms. Burne-Jones."

"I assume we live in two entirely different worlds, Mr. Isherwood," she stated.

"You assume correctly."

"For which I am grateful," she added.

"Your world would not exist but for my world," he snapped a little testily, losing his composure for the first time. "It is my world which makes your world possible."

Georgiana scoffed, "I don't believe that."

Snakelike eyes narrowed. "Believe it."

She shuddered. "In your world twelve men were your jury, your judge and your executioner."

"I see you have it all worked out."

"I've had a lot of time to think about it in the past week," Georgiana told him.

"I know," he said casually. "I've been watching you."

Georgiana made a disparaging sound. "If that's the case, then you're nothing more than a Peeping Tom."

His reply was a sly one. "Oh, I'm much more than a Peeping Tom, I assure you."

She was fearless and a little indignant, Cole thought as he carefully, painstakingly moved his feet another inch. If Georgiana could just keep Isherwood talking a little longer, he might be able to draw the gunman's line of fire away from her. Then he could make his move.

"What are you, then, Mr. Isherwood?" she asked.

"I'm a professional," he answered.

"A professional *what*?"

He brandished his fancy gun at her. "Killer. Hit man." A furrow momentarily appeared between his brown eyebrows. "Although I prefer the term *assassin*."

Georgiana was not in the least bit discreet. "In other words, you kill people for money."

Isherwood shook his head. "I kill people as one of the services I offer to a select clientele. I am, I will freely admit, handsomely compensated for my services."

"If you're a professional assassin"—she was deliberately using the term Isherwood had said he preferred, Cole was willing to bet on it—"then why try to implicate an innocent person like myself for the murder of your cousin Vinny?"

The man shook his head from side to side. "You still don't see the whole picture, do you, Ms. Burne-Jones?"

She appeared obtuse. "Perhaps you would be so good as to fill me in, Mr. Isherwood."

"I am a professional," Paul Isherwood began.

"You've already told me that," she indicated.

"I'm not the only professional in the line of work I do, of course," he elaborated.

"I assumed as much."

"Like any other group of professionals, we have our standards, our codes and our own kind of organization."

"Do you also attend monthly meetings and pay yearly dues?" she inquired.

"Sarcasm is not becoming of you, Ms. Burne-Jones," Isherwood retaliated.

"My apologies," she said insincerely.

Cole moved half an inch.

Paul Isherwood was becoming downright verbose. "I've always been something of a maverick. But in the past year I have accepted certain commissions, if you will, that did not meet with the approval of my brother assassins."

"So they kicked you out of the club, did they?" Georgiana speculated.

"I'm afraid there is only one way out," the man informed her with a sigh.

Cole saw the instant it dawned on her.

So did Isherwood.

Her gasp was soft and horrified. "You're either in the club or you're dead."

"I see you now comprehend the reason Paul Isherwood had to be found murdered in his suite at the Sonoran."

"And I was set up as the scapegoat because you could hardly take 'credit' for killing yourself."

"In a nutshell, yes."

"That wasn't very nice of you, Mr. Isherwood," she said, scolding him.

"No, it wasn't," he agreed. "But it was necessary. Paul Isherwood had to be eliminated. Someone had to take the blame. You were the logical choice. In fact, you were the perfect choice."

"Since everything went according to your plans, what are you doing here?"

"There were several unexpected departures from my plan, actually."

"I escaped."

"You ran away."

"And I didn't escape alone."

Isherwood expounded, "You were supposed to be caught that same night by the police, arrested for my murder and hauled off to jail. I was prepared to go my own way, which included a stop in California for a bit of plastic surgery and a new identity. Instead, I was forced to change my travel plans."

"Sorry."

"Your apology is not acceptable," the former Sonoran guest said in something of a snit.

Cole could see that Georgiana almost said sorry again, but caught herself in time.

Soon, it would all be a moot point. He had nearly reached his objective. He had another inch or two to go at the most. Then when he made his move, Isherwood would have to choose between his targets. Cole was certain—well, almost certain—that the gunman would instinctively go for the moving target: Cole.

"I don't like loose ends. They can quickly become liabilities," Isherwood was explaining to her. "Besides, I always make a habit of tidying up after myself."

Georgiana sought verification. "Tidying up?"

"I regret that you and Mr. Worth must go."

"Go where?"

"Into the water."

Georgiana pointed toward the icy blue Pacific. "You mean that water?"

"Yes."

"But we'll die from hypothermia."

"The cold water temperature won't matter," he assured her.

"Why not?"

"You'll already be dead." Then Isherwood laughed. It was not a pleasant sound.

For the first time since Georgiana had spotted Paul Isherwood, Cole was afraid she was losing her nerve. She'd been so brave and she'd done so well. But she had gone pale when the gunman made it clear there was no escape.

He had to act, and now.

"I don't see any reason for the scum of the earth like you to threaten a lady like Ms. Burne-Jones," Cole spoke up, instilling every ounce of disdain he could into his voice and manner.

Georgiana's eyes flew to Cole's in alarm.

He definitely had Isherwood's attention, as well.

"I was going to kill Ms. Burne-Jones first and make you watch, Worth. But I've changed my mind. I think I'll shoot you first," the assassin announced.

Cole got ready.

"So shoot me," he said, issuing his dare.

It all happened very quickly after that. Cole drew the line of fire from Georgiana. Then he threw himself at Isherwood's feet and managed to get a secure hold on the man's ankle. The assassin teetered for a moment, and was finally tackled to the ground.

The gun in his hand went flying through the air. Georgiana had the presence of mind to make a grab for it as Cole managed to get back on his feet, seize the smaller man's arm and twist it behind his back.

Cole stood there, breathing deeply, and glared down at Isherwood. "I don't like being threatened. And I don't like my woman being threatened." He issued his edict. "From now on, Isherwood, we're doing this my way."

Thirty

She didn't like guns.

Suddenly she was the one with the gun.

Georgiana wondered what in the world she was supposed to do with it. It wasn't as if she knew the first, or even the second, thing about firearms. She knew nothing about them.

She did know one thing for certain: Cole had deliberately taunted Isherwood. Then he had bravely launched himself at the professional assassin—who possessed at least some human foibles, pride and a temper among them, not to mention a complete disregard for life—and had tackled him to the ground.

The piece of black, shiny metal had gone sailing through the air and landed with a soft thud in a bed of pine needles and loam. There had been a second or two—or perhaps even longer—when Georgiana had watched, transfixed, frozen to the spot where she stood. But at least she'd had the presence of mind to finally move, to grab the weapon, to hold it up in her hand and point it at Mr. Isherwood, although it felt cold and awkward and foreign in her grasp.

Paul Isherwood was a cool customer. "You'd better be careful with that, Ms. Burne-Jones. A beautiful gun is like a Stradivarius: it takes an artist, a genius, if you will, to play it as it was meant to be played. The 'instrument' in your hand was crafted to my specifications, especially for me, to the precise width of my palm and the length of my fingers. She won't like being handled by a stranger. She's got a hair trigger and she could go off at the merest provocation."

Cole obviously didn't care for what he was hearing. "Be damned careful, honey," he admonished.

Her voice quavered. "I will."

"Don't be afraid," Cole said, trying to boost her spirits and her self-confidence. "You're doing great."

Isherwood gave a smirk. "For someone who has obviously never handled a lethal weapon before." He went on in that irritating, high-pitched voice of his, "You haven't, have you, Ms. Burne-Jones? You've never held a gun in your hand until this moment."

"That isn't true," she said hotly. "I held a gun on those three men last night."

"Ah, yes. Flopsy, Mopsy and Cottontail," he said with an icy, knowing smile.

Her eyes widened. "Flopsy, Mopsy and Cottontail?"

Isherwood made himself only partially understood. "Don't look so surprised, Ms. Burne-Jones. Like all men, I was a boy once. I had my bedtime stories read to me."

Georgiana wondered what could have gone wrong in that boy's life. How had he grown up to be a professional killer? What had warped him into the horrible parody of a human being that he was?

"Those three incompetent goons actually did me a favor," he claimed.

"How do you figure that?" Cole asked, keeping a firm grip on Isherwood's arm.

"They created a welcome, even amusing diversion." He laughed from his throat. "You were so busy keeping an eye on them, Worth, that you forgot to watch out for me."

"We didn't know you were alive," Georgiana pointed out. "You were supposed to be dead."

"I was, wasn't I?" Isherwood laughed heartily this time and shook his head as if he found the whole incident vastly amusing.

Then he began to cough. It was a horrible, anemic rattle coming from his lungs. He suddenly dropped his head and bent over at the waist as if the pain had doubled him over.

Georgiana was suddenly afraid.

She had good reason to be. When the seemingly slight and infirm man straightened a moment later, he had a gun—a second and slightly smaller version of the one in her possession—clutched in his free hand. Before she knew what had happened, the barrel was pressed against Cole's chin.

"If I fire from this precise position, Mr. Worth, the bullet will travel straight through the roof of your mouth, along your nasal cavities and into your cerebral cortex. There it will explode. Your brains will be splattered from here to China," Isherwood promised.

"Shit!" Cole was furious with himself.

Georgiana was stunned.

"Now who has the upper hand, Mr. Worth?" inquired the man in a voice like death.

Cole straightened. Then he looked across the no more than fifteen feet that separated them and directly into Georgiana's eyes. "Shoot Isherwood," he ordered. "Shoot him now."

He couldn't mean it.

"I can't," she cried out.

Cole's handsome face was carved from solid stone; his features were without expression. "Why not?"

Surely the reason was obvious to him, to all of them. "Because he'll kill you."

There was no inflection in Cole's voice; he had even lost his Texas drawl. It was almost as if the man had already accepted his fate. "It doesn't matter."

She wanted to scream at him. How could he think it didn't matter? It was the only thing that did matter.

Georgiana didn't recognize her own voice when she said, "Of course it matters."

Under the circumstances, Cole couldn't shake his head. "You must save yourself."

She could be just as determined, just as stubborn, as he was. "Not if it means losing you."

His eyes were the color of the midnight sky. "Georgiana, shoot to kill."

Oh, God.

Her heart was wedged in her throat. Her lungs were empty of air. She couldn't breathe. She didn't care. "Please, Cole, don't ask me to do this."

He was a man on the edge. He was a man who had gazed down into the great abyss and knew what awaited him. "I'm not asking you. I'm telling you."

There were no tears; she was even too frightened to cry. "How could I live with myself?"

His voice softened ever so slightly. "The important thing is that you live."

Georgiana knew that wasn't always true. "That isn't always the most important."

Paul Isherwood had been listening to their exchange with a certain vicarious and prurient interest. "While I find this emotional outpouring between the two of you very touching, it is growing wearisome.'' He snapped, ''Drop the gun, Ms. Burne-Jones.''

Cole made one more attempt to convince her. ''Georgiana, don't put the gun down. It's your only chance.''

Her heart was racing, but she did as Isherwood had ordered. She carefully placed the gun on the ground at her feet, very much like she had found it.

Isherwood was suddenly in a frenzy of energetic activity. ''Let's get this over and done with. I have allowed the two of you to vex and annoy me long enough.''

Georgiana met and held Cole's gaze. She saw only his eyes. She thought only of the things she could have said to him and should have told him in the past few days. She wasn't going to have a chance to tell him now.

Time had run out for them.

With his gun pressed to their backs, Isherwood marched them to the edge of the rocky cliff that overlooked the huge blue expanse of the Pacific far below.

''You can say good-bye to each other now,'' he announced as if he were being magnanimous.

Georgiana turned to Cole. His face was gaunt. The skin was drawn tightly across his sharp features. He was drawn in on himself. ''This won't be good-bye,'' she vowed. ''I have to believe that.''

''Don't worry,'' came a voice from directly behind them. ''It won't be good-bye.''

They turned as one.

It happened in the blink of an eye. Georgiana watched with horror and a certain morbid fascination as Isherwood pivoted on his feet and pointed his weapon at Detective Mallory.

Appearances were deceptive.

Apparently Detective Mallory was the perfect example. He was like a bolt of lightning. In fact, his hand—the one with the standard-issue police revolver grasped in it—struck so quickly that the fact barely had time to register in Georgiana's brain.

Isherwood got the oddest expression on his nondescript features. Then she saw the small, neat round hole that had suddenly appeared in the middle of his forehead.

His fist opened. The gun in his hand dropped to the ground. His slender form seemed suspended on the edge of the rocky cliff for a moment, then he toppled backward and went over the side. It was several hundred feet straight down. When his body hit, there was only the smallest splash on the otherwise placid surface of the water as he disappeared into the dark, deep, icy cold depths.

Detective Mallory was the first to speak. "Good riddance to bad rubbish," he muttered.

"This time the right Isherwood is dead," Mallory observed with a certain grim satisfaction in his gravelly voice as the three of them stared down at the cold waters of the Pacific. "Not that Vinny Isherwood was a man with a spotless reputation. In fact, he had a rap sheet a mile long and was suspected of being personally involved in more than one murder himself."

Cole was still willing his heart to stop pounding in his chest. It wasn't the prospect of his own death that had frightened him; it was the realization that Georgiana . . .

He didn't finish the thought.

He turned to the detective and said in his Texas drawl, "Nice people, the Isherwoods."

Mallory replaced his weapon in the shoulder holster under his rumpled suit jacket. "Assuming Isherwood was their real name. I suspect if we knew where to search we'd find a dozen aliases and nearly as many bank accounts.''

Georgiana stood with her arms wrapped tightly around herself. Her voice contained a brittle calm; it was like a piece of fragile glass that might shatter at the slightest provocation. ''Unfortunately the one man who could have proven my innocence in Vinny Isherwood's murder has just gone over the cliff.''

''That is not going to be a problem, Ms. Burne-Jones,'' the police detective assured her.

Her eyes were clouded over. ''I'm afraid I don't understand,'' she admitted.

''The so-called professional organization that Isherwood was a member of believe that he was taken out by his cousin . . . instead of the other way around. Not that it matters. Those gentlemen will now go about business as usual.''

Her shoulders slumped. ''But my fingerprints are on the steak knife,'' she blurted out.

Mallory shook his head. ''There were no fingerprints on the steak knife,'' he stated.

She slowly uncrossed her arms. ''But . . .''

''I had the forensics report sent directly to me. I know what I'm talking about, Ms. Burne-Jones. There were no fingerprints. The killer was a professional; he wore gloves.'' Mallory expanded on his personal theory. ''I believe the killer had to be experienced at this method of execution. He knew just where to stab a man in the chest to make sure the wound killed him.''

Georgiana pressed her hands against the flat of her stomach. Cole could imagine what her insides were doing at the moment. He knew what his felt like.

''I don't like violence,'' she declared to no one in particular.

''We know,'' Detective Mallory said with almost paternal concern. "That's why we're hoping and praying that you are never innocently involved in something like this again."

Cole wanted to clear up a few of the necessary details. "What will the police report say?" he asked.

"The official record on this case will show that Ms. Burne-Jones served dinner to Paul Isherwood, at his request, and never returned to his suite again that evening. Person or persons unknown then entered the suite, stabbing Paul Isherwood with the steak knife from his own dinner table. The murder was probably a contract killing within his own unsavory organization."

Georgiana apparently felt it was necessary to remind Detective Mallory of several facts. "When I telephoned my mother and father they said that policemen had been to the house, and police detectives and even federal agents."

"It was thanks to that call, by the way, that I was able to get a lead on where you two had skedaddled."

Cole raised a skeptical eyebrow. "A legal wiretap?"

Mallory was evasive on the subject. "I wouldn't want to say." He took a pack of cigarettes from his pocket, shook one out, popped it between his lips and lit it. "Officially we were treating Ms. Burne-Jones as a missing person."

"A missing person?"

"Mr. Regen, her immediate superior at the Sonoran, was fearful that she had been abducted."

"Is that how you intend to explain my sudden disappearance?" she asked.

"Nope."

Cole was just as curious as Georgiana. "How do you intend to explain it, then?"

"Ms. Burne-Jones's sudden disappearance came about because she lost her head and her heart over a handsome son-of-a-gun and ran off with him for a few days of fun in the sun.''

Georgiana's mouth opened and closed.

Cole's did the same.

''Since the lady was in the back of beyond . . .''

''Is that anything like the middle of nowhere?'' Cole said, feeling a certain relief descend on him.

''That's exactly what's it like,'' Mallory replied, puffing on his cigarette.

''As you were saying . . .'' Georgiana prompted.

''Since the lady was incommunicado, she was unaware that anyone was looking for her.'' Mallory glanced meaningfully at Cole. ''If there is ever any question raised about the identity of the handsome son-of-a-gun, you get to play the role of the boyfriend. Agreed?''

''Agreed,'' Cole assured him.

''Yup, the lady went away for a few quiet and isolated days with her boyfriend.'' Mallory took a gander around the area. ''And this place sure is isolated.''

''I'd like to keep it that way,'' Cole said pointedly.

''It will be.'' Mallory dropped his cigarette to the ground and rubbed it out with the worn toe of his shoe. ''As a matter of fact, I never followed you two up here. None of us ever laid eyes on Isherwood. Everything that has happened in the past hour is going to be kept permanently between the three of us.''

Georgiana got the most incredible expression of hope on her lovely face. ''Can you really do that?''

The man gave her shoulder a fatherly pat. ''Justice is sometimes best served when we remember that the law is supposed to protect the innocent, Ms. Burne-Jones. I'm due to retire in a couple of years. I couldn't live with myself if doing my so-called duty required me to drag your name and your reputation through the mud for what I know in my heart and soul is no good reason.''

"You're a good man, Mallory," Cole said gratefully.

"Which isn't always the same thing as being a good police detective, but I can live with that."

"What about Isherwood?"

"If his body is ever found, the currents will have carried it hundreds of miles from here. But, frankly, I doubt if it will ever surface again." Mallory added philosophically, "If a man lives by the sword, he's more than likely going to die by the sword."

"I don't know how to express my gratitude," Georgiana murmured as she grasped the man's hand for a moment.

"Thank you, Mallory," Cole said simply, shaking that same hand a moment later.

Mallory turned and started to walk away. Then he stopped and looked back at Coleman for an instant. "Tell me one thing. Was she in your suite that night?"

Cole just smiled. "A gentleman never kisses and tells."

Detective Mallory shook his head and laughed. "I'd better be on my way. I've got an investigation to wrap up."

Georgiana called out, "How can we ever thank you?"

The gentleman threw back over his slightly stooped shoulder, "Invite me to the wedding."

Thirty-One

The worst was over, Georgiana reflected as she cradled a cup of very strong black coffee, laced with medicinal brandy, between her hands. She occasionally raised the cup to her lips and took a sip.

"I have a confession to make," Cole told her as the two of them quietly sat before the fireplace in the cabin.

With the setting sun, the evening had turned surprisingly cool. The warmth of a log fire burning brightly in the old stone hearth was more than welcome.

The past twenty-four hours had been the longest and the most unusual of her life, Georgiana reflected. But the night was clear and cool, and tomorrow promised to be a particularly fine day, perhaps the finest of the spring.

Detective Mallory had come and gone, of course. And they were once more alone. It was the first time since they'd met that she and Cole weren't facing some kind of danger.

Or at least the danger they were presently facing was of an entirely different kind.

Cole cleared his throat and started again. "I have to

confess that I was caught off guard by Isherwood.''

Georgiana reassured him, ''It could happen to any-one.''

The man sitting beside her scowled and vehemently declared, ''Not to me.''

Georgiana was too emotionally exhausted to be diplomatic. ''Yes, Cole, even to you.'' She gazed into the heart of the fire. ''You are an amazing man, probably the most amazing man I have ever met, but no man is superhuman''—she smiled fleetingly to herself—''not even one from Texas.''

Cole took a long swallow of alcohol-laced coffee and stared straight ahead. ''I did a lousy job of protecting you.''

Georgiana's mind searched back over the events of the past ten days. Had it only been a little more than a week since that fateful night when she had burst into his suite at the Sonoran?

''That's not true. If it hadn't been for you, I would be rotting in jail right this minute.''

Cole's mouth disappeared altogether. ''You would have been safer in jail.''

She was forthright. ''Even Detective Mallory couldn't have saved me the way you did.'' She traced the rim of the coffee mug with the tip of her finger. ''I don't know how I'll ever be able to thank you.''

He got a strange look on his handsome face and re-peated the words that Mallory had tossed over his shoul-der as he'd left: ''Invite me to the wedding.''

There was silence.

It was broken by Cole. ''We have to talk.''

''We have been talking,'' Georgiana pointed out, de-liberately keeping her tone light.

''I mean really talk.''

She knew what he meant. ''Okay.''

"I'm not an articulate man," he said for starters.

Georgiana couldn't help herself. She hooted. "Are you bullfrogging me?"

Cole shook his head.

She explained the source of her amusement. "You're the head of a huge corporation that you built from the ground up with your own two hands, your brains, your hard work and determination and your incredible ability to talk people into doing whatever you want them to do, and you sit there and claim that you aren't an articulate man."

Cole appeared sheepish and corrected his statement. "I'm very good in large groups."

"What about small groups?"

"I'm good in small groups, too." He finished off his coffee and set the mug down beside his hand-tied twig chair. "It's one on one where I have a problem."

"Is this a general or a specific problem?"

"It's a problem only when I try to talk to you."

"But that's all we've done for the past ten days," Georgiana declared, astonished by his claim.

"That's not all we've done," he reminded her.

"It's what we've mostly done," she fine-tuned.

"But it wasn't until this evening when Isherwood was about to shoot us that I realized there was so much I wanted to say to you, needed to say to you that I hadn't said."

Georgiana reached across the short distance between their two chairs and patted his hand. "I know. I felt the same way."

Cole took in a deep breath and slowly released it. He gave the impression that he was about to take not a step, but a leap of faith. "I never thought I was the marrying kind."

"I never thought you were, either."

That brought a raised masculine eyebrow. "You didn't?"

"Nope."

He scowled. "Why not?"

Georgiana was straightforward. "I could list a dozen reasons. Where would you like me to start?"

Cole was perfectly serious. "With the first one."

Georgiana ticked the reasons off one by one on her fingers. "You're thirty-seven years old and still a bachelor."

"So?"

"So, most men of thirty-seven are already married if they intend to ever get married."

"I know a number of men my age who aren't married," Cole stated in defense of his entire sex.

She didn't mince words. "How many are straight? How many were married and are now divorced? How many are seriously involved in a relationship?"

There was no response from the man sitting beside her.

Georgiana plunged ahead. "I think you still carry the scars of your childhood. You don't trust people in general or women in particular, and I can't say that I blame you for feeling that way."

They both knew she was referring to his mother's abandonment of him at birth.

After clearing his throat, Cole said, "I told you the past is dead and buried."

She couldn't prevent the wistful sigh that slipped out from between her lips. "Is it, Cole?"

"I want it to be," he said earnestly. "I'm working on it."

"I know you are."

"Are there any other reasons you think I'm not the marrying kind?" he asked.

Georgiana nodded her head. "Just one more."

"What is it?"

"I don't think you've ever told anyone—man, woman or child—that you love them," Georgiana ventured, knowing that the sadness in her tone was apparent to both of them.

Life was no longer predictable.

It hadn't been predictable since that fateful moment when Georgiana Burne-Jones had literally burst unannounced and uninvited into his back hallway, his suite, his life.

Life was no longer a game.

He had taken sabbaticals from the rest of civilization to test himself, to create a diversion, to relieve his boredom. Yet it was this woman who was proving to be an endless challenge. One moment he was certain that he had her all figured out; the next he didn't have a clue. Something told Coleman Worth that wouldn't change in a year, in ten years, in a hundred years.

He had always come back from his previous sabbaticals a new man. Or so he had thought.

This time he had changed.

This time he was a different man.

This time he was a new man.

And it was all because of Georgiana.

He had to tell her. He had to find the words. He had to make her believe him. But where in the hell should he start? What were the magic words that would convince her?

Cole opened his mouth. "I want to marry you."

Beside him, Georgiana froze.

"You don't have to give me an answer right away," he quickly went on to assure her. "You can take as much time as you want to think it over."

"I don't need to think it over," she said softly.

He was taken aback. "You don't?"

Georgiana moved her head slightly. He couldn't tell if it was a yes or a no. "I know what my answer is."

Was she going to keep it to herself or share it with him? "What is it?"

"No."

Cole's heart stopped beating for a count of three. His mouth disappeared. It was a minute or two before he could speak. "Is it because you don't love me?"

Georgiana turned and her face revealed everything. "Of course I love you."

She loved him.

She loved him.

It became the words to his favorite song.

Then he puzzled: if Georgiana loved him, then why wouldn't she marry him?

Cole tried again. He reached for her hand, held it in his and gazed down into her eyes. "I haven't said the words that you want to hear or need to hear, but I'll try." He took in a sustaining breath. "I love you, Georgiana. I've never said that to a woman before. I've never said it to anyone before."

Green eyes welled with tears. "I know," she said on a hiccup.

The answer was still no, and he needed to know why. "Why won't you marry me?"

It was some time before she told him. "Because you'll always wonder if I married you for your money."

Cole was stunned.

"I don't care," he finally told her.

"But I do," Georgiana stated in a tone that would brook no argument. "I'll be your friend. I'll be your lover. I'll live with you. I'll stay with you forever. But I won't marry you, Cole."

"Because of the money."

"That's right."

"Because I have money and you don't," he clarified. She nodded.

He stood and paced the small cabin for a few minutes. Then he stopped in his tracks and looked down at her. "All right."

"All right, what?"

"I'll give it all away," he announced.

Georgiana's mouth dropped open. "You aren't serious."

"I am serious." Cole had never been more damned serious in his whole damned life. "If that's what it will take for you to say yes to marrying me, then that's what I'll do."

Georgiana was speechless. "You can't."

"I can."

She sputtered, "But you've worked hard all of your life for that money. That money is your life."

"If you believe that, then I am a poor man, indeed."

"I don't know what to say."

"Tell me that you love me whether I'm a rich man or a poor man. Tell me that the money doesn't matter because you love me for the man I am inside, the man that only you know. Tell me that we both found the truth and saw the light that afternoon in each other's arms. Tell me that sometimes the wrong man and the wrong woman can fall in love with each other and that love makes everything right."

Georgiana slowly rose to her feet and came to him. She wrapped her arms around him and placed her ear on the spot directly above his heart. "I can hear your heart beating."

"Hmmm," was all Cole said.

"It beats strong and brave and true," she whispered.

"It beats only for you."

"I will care for it as if it were mine," she vowed.

"It is yours," he told her.

She raised her eyes to Cole's. "I've never been to Texas."

The tension started to ease from his mind and body. "I think you'll like it. It's . . ."

"Big," she finished for him. Her heart came to a standstill. "I love you, Coleman Worth."

Dark, intent eyes found hers. "I love you, Georgiana Burne-Jones. I want you. I need you. I adore you. You're the right woman for me. You're the perfect woman for me. You're the only woman for me. I can't live without you. You have shown me the way out of the darkness and into the light. Without you I have nothing. With you I have everything."

Those were all the right reasons, Georgiana decided.

Cole was suddenly down on one knee in front of her. "I want to make it official. Will you marry me?"

Georgiana blinked away the tears of happiness and replied, "I will marry you." She bent over and dropped a kiss on the hard line of his jaw. "I want to spend the rest of my life with you. I want you to be my best friend, my lover, my husband and the father of my children."

"There will be so much to see to," Georgiana began to fret some time later, a long time. It was nearly dawn again and they had been making love all night long.

"What needs to be seen to?"

"Well, for one thing we have to return Bessie to that sweet young couple in Arizona."

"Return Bessie," Cole repeated as if he were making a mental note of it.

"I was wondering if we could perhaps arrange for them to have the honeymoon they talked about that night at Hal's House of Honky Tonk," she mentioned. "Well, I assume you intend to give away at least some of your money."

"I thought we might like to invest in a small business in Prescott, as well," Cole said.

"An excellent idea, Mr. Worth, and a wise investment," Georgiana murmured, and her happiness was almost a tangible thing he could reach out and touch.

"About the three thousand dollars," he brought up.

"Ohmigod." Her hand flew to her mouth. "I forgot all about the three thousand."

"The Policemen's Benevolent Fund?"

She laughed and nodded.

Cole grew serious for a moment. "I'm glad I waited."

"For what?"

"For you," he said, as he dropped a kiss on her bare shoulder and began to settle himself again between her thighs.

"Why?" Georgiana whispered as he came to her.

"Because good things come to those who wait," he promised.

Like all the other promises Cole would make to her, it was a promise he kept.

Author's Note

There are special places for each of us in this world. I can recall a hundred.

I will name only a few.

A harsh, craggy jut of rock on the coast of Massachusetts where I stood alone and looked out at the cold winter Atlantic: I was sixteen at the time.

The shadow and mystery of the Catskill Mountains. Surely, as a child, I had heard the quavering voice of Rip Van Winkle and the rumblings of the legendary game of ninepins.

A warm, cozy corner tucked away on the third floor of the old library (it had once been a mansion; libraries often were in those days), sunlight streaming in through the stained-glass windows, the air filled with the smell of leather and books and dust.

And, of course, that first night in Arizona—there have been so very many nights since—when I walked beneath the palm trees and inhaled the wondrous scent of the orange blossoms.

The Room of Light is real, but I am not going to tell you where it is. It is enough to know that such a place exists. Besides, I believe that each of us must discover the special places for ourselves.

So, sometimes, when the memory starts to fade a little for me, I sit quietly, close my eyes and remember. That is when the sight, the smell, the feelings come flooding back into me and I am, once again, filled with light.

Survey

TELL US WHAT YOU THINK AND YOU COULD WIN

A YEAR OF ROMANCE!
(That's 12 books!)

Fill out the survey below, send it back to us, and you'll be eligible
to win a year's worth of romance novels. That's one book a month
for a year—from St. Martin's Paperbacks.

Name _____

Street Address _____

City, State, Zip Code _____

Email address _____

1. How many romance books have you bought in the last year?
   (Check one.)
   __0-3
   __4-7
   __8-12
   __13-20
   __20 or more

2. Where do you MOST often buy books? *(limit to two choices)*
   __Independent bookstore
   __Chain stores *(Please specify)*
       __Barnes and Noble
       __B. Dalton
       __Books-a-Million
       __Borders
       __Crown
       __Lauriat's
       __Media Play
       __Waldenbooks
   __Supermarket
   __Department store *(Please specify)*
       __Caldor
       __Target
       __Kmart
       __Walmart
   __Pharmacy/Drug store
   __Warehouse Club
   __Airport

3. Which of the following promotions would MOST influence your
   decision to purchase a ROMANCE paperback? *(Check one.)*
   __Discount coupon

__Free preview of the first chapter
__Second book at half price
__Contribution to charity
__Sweepstakes or contest

4. Which promotions would LEAST influence your decision to purchase a ROMANCE book? (Check one.)
        __Discount coupon
        __Free preview of the first chapter
        __Second book at half price
        __Contribution to charity
        __Sweepstakes or contest

5. When a new ROMANCE paperback is released, what is MOST influential in your finding out about the book and in helping you to decide to buy the book? (Check one.)
        __TV advertisement
        __Radio advertisement
        __Print advertising in newspaper or magazine
        __Book review in newspaper or magazine
        __Author interview in newspaper or magazine
        __Author interview on radio
        __Author appearance on TV
        __Personal appearance by author at bookstore
        __In-store publicity (poster, flyer, floor display, etc.)
        __Online promotion (author feature, banner advertising, giveaway)
        __Word of Mouth
        __Other (please specify)_____

6. Have you ever purchased a book online?
        __Yes
        __No

7. Have you visited our website?
        __Yes
        __No

8. Would you visit our website in the future to find out about new releases or author interviews?
        __Yes
        __No

9. What publication do you read most?
        __Newspapers *(check one)*
          __*USA Today*
          __*New York Times*
          __Your local newspaper
        __Magazines *(check one)*

__People
__Entertainment Weekly
__Women's magazine *(Please specify:_____)*
__Romantic Times
__Romance newsletters

10. What type of TV program do you watch most? *(Check one.)*
    __Morning News Programs (ie. "Today Show")
    (Please specify:_____)
    __Afternoon Talk Shows (ie. "Oprah")
    (Please specify: _____)
    __All news (such as CNN)
    __Soap operas   *(Please specify: _____)*
    __Lifetime cable station
    __E! cable station
    __Evening magazine programs (ie. "Entertainment Tonight")
    (Please specify: _____)
    __Your local news

11. What radio stations do you listen to most? *(Check one.)*
    __Talk Radio
    __Easy Listening/Classical
    __Top 40
    __Country
    __Rock
    __Lite rock/Adult contemporary
    __CBS radio network
    __National Public Radio
    __WESTWOOD ONE radio network

12. What time of day do you listen to the radio MOST?
    __6am-10am
    __10am-noon
    __Noon-4pm
    __4pm-7pm
    __7pm-10pm
    __10pm-midnight
    __Midnight-6am

13. Would you like to receive email announcing new releases and special promotions?
    __Yes
    __No

14. Would you like to receive postcards announcing new releases and special promotions?
    __Yes
    __No

15. Who is your favorite romance author? _____

WIN A YEAR OF ROMANCE FROM SMP
(That's 12 Books!)
No Purchase Necessary

OFFICIAL RULES

1. To Enter: Complete the Official Entry Form and Survey and mail it to: Win a Year of Romance from SMP Sweepstakes, c/o St. Martin's Paperbacks, 175 Fifth Avenue, Suite 1615, New York, NY 10010-7848, Attention JP. For a copy of the Official Entry Form and Survey, send a self-addressed, stamped envelope to: Entry Form/Survey, c/o St. Martin's Paperbacks at the address stated above. Entries with the completed surveys must be received by February 1, 2000 (February 22, 2000 for entry forms requested by mail). Limit one entry per person. No mechanically reproduced or illegible entries accepted. Not responsible for lost, misdirected, mutilated or late entries.

2. Random Drawing. Winner will be determined in a random drawing to be held on or about March 1, 2000 from all eligible entries received. Odds of winning depend on the number of eligible entries received. Potential winner will be notified by mail on or about March 22, 2000 and will be asked to execute and return an Affidavit of Eligibility/Release/Prize Acceptance Form within fourteen (14) days of attempted notification. Non-compliance within this time may result in disqualification and the selection of an alternate winner. Return of any prize/prize notification as undeliverable will result in disqualification and an alternate winner will be selected.

3. Prize and approximate Retail Value: Winner will receive a copy of a different romance novel each month from April 2000 through March 2001. Approximate retail value $84.00 (U.S. dollars).

4. Eligibility. Open to U.S. and Canadian residents (excluding residents of the province of Quebec) who are 18 at the time of entry. Employees of St. Martin's and its parent, affiliates and subsidiaries, its and their directors, officers and agents, and their immediate families or those living in the same household, are ineligible to enter. Potential Canadian winners will be required to correctly answer a time-limited arithmetic skill question by mail. Void in Puerto Rico and wherever else prohibited by law.

5. General Conditions: Winner is responsible for all federal, state and local taxes. No substitution or cash redemption of prize permitted by winner. Prize is not transferable. Acceptance of prize constitutes permission to use the winner's name, photograph and likeness for purposes of advertising and promotion without additional compensation or permission, unless prohibited by law.

6. All entries become the property of sponsor, and will not be returned. By participating in this sweepstakes, entrants agree to be bound by these official rules and the decision of the judges, which are final in all respects.

7. For the name of the winner, available after March 22, 2000, send by May 1, 2000 a stamped, self-addressed envelope to Winner's List, Win a Year of Romance from SMP Sweepstakes, St. Martin's Paperbacks, 175 Fifth Avenue, Suite 1615, New York, NY 10010-7848, Attention JP.